EDITED BY
ANTHONY GIANGREGORIO

OTHER LIVING DEAD PRESS BOOKS

LIVING DEAD PRESS PRESENTS: A HORROR MAGAZINE
THE BABYLONIAN CURSE
ONLY THE YOUNG SURVIVE
ZOMBIES AND POWER TOOLS
SEX IN THE TIME OF ZOMBIES
ZOMBIE EROTICA: AN UNDEAD ANTHOLOGY ABOUT SEX
THE TURNING: A STORY OF THE LIVING DEAD
THE DEAD OF SPACE BOOK 1 AND 2
PLAYING GOD: A ZOMBIE NOVEL * THE JUNKYARD
PLANET OF THE DEAD * THE HAUNTED THEATRE
ZOMBIES IN OUR HOMETOWN
THE HAUNTED THEATRE
NIGHT OF THE WOLF: A WEREWOLF ANTHOLOGY
JUST BEFORE NIGHT: A ZOMBIE ANTHOLOGY
THE BOOK OF HORROR VOL.1 * KNIGHT SYNDROME
THE WAR AGAINST THEM: A ZOMBIE NOVEL
CHILDREN OF THE VOID * DARK DREAMS
BLOOD RAGE & DEAD RAGE (BOOK 1& 2 OF THE RAGE VIRUS SERIES)
DEAD MOURNING: A ZOMBIE HORROR STORY
BOOK OF THE DEAD: A ZOMBIE ANTHOLOGY VOLUME 1-6
LOVE IS DEAD: A ZOMBIE ANTHOLOGY
ETERNAL NIGHT: A VAMPIRE ANTHOLOGY
END OF DAYS: AN APOCALYPTIC ANTHOLOGY VOLUME 1-5
DEAD HOUSE: A ZOMBIE GHOST STORY
THE ZOMBIE IN THE BASEMENT (FOR ALL AGES)
THE LAZARUS CULTURE: A ZOMBIE NOVEL
DEAD WORLDS: UNDEAD STORIES VOLUMES 1-7
FAMILY OF THE DEAD, REVOLUTION OF THE DEAD
RANDY AND WALTER: PORTRAIT OF TWO KILLERS
KINGDOM OF THE DEAD * DEAD HISTORY
THE MONSTER UNDER THE BED * DEAD THINGS
DEAD TALES: SHORT STORIES TO DIE FOR
ROAD KILL: A ZOMBIE TALE * DEADFREEZE * DEADFALL
SOUL EATER * THE DARK * RISE OF THE DEAD
DEAD END: A ZOMBIE NOVEL * VISIONS OF THE DEAD
MISADVENTURES OF THE DEAD
INSIDE THE PERIMETER: SCAVENGERS OF THE DEAD
BOOK OF CANNIBALS VOLUME 1 * CHRISTMAS IS DEAD…AGAIN
EMAILS OF THE DEAD * EMPIRE OF DIRT
THE CHRONICLES OF JACK PRIMUS

THE DEADWATER SERIES

DEADWATER * DEADWATER: Expanded Edition
DEADRAIN * DEADCITY * DEADWAVE * DEAD HARVEST
DEAD UNION * DEAD VALLEY * DEAD TOWN * DEAD GRAVE
DEAD SALVATION * DEAD ARMY (Deadwater series book 10)

BOOK OF HORROR
2

BOOK OF HORROR 2

Table of Contents

RED

JOHN C. FOSTER

59:00 to Zero Hour

The walking man, called Red—though he didn't think of himself in that way—stepped off the pitted road and started across a parking lot. The building was less a restaurant than a roadhouse, with pickup trucks huddled close like suckling pigs. There were three light posts around the lot but only one possessed an intact bulb. The dark night was beating it handily.

Red was tall and lean, with only a faded denim jacket, work shirt and blue jeans to ward off the late October chill. His was the kind of face that smiled a lot, open and friendly as the best American faces are. The wind whipped at his ruddy curls, but he didn't seem to mind and his smile never faltered.

No one inside the roadhouse noticed as Red strolled around to the back of the building, feet crunching across the gravel lot.

A dumpster squatted in shadow.

Red made a simple calculation and pulled a folding Buck knife from his belt.

He knelt down on one knee and pressed the palm of his left hand flat against the gravel, spreading his fingers wide. Then he took the dependable blade of the Buck and dug it into the root of his smallest finger, bearing down with his weight until the knife cut through with a wet pop.

Brackish liquid pulsed from his knuckle as the digit bounced free. He knotted a handkerchief around the violated hand before picking up the finger and tossing it into the dumpster. The digit fell across the mounds of food and refuse until it nestled down deep among the sedimentary layers.

Red walked around to the front of the building and opened the door, letting the warmth and noise of drinking men roll across him. When the waitress asked him if he wanted a table, he gave the same easy smile worn while sawing off his little finger.

He thought he might try to hitch a ride north. It was time to spread out.

57:13 to Zero Hour

"I've never seen anything like it," muttered the slack-jawed farmer standing behind Cain.

Cain cupped his hands around the tip of a cigarette and lit it with a paper match. He drew in, enjoying the scratching smoke, letting it trickle from his nostrils. He held the cigarette reversed, with the glowing end cupped in his palm like a convict.

His face wasn't so much shaped as it was carved and his eyes lurked remotely in shadows beneath a heavy brow. He rarely smiled and it was hard to imagine him ever laughing. Cain wore his ugliness like a coral snake wore its coloring.

"Have you seen this before? I mean, is that why they sent you?" the farmer asked.

A circle of ground was coated with a thin, caramelized crust roughly thirty meters in diameter. The corn stalks had vanished completely from within the circle, though they stood tall all around the space, dry and crackling in the wind.

Cain pulled a small sensor from his belt. He didn't bother explaining it to the farmer as he held it over the ground and thumbed the button.

He followed its low thrumming like a dowser with a hickory rod, until the device led him to the exact center of the circle, allowing its signal to lead him to the edge of the towering corn stalks. Several were recently broken and pushed aside.

Cain lifted a small burst transmitter to his mouth.

"Crop circle is approximately thirty meters in diameter and demonstrates unusual characteristics. A thin, caramelized crust coats the dirt within the circle. Appears to be organic material residue." He paused, then continued. "This one is different."

The farmer tapped him on the shoulder. "Hey, did you hear me talking to you?"

Cain turned his head and let his eyes do their thing. The farmer dropped his hand and Cain lifted the device again.

"Subject is not in immediate vicinity and has made no effort to conceal direction of travel, suggesting two possibilities. One, the subject is unaware that its entry was detected. Two, the subject is not concerned that its entry was detected."

A cold dread settled deep into his gut and he looked up at the clear night sky above, his gaze pushing into the deep, dark spaces between the sparkling stars.

"Cain tracking," he said, then pressed a button to send the burst transmission.

56:00 to Zero Hour
The black Chevy Suburban roared east, goaded by Cain's heavy foot on the accelerator. A barely cracked window sucked the cloud of cigarette smoke away from his face as he pulled several items from the glove compartment.

He barely noticed as the speedometer raced past 105 mph.

The first and second items were both cell phones, which he thumbed on and preset to a number in the 202 area code—Washington, D.C. If the unthinkable happened he would call the number and say two words, "Option bravo."

Plan B. It was a just a precaution.

The speedometer needle bounced against the pin as he passed 120 mph.

He laced one phone on the passenger seat and slipped the second into a coat pocket.

The third item from the glove box was a black pistol, an ugly semi-automatic, .45 caliber, loaded with seven rounds. He slipped the pistol into his shoulder holster, beneath his coat. He slid two loaded clips into holders beneath the pistol.

A police siren started screaming and he glanced into his rear-view mirror. A pair of headlights topped by a revolving blue strobe skidded up an onramp a hundred yards back, overshot, then gained control and began to chase him.

Cain picked up the spare phone from the seat and thumbed the preset for a different number, not slowing as the cruiser struggled to gain on him.

"Operative Cain, voice ident." He waited for two answering tones. "Send out an APB to all Illinois police units, state, highway and local townships. Leave me the fuck alone."

He disconnected and redialed the 202 number, tossing the phone back onto the seat.

A minute later the siren cut off in mid-wail and the lights disappeared.

Cain stubbed out the ashy butt of his cigarette and ground his foot on the gas pedal. Without looking, he fished a new Camel from his pack, lipped it, lit it, and smoked it.

The sensor on his dash was giving coordinates now, which meant he'd closed to within twenty miles of his quarry.

53:22 to Zero Hour

The trucker snuck a glance at his passenger's hand again. A stained rag knotted around his fist couldn't hide the fact that he was missing a finger. But he seemed pretty damn easy about it. He was smiling, even though they hadn't exchanged a word in the last five minutes. Maybe he was stoned.

"Mind if I turn on the radio? We should be in range of a good oldies station now," the trucker said.

"I don't mind," Red replied. He relaxed into the worn seat in the cab of the semi. They were making good time, the trucker having told him earlier they would reach Chicago before dawn.

The radio kicked in with some static-laden rock.

"Well, that sucks," the trucker muttered as he began the complicated process of downshifting his big rig.

"What are you doing?" Red asked as he sat up.

"Cold night for a break down. Gonna see if these folks need a lift to the next town."

Red followed the trucker's gesture and saw the red gleam of road flares spaced around an SUV up ahead.

The trucker pulled in behind the ring of flares. "Yuppie trucks are all show and no go."

Red saw the big vehicle sitting on the side of the road with its hood up. Steam was boiling up from the engine and he could see a man in a long coat working under the hood. The SUV's blinking hazard lights intermittently lit up trees and bushes bordering the road. The trucker engaged the parking break and opened the door, lowering himself heavily to the road. Red cracked open his door and slid out to the pavement as well.

"Hey, fella, got a problem?"

Cain looked up from the Suburban's engine as the trucker lumbered forward. "Looks like a hose popped loose. I'm letting it cool down before I try to re-attach it."

The trucker nodded. "Want me to take a look?"

Cain straightened up but didn't step away from the open hood. The trucker and the red-haired man couldn't see the long object wrapped in cloth resting on the hissing engine.

Cain looked them both over and suddenly craved a cigarette, but when he reached inside his coat, he pulled out the .45, not his Camels.

"So which one of you shoddy motherfuckers is an alien?" Cain asked calmly.

The trucker gaped and said, "What?"

Suddenly Red was behind the trucker, his arms snaking around the man's neck in a strangle hold. The trucker was a big man and he bucked back hard, but it was like ramming a brick wall for all the effect it had on Red. The arms tightened.

Cain lifted his pistol and sighted down his arm. He couldn't get a clear bead as the red-headed man dragged the trucker back towards the idling truck.

He aimed low and fired, blowing a hole in the trucker's thigh. The man screamed and collapsed, jerking Red forward with sheer weight. Cain was already moving into a Weaver stance, aiming high. The semi-automatic barked and a .45 slug slammed into the now-exposed mass of red curls.

The trucker fell hard onto his face, bellowing.

Red backpedaled and bounced off the steel grille of the semi, his head whip-lashing to fling a streamer of black liquid up onto the windshield. Cain drilled two more shots into Red's chest and he spun at the impacts, then rushed forward at Cain with shocking speed.

Cain sprang backwards, dropped his pistol and snatched the wrapped bundle off the engine, ripping at the cloth.

Red hurtled at him, arms wide, and leaped.

Cain shucked the wrapping free and braced the blunt length of a Benelli combat shotgun against his shoulder. He didn't aim, just fired.

A full load blasted into Red's chest from a distance of three paces. Nine .32 caliber pellets traveling at thousands of feet per second with enough force to kill an elephant.

Red somersaulted backwards and hit the ground hard.

Cain pumped the shotgun's slide.

Red lurched up to his feet.

Cain stepped in and rammed the smoking barrel against Red's still grinning face. He fired.

Red's head disintegrated and his body staggered back in a drunken wobble.

Cain racked the slide and blasted Red's right arm off. The body spun around and lost balance, then fell. Cain pinned the eviscerated chest with his foot and blew off Red's right leg. Then his left leg. Plastic shell casings bounced across the tar as they ejected from the shotgun.

Cain used his last round to blow off Red's left arm.

The echoing blast rolled away and again the night was quiet except for the idling truck. Cain stepped back, breathing through his teeth. He fumbled more shells from his coat pocket and slid them into the shotgun's tube.

The shattered, oozing mass twitched and smoked, scorched by point-blank muzzle blasts. Cain edged closer, then fired six more shots into the body as fast as he could pump the slide and squeeze the trigger.

Soon, the body was no longer recognizable as such and it damned sure didn't twitch.

Cain leaned his shotgun against the Chevy and fished out his cigarettes. The tip was rock-steady as he held the fragile match flame against it. The trucker moaned and slid into a fetal position on the road. Cain fetched a first aid kit from the Chevy and approached the downed man, skirting a spreading pool of blood beneath the thigh wound.

"I'm shot," the trucker gasped. First timers always said that.

"Yeah, I know." Cain knelt down and cut open the man's pants around the wound.

"Who...who are you? What happened?"

Cain slapped a bandage over the hole and the wounded man jerked in pain. Cain pulled an Illinois State Police badge out of his left rear pocket and flashed it. He had other badges in different pockets for various occasions.

"You're lucky," Cain said as he helped the wounded man sit up and lean back against the semi. "Laughing boy was a serial killer wanted in four states. His M.O. was hitchhiking."

The trucker shivered. "Jesus."

Cain stood up and pulled on rubber gloves as he walked over to Red's shattered remains.

"Hey, where you going?"

Cain ignored the trucker and began shoveling the body parts into a plastic hazardous materials bag. He was quick but careful. The trucker's moans faded to background noise.

Cain sealed the bag shut.

"Officer, I can't feel my leg," the trucker whispered, weakening.

Cain ignored the trucker as he tossed the bag into the Suburban's back seat and climbed in. He closed the door and cut off a last "Hey officer…"

As he pulled out onto the road, he dialed 9-1-1 and offered an anonymous tip about a shooting.

41:00 to Zero Hour

The conference room was antiseptic and precise with its steel table and soundproofed walls. A large screen came down out of the ceiling and began to show footage of the onsite lab. Figures in clumsy bio-suits trailing hoses were using forceps to pluck objects off an examining table and place them in the receptacle of an electron microscope.

Cain hunched deeper into his chair and watched. He hadn't slept in almost twenty-four hours and was exhausted. He lit a cigarette before the bald man, Fortier, noticed what he was doing.

"There's no smoking in here," Fortier said.

Cain looked at him and Fortier essayed a smile.

"Perhaps you didn't notice the signs?"

Cain let the smoke trickle out between his teeth.

"You were right about the caramelized substance being biologic in origin. It's an inert version of what we found in the subject," Fortier said.

Cain watched the scurrying scientists on the big screen. "So it was alive? We thought it would be a machine."

Fortier leaned forward and said, "Well, yes and no. Once it was broken down to the cellular level we found something interesting." Fortier thumbed a switch on the table and the screen flashed to a new image. Rows of microorganisms quivered. "The basic building blocks bear a striking resemblance to cellulose."

Cain sat up. "It's a plant?"

"No, it is a machine…a brilliantly designed collection of nano-robots constructed out of biological materials."

"Nano-robots," Cain said.

"Exactly. Complex robots built on a microscopic scale, not even measurable in micrograms. Entire colonies of them."

"Why biological materials?" Cain asked.

"Because it's a self-replicating organism," Fortier said as he folded his hands, pleased at having finally elicited interest from the taciturn field operative.

"Explain," Cain said.

"Our initial detection of the landing indicated an object of microscopic size. The current theory is that the initial landing vehicle was a single nano-robot. It intentionally landed in a region with a large quantity of available bio-materials."

"The cornfield," Cain stated, stubbing out his cigarette on the table.

"Correct. The crop circle was created when the single nano-robot consumed raw materials and began a process of self-replication. It grew into a collection of literally billions of nano-robots."

"Until it looked like a man."

"Exactly. Did you now that the clothes it wore weren't really clothes at all? It simply shifted the appropriate part of its exterior to resemble clothing that would elicit minimal attention."

"It looked like it had just stepped out of a Norman Rockwell painting," Cain said, remembering.

Fortier nodded. "An appearance calculated to be non-threatening to us."

A terrible chain of thoughts began in Cain's head and he lit another cigarette without noticing the other man's grimace.

Fortier cleared his throat and continued. "The prevailing theory for this is that it wanted to avoid confrontation. From that we deduce a level of concern for its vulnerability. Psych says it may indicate that *they* aren't confident of the outcome in a direct confrontation..."

Cain interrupted him. "It was missing a finger. Why?"

"Ahh...we're not sure yet."

"Can the nano-robots replicate into anything besides the red-haired man?"

Fortier frowned. "Unknown."

"If I hadn't killed it, how many times could it have self-replicated?"

Fortier's frown deepened. "We're not certain. Assuming there's enough biologic material on hand to use in the process..." Fortier interrupted himself and closed a mental file on the thought. "We're not certain."

Cain leaned back and closed his eyes, replaying the scene on the Illinois road. The way the red-haired man had soaked up bullets and came at him so *fast*.

Fortier was speaking but he ignored him. He knew he was nowhere near as intelligent as the scientists dissecting the body. Probably not even as intelligent as Fortier, but they were trained as scientists and bureaucrats, while he was trained as a soldier—more accurately, as a killer. A tiger doesn't wear stripes because it's afraid of its prey. It uses camouflage and stealth because they make killing more efficient.

Cain stubbed out his second cigarette. "It wasn't afraid of confrontation."

"The psychological department begs to differ."

Cain felt fatigue wash over him again. He shook his head. "What do the psych boys say about its finger?"

Fortier stood up. "They have several different theories."

Cain stood as well.

"Thank you for your report, Operative Cain. We'll contact you if further input is needed," Fortier said, dismissing Cain from his office.

35:24 to Zero Hour

Cain's wife was screaming and he couldn't do anything to help her. Then he woke up and realized that the shrill keening came from his phone. If his wife was screaming, he would never know. She'd left him four years ago and moved to Boston with an architect. He sat up in bed, groggy; exhausted down to his bones.

He worked his dry mouth and picked up the phone to silence its noise. His throat managed one word, "Cain."

The voice on the other end was devoid of emotion and its very lack of excitement sent a burst of adrenaline into Cain's bloodstream. It was the dispatcher at Operations.

"Orange six," the disaffected voice said.

"Copy, orange six," Cain replied and hung up the phone.

Orange indicated the situation level as a serious threat. *Six* pointed back to his last operational zone. Cain got up and began to dress.

28:30 to Zero Hour
The fry cook's name was Jerome and he had forgotten to lock the front door again after he came in. He turned at the sound of the chime.

"Sorry, fellas, we're not gonna start serving till 6:30 this morning," Jerome said as he walked from the kitchen into the main room and saw three men. Then his eyes grew big and he stopped.

The three red-haired men in denim smiled easily at him. They were triplets. Identical in appearance except for one, who wore a bandage over what appeared to be a missing ear. That one pulled a Buck knife from his belt and slid open the blade. It gleamed.

"Sweet Jesus," Jerome said.

They rushed him.

26:14 to Zero Hour
Mary's heel beat against the kitchen floor as she twitched during the seven seconds it took the massive cranial trauma to kill her.

Red smiled and dropped the hammer he'd liberated from the garage.

He knelt beside the dead woman and placed his palm on the linoleum floor, spreading his fingers...the three remaining on that hand.

The Buck knife made its appearance and took off a finger at the knuckle. Red didn't bother binding the wound and brackish liquid dripped in viscous strings from his knuckle. Stealth was less important than speed at this phase.

Still kneeling, Red took the severed finger and placed it in Mary's mouth, shoving it down deep into her throat.

He stood and looked down at her, judging her body mass to be under by perhaps twenty pounds. Searching the kitchen, he found two sacks of potatoes in the cupboard and decided they would do nicely. He upended both sacks over her corpse. A few potatoes rolled away and he retrieved them, stacking them atop her wide middle.

Then Red departed and left the nano-robots to do their work.

21:00 to Zero Hour

Wind whipped the yellow police tape strung around the spot where he had gunned down the subject.

Cain ducked under the tape and glanced at the State Police cars parked at the scene, roof-lights flashing. He knew that the dour men inside were no more Illinois cops than he was.

"Cain?" A big man in a suit approached. Cain shook the man's hand and nodded as the other added, "I'm Leonard."

Cain wasn't sure if Leonard was a first or a last name, but didn't care enough to ask as he followed him to several holes in the grass around a large tree.

"We were told to secure the site until you arrived," Leonard said, his look probing.

Cain ignored the unasked question and knelt by one hole. It was a foot deep in the earth and four feet wide. Grass and a dense root structure appeared to have been eaten away, as if by acid. Cain put on rubber gloves and fingered the crispy, caramelized layer.

"Are these the only three holes?" Cain asked.

"Yes," Leonard said.

Cain squat-walked to another hole, closer to the tree. He tapped the trunk and noted the hollow sound. Standing, he kicked the tree hard, his foot plunging in up to the ankle.

"What the hell?" Leonard said. "Something ate out the inside of the tree?"

Cain wiggled his foot free and plucked splinters from his sock.

He walked away from Leonard's questions and raked his gaze over the surrounding countryside. With all those shotgun blasts, maybe he had sent an ear or chunk of bone flying away from the body.

He turned back to Leonard. "Call Fortier. Tell him they can self-replicate multiple times and I'm tracking up to three new subjects."

"Yes, sir," Leonard said as he pulled an encrypted satellite phone from his belt.

Cain climbed into his big Suburban and activated the sensor. A tone came on and the LED's flashed, but it wasn't giving him coordinates.

The subjects were already more than twenty miles away.

17:10 to Zero Hour
The only outward signs of Fortier's sudden nausea were a slight paling and a bead of sweat on his upper lip. On the screen, Fortier watched the computer model as it replicated over and over until it filled the entire picture.

The first scientist held up a laser pointer, using the red dot to trace a pattern as he spoke. "As you can see, growth is at a geometric rate. One becomes two, two become four, four become sixteen, which become two hundred and fifty-six and so on."

The second scientist nodded gravely. "The growth is very fast, but seems to be limited to a set pattern."

"So the subject, or subjects, will be identical in appearance," added the first.

"We thought they'd be smarter than that," Fortier muttered.

"On the contrary, their technology indicates immense, yet utterly alien intelligence. As a poor example, have you ever looked at a barnacle? They look identical, right? To us at least. Now imagine that your sensory equipment wasn't even optical, what if it was only auditory...how different do barnacles sound from each other?"

"Right," Fortier said as he wiped the sweat off his lip and straightened his jacket. "We've located what we believe to be the residue of three more subjects, possibly dislodged from the initial subject when our operative terminated it."

Both scientists stilled, and one glanced at the explosive growth progression on the screen.

"We don't want to be creating new ones every time we terminate a subject," Fortier continued. "We need recommendations for a more sterile method."

The first scientist opened his mouth but Fortier raised a hand. "This method must work in the field, gentlemen."

The scientists spoke at the same time.

"Fire."

14:30 to Zero Hour
The county worker cursed and stabbed his finger at the kill switch for the garbage masher. Then he clambered up the side of

the huge garbage truck and stopped beside the metal dumpster held high in the truck's hydraulic arms, only half emptied.

"Son-of-a-bitch," he whispered, staring down into the bowels of the trash compartment. White and limp, a hand protruded from the refuse.

The county worker jumped down to the gravel and ran towards the roadhouse, shouting. "Help! Call 9-1-1!"

Inside the trash compartment, Red stirred and sat up, garbage rolling off his head and shoulders. He thought about pursuing the county worker but decided that distance and speed were his immediate tactical concerns.

They were at a delicate phase right now.

Red sprang from the bowels of the trash compartment and landed in the parking lot. Then he swung himself through the open door of the garbage truck and keyed the ignition.

The county worker ran out from inside the roadhouse in time to see the red-haired man drive off with a smile on his face.

14:00 to Zero Hour

Cain kicked in the door of Mary Simms' house with his shotgun gripped in one fist, and a gallon can of gasoline in the other. Operations had already filled him in on the recommended termination method but Cain couldn't wait for the delivery of a flamethrower.

The window shades had been pulled and the inside smelled of rotting vegetables.

An officer of the law would have called out for the owner of the house, but Cain just crept as quietly as possible through the living room. He walked on the edges of his shoes, reducing impact noise. Rather than darting about, his eyes were focused on non-space. His training told him he would react fastest to a peripheral cue.

A quiet *drag-thump, drag-thump* from the direction of the kitchen, caught his attention. He moved until his back was against the wall near the entryway.

The sound stopped.

Cain breathed.

The sound didn't repeat.

He hoped the subject wasn't pressed against the wall inside the kitchen, mirroring him, also waiting.

It was quiet as a church.

Cain bit back a curse and rushed through the entryway, hurling his body at the far wall as he spun. His shoulder slammed into a big white Frigidaire and a cascade of magnets and postcards rained down as he dropped to a crouch.

A dark shadow moved in the corner and the thick smell enveloped him. He straightened up, keeping his shotgun trained on the moving form as he set the gas can on the counter. He flicked on the kitchen light and squinted, protecting his eyes against the sudden glare and the grotesquerie in the corner.

"You're smart enough to fly halfway across the galaxy and drop nano-bots on us, but you're not smart enough to hide in the fucking closet until you finish replicating?" Cain asked.

It regarded him hideously and Cain forced himself to hold its gaze. A nose was pushing its way out of Mary Simms' face—a man's nose. Her hair was still long but her head sat atop the body of an almost man. One half of the torso was clad in faded blue denim, the other half was bare, a female breast slowly sinking down into a swirl of fleshy quicksand. One of its legs seemed to be consuming the other.

"So how many of you are there?" Cain asked.

A shudder ran through it and flesh bulged strangely.

Cain unscrewed the gas can lid and said, "Let me guess. You guys found Voyager, right? A nice welcome message?" He stepped closer, though still out of its reach, and splashed acrid yellow fluid over the subject. It shifted sluggishly, its one good leg digging in a heel for purchase on the linoleum.

"Well, we changed our mind," Cain said.

Its eyes focused on him and glittered in the harsh kitchen light. Cain dropped the can and stepped back to where his shotgun rested on the counter. He placed a Camel in his mouth and fished a matchbook from his pocket. He lit the cigarette.

Abruptly, the thing in the corner sat up straight.

Cain flicked his match across the room and what was once Mary Simms burst into flames with a keening wail.

"We revoke our invitation," Cain said flatly as fire consumed the flopping form and spread to the walls and floor.

He was gone fifteen minutes before the first fire truck arrived.

An hour later, he caught another subject almost completely replicated in a diner. He burned the entire building down with a flamethrower.

12:50 to Zero Hour

Fortier stood in front of his superior's desk and waited. General Adam Laird was the highest-ranking scientist of the United States Air Force and chief defense analyst for Joint Space Command. Until less than two years ago, his job was largely theoretical and it was to his credit that he commissioned the Operations Directorate.

Laird steepled his hands and said, "If they can use plant and other organic materials to replicate, why are they using human hosts?"

"We don't know," Fortier said.

"Is it a preferred biology? A psychological strategy to frighten us?" Laird felt his frustration increase. "Do we just taste good?"

"We don't know," Fortier repeated, quieter.

Laird looked at a wall map. Red pins indicated points of contact and a barely emerging pattern.

"Alert the FBI and Illinois State Police. We'll disseminate a complete briefing and tactical plan immediately," Laird said.

Fortier felt the surge of nausea again. "But sir..."

Laird cut him off. "Until they receive the tac-package, all units are ordered to shoot on sight. We've got to slow them down until our operatives can arrive on scene and sterilize the subjects."

"Yes, sir," Fortier said before hurrying from the office to issue the new directives, not realizing that the orders were coming too late.

4:07 to Zero Hour

Cain's police band scanner picked up the panicked calls from the St. Lawrence police.

"Repeat! *Officer down!* Request immediate backup!"

From the rest of the conversation, he knew the small town cops were engaged with several of Cain's targets. St. Lawrence was less than four miles away...and only ten miles from Chicago's south side.

Six minutes later, Cain stomped hard on the brakes but the Chevy Suburban still plowed into the police cruiser blockading Main Street.

There were bodies in the streets of St. Lawrence—police officers and civilians.

Cain kicked open his door and jumped out, running around back to throw open the rear door. Every effort drew complaints from his joints and muscles. His eyelids felt like they had sand beneath them. He shucked his coat and threw the flamethrower harness over his shoulders, buckling it as he ran towards the shooting.

Around the corner, a blood-spattered cop was firing his 9mm Glock into a building through an open doorway and screaming at the top of his lungs. "Come out, you motherfucker! C'mon outta there!"

Cain slowed until the Glock ran empty and the young officer fumbled through his reload, then Cain ran up to him.

He couldn't see anything through the open doorway. It was some sort of rooming house. "Officer, how many subjects inside?" he asked.

"Huh? They're in there! I know I hit one but—who the fuck are you?"

Cain flashed an FBI badge. "How many civilians are in there?"

The cop's eyes rolled wildly and he finished reloading with a snap. He didn't know.

"Goddammit," Cain said. "Follow me and keep your eyes open."

Cain triggered the flamethrower and a blue flame began hissing from its barrel. He stepped onto the front porch, then turned to look back at the cop.

"Alert but calm. Don't trip and shoot me in the back," Cain said.

The cop nodded and hair flopped over his forehead, making him look even younger.

The building's foyer was ripped and tattered from a dozen gunshots. Cain found the landlord behind the front desk, on the floor with a broken neck.

He didn't know how long until the replication process started, but he believed in precautions.

"Fire in the hole," he said and roasted the corpse with jellied gasoline.

"What the hell..." the cop said but Cain was already in the hall and heading for the stairs.

Someone started screaming from outside but Cain ignored it. He could hear sirens approaching, too. He began edging upward, following the questing snout of the flamethrower up the stairs. He wanted to recon-by-fire, to light up everything in his path and then move in to mop up, but couldn't; there might still be civilians in the building.

"Hey, kid, I want you to..." Cain began, but then the cop was shooting and Cain spun around.

The figure was in the first floor hallway and running at the stairs. The barrage of 9mm rounds made it shudder but barely slowed its charge.

"Get down!" Cain bellowed and the young officer was quick, dropping hard onto his belly as Cain let loose a stream of fire right over him. The burning mass hit the subject square in his grinning face and lit it up like a sparkler.

Flames snapped and popped, and the form reeled back, clawing at its burning head.

Cain was shifting for better aim when a weight slammed into his shoulders, ripping at the fuel tank on his back.

"Behind you!" The St. Lawrence policeman was on his feet, trying to aim past Cain, who dropped and twisted, then cannoned up with his full body weight and leverage, driving Red into the wall. Plaster rained down around them.

Cain reversed and drove a knee into Red's groin before jabbing stiffened fingers into his throat.

Red grinned widely and struck incredibly fast with tremendous force.

Cain careened backwards and crashed through the railing. He heard the *pop-pop-pop* of the cop's Glock as he was falling.

Something hit him and he couldn't breathe and then everything went away.

27 Minutes to Zero Hour

Machines hummed and something was digging into Cain's forearm. There was a low, mechanical chirping sound nearby.

The front of his face felt swollen and cracked, and he knew his nose was broken. His tongue probed gently, finding the gap where his two upper front teeth had recently been.

The skin of his cheeks was so puffy and enlarged that opening his eyes was difficult, so he didn't.

Memory slowly swam back against the current. The smell of burning meat and the high velocity cracks of the police officer's pistol.

He was in tremendous pain. His nose and mouth. Muscle pulls. Abrasions. Worst was the sharp ache from his back where ribs were cracked. He opened his eyes a slit, closed them and waited for moisture to rebuild, then opened them again.

Greenish shapes moved around him, occasionally blocking the overhead lights.

Vision focused and the greenish shapes almost became doctors in bulky surgical scrubs. His vision blurred again.

"Mr. Cain? Are you awake?"

Cain focused on the kind eyes behind the surgical mask and managed a nod.

"Pain..." he whispered, unable to get out the word '...killers.'

The doctor hovered closely. "It hurts here?" The doctor pressed against Cain's lower rib cage, and he convulsed, the agony cutting through the fog.

"Don't...dammit..." He panted heavily and clarity returned. "Where am I?"

"You're in Chicago Memorial. You suffered extensive structural damage," the doctor said, stepping back among his colleagues.

Cain had a thought then, but said, "Who brought me here?"

"You were brought here by police officers," the doctor said, stepping closer. "The police officers were surprised you were able to detect the invasion units. How were you able to accomplish this?"

Cain sagged deeper into the bed and his head rolled slightly to the left. "Closer," he whispered.

The doctor leaned over him helpfully. "Is this better?"

Ignoring the pain, Cain abruptly snatched the surgical mask from the doctor's face. He shrank back from the kind smile greeting him. He tried to lunge from the bed but realized too late that plastic straps restrained his feet.

Another doctor spoke. "We have recorded your involvement. Your level of effectiveness was unanticipated, as was your survival."

As one, the doctor's pulled down their masks to reveal identical friendly faces. Cain realized that their scrubs were so bulky because they had been pulled on over denim jackets.

He cast about wildly for escape but two of the red-haired men moved in and grabbed his arms, pressing him to the mattress. It was then that Cain noticed a severed ear lying in a metal dish.

They began questioning him. One would start speaking and another would finish the thought, as if a single intelligence drove them. They applied pressure to his wounds and created new ones. He felt something snap in his middle and tasted copper. When one of them levered his mouth open and another tried to shove the ear down his throat, he began talking.

He told them about the tracking devices, about Fortier, Laird and the Operations Directorate. They kept working on him and he told them almost everything he could think of.

When they stepped back, he struggled to suck in air. He felt the blood filling his middle and blackness scratching around the edge of his thinking.

Shame flooded through him, and he couldn't stop himself as he moaned from the pain.

He rolled his vision over to the disembodied ear waiting for him in its antiseptic metal tray. He had a sudden image of hundreds of other patients in the hospital, all strapped to their beds—changing.

He heard voices in the hall and they were all the *same* voices.

"We wish to open communications," said one grinning fellow.

Another held a phone up to Cain.

"Your command system is extremely disorganized. You will use your security clearance to open a high level channel for us."

Cain nodded. "They'll need..." He coughed and his vision swam from the agony. "My voice identification..."

The phone was pressed to his ear. His arm was lifted and his finger weakly touched the numbers he remembered.

The darkness was closing in on him, blotting out more and more of his thinking. Seconds ticked by and he heard a tone. "Operative Cain, voice ident," he said.

It felt like years but it was only a moment later that two tones answered him.

Cain turned slightly and looked at the man holding the phone as he spoke two words into the receiver. "Option bravo."

Then the phone was snatched away and they moved in with their questions and their pain, trying to determine what he had just done.

Five minutes later, they were still working on him and he was screaming, dying, trying not to tell them.

Then everything went white, so impossibly white, and nuclear fire swept the entire state of Illinois.

Zero Hour Plus 24:00
The two college students in the van were listening to the unbelievable story out of Illinois. The nuclear weapons accident. The National Guard shutting down the Midwest. Mushroom clouds people could see in Michigan.

It was getting towards dark when they passed a small town hugging the edge of the Mojave Desert. A hitchhiker was strolling beside the road and they gave each other a look before pulling over. The man wasn't carrying any gear but he was dressed for walking in denim and boots.

"You need a lift?"

The red-haired hitchhiker climbed into the back seat of the van and smiled. "Thanks."

They passed a sign a little while later. **Welcome to California**.

KILLER CAREER MOVE

DAVID BERNSTEIN

Margaret Atwood sat in class having just finished her algebra test. She was a brilliant fourteen year old girl, always getting A's on her tests regardless of the subject. She glanced at the clock and smiled; fifteen minutes until the end of the period.

Margaret was always done before anyone else and never content with finishing quietly. She would raise her hand and ask to use the restroom, her way of announcing that she had won.

She rarely had to use the facilities and usually wound up sitting on a toilet and carving a poem into one of the stall's walls with her straight razor—magic marker seemed so vagrant-like and was easily removed. Her mother constantly preached that horrible things could happen to little girls if they weren't careful but Margaret had decided at the age of nine that careful wasn't enough.

She added 'peace of mind' by carrying her razor; a smooth to the touch blade made of surgical steel, giving her a sense of hidden power. If ever needed, it could cut off a man's balls with but a flick of her wrist. The instrument's easy gliding motion and scalpel-like edge were something to admire.

To Margaret, school was always a competition. Her parents enforced the desire to achieve greatness and that nothing should ever get in her way to achieve it. Family, kids, and frivolous material items would all come to her if she was the best, but she had to be honest.

Cheaters were vile creatures and would eventually pay the price for their putrid acts. Cheating was stealing, and hard work was a priceless commodity. Margaret, along with making sure she was the best, had to watch out for cheaters and make sure she kept them from robbing her most vital achievements.

Margaret, having achieved another A for sure, was about to raise her neatly manicured hand in signature fashion when Brian Avine beat her to it.

"Mrs. Morgan," he said. "Can I use the bathroom?"

Heads that had been slanted down at a northwest position—except for the lefties, they screwed up the uniformity—had suddenly lifted from their unison positions and turned to stare at Brian.

Margaret was dumbfounded.

No, not dumbfounded...flabbergasted. No one had ever asked to use the restroom before her. The heads turned to the teacher awaiting her return volley. What was Brian up to? No one was allowed to leave the classroom until that person had finished their test and handed it in.

"Brian, dear," Mrs. Morgan began, seeming tired and wanting nothing more than to be whisked away by some twenty-year-old with a yacht and an endless supply of caviar. "No bathroom until you've completed your test. You know the rules."

The return was an ace, a shot so perfect that the volley was over. Students began shaking their heads in disappointment as they returned to work. Margaret smiled, as she would be the one to walk slowly up to the front of the classroom to hand in her test. She'd stop on her way, grab her crotch, stick out her tongue, and mock Brian for trying to ruin her record.

"But, I am done," Brian said. Again, all the heads turned to gawk at him.

Margaret felt as if she'd been struck by a magic frost bolt. Her breathing had stopped and she was clearly going into shock, frozen and unable to join in the class' staring. Someone had finished before her, but as logic began to enter its way back into her brain, she realized something was askew.

It couldn't be that someone had bested her, let alone stupid Brian Avine. He was a D student, who maybe achieved a C when he was fortunate enough to cheat off of a neighbor's paper. Margaret began to formulate her own hypothesis as to what was happening.

Brian, the loser, jealous of her constant winnings, decided he couldn't pass the test anyway and would take an F just so he could hand it in and ruin her consecutive winning streak.

"You've answered all the questions?" Mrs. Morgan asked, peering up from her newspaper. Her eyeglass chain drooped low, accentuating her flabby cheeks and making her look like an old bulldog. "Are you sure you don't want to take the extra time to go over your answers?" The test had become a secondary thought as the class was entrenched with Mrs. Morgan and Brian's rapport, something hardly ever seen.

"Nope, no need, this one's an A," Brian said with a confidence that bellowed throughout the room.

Margaret couldn't believe how big of a dissident Brian Avine was, flat out lying to the teacher in order to win. He had to be disqualified, he was cheating. There'd be a huge asterisk by this one and, as far as she was concerned, her record was intact.

Margaret had never liked Brian and only sat in front of him because of Mrs. Morgan's alphabetical order policy. She tolerated his gross burping and farting, but ruining her record, her satisfaction, and her accomplishments, was inexcusable.

Margaret heard screeching as Brian's chair slid along the tile floor. He was getting up. It should've been her chair making that annoying sound, not his. He walked by her, brushing his hip against her desk and letting go a nasty fart. Halfway up the aisle he turned, grabbed his crotch, stuck out his tongue, then left the room after handing in his test.

Margaret seethed in her seat as she replayed Brian's arrogance and brash behavior. He did exactly what she had planned to do. She wanted to hand in her test and go to the restroom where she could confront Brian face to face, but Mrs. Morgan's rules only allowed one person to leave the classroom at a time.

She raised her hand anyway, and seeing Mrs. Morgan was about to repeat the rules, Margaret spoke first. "I just want to hand in my test, Mrs. Morgan. I'll wait until Brian gets back before I go to the restroom." She begrudgingly walked up to Mrs. Morgan's desk and handed in her exam before returning to her seat.

Margaret watched as the second hand ticked by on the white circular clock hanging above the doorway. Brian was taking his sweet time—Margaret's time. Her insides grew heavy with depression as if her organs were sponges sopping up all of the debilitating emotion. With shoulders propped at attention, chest pushed out and spine straight as if sitting against a wall, Margaret managed to maintain her normally proud posture.

Brian finally returned after having been gone an excruciating ten minutes. The period had five minutes remaining so Margaret, for the first time since she could remember, decided to skip the bathroom visit.

The next day Mrs. Morgan handed back the exams. Margaret's depressed state was gone, replaced by a simmering anger, but seeing an A on her paper and an F on Brian's paper would surly lighten her mood.

"Good job as always Margaret," the teacher said before continuing onto Brian.

Margaret itched with excitement as she waited for Mrs. Morgan's gleeful words. Brian wouldn't care about the F, but at least the class would know what a loser he was by handing in a test way too early. Losers like Brian didn't give a rat's ass about grades, they only cared about being shown up which was precisely what she had in mind. She was about to turn around, give a wink and a smile, when something Mrs. Morgan said made her want to vomit.

"Great job, Brian. Keep it up."

The room began to shift as if Margaret was being sucked out of existence. She was suddenly brought back to reality, feeling like she might puke. The emotional sponges in her stomach were being rung, releasing whatever dastardly sensations they held. Emotions swam around her belly, ones she'd never known or felt before, causing her to upchuck a minute amount of warm bile, before quickly swallowing it back down.

She wanted to run to the water fountain in the hall and wash the horrible taste from her mouth, but instead pinched herself. After all, it was what people did during nightmare like events, wasn't it? She applied further force and pinched harder when she didn't wake, then dug her nails in deep, drawing blood.

She had to turn around, to see with her own eyes and make sure her mind hadn't deceived her. She needn't hurry, as Brian would leave the exam out in the open for all to see, especially her.

She turned around slowly in her seat like a Sherman tank readying to fire on a new target. Brian met her eyes; he was waiting. She smiled.

"That's right," he said. "An A." He looked smug and had a grin that could rival a circus clown's.

Margaret glared down at the exam, which was positioned nicely in her direction, again indicating how much Brian was enjoying himself. It was true. Brian had received an A. She suddenly felt sick again, wanting to run out of the room.

"Not feeling so hot?" Brian asked.

Margaret's nausea passed quickly as if icy water had been thrown on her. She looked up from his exam paper, meeting his vacant eyes, except this time they had something in them. She peered in, making Brian move back.

There was something there she'd never seen before, he had life in them. Where the hell did he get it? Shallow minded hollow heads like Brian didn't have that inner flame within them. He was as vacant as a freshly raided whore house on Christmas Eve.

"What?" he asked nervously.

"You cheated," Margaret said softly so only Brian could hear. "Prove it."

Margaret tried keeping her composure, but the rage swimming throughout her needed its freedom. She smashed Brian's desk with her fist, making him jump back further.

"What was that?" Mrs. Morgan asked from a few aisles away.

"Nothing," Brian said swiftly. "My hand slipped as I was stretching."

Mrs. Morgan shook her head and continued handing back the exams.

Margaret regained her control, but was still enraged. "You're a big, hollow cow and a no good loser. There's no way you could have received an A without cheating."

Brian seemed to have regained his swagger. "There's a new top dog in class, so get used to it, twat."

Margaret had been called plenty of names on the playground and in gym class—or as she liked to call it, Neanderthal hour—but the classroom was a sanctuary, a place for civility. Brian's words were flat out blasphemous and criminal.

Her eyes became slits, her jaw muscles rippling her cheeks. "I'll find out what you did and when I do, I'll make sure you get expelled." She spoke softly through clenched teeth, but held a firm tone to her voice. "I shouldn't have to deal with trash like you."

Red blotches began sprouting on Brian's cheeks, camouflaging his many freckles, before spreading throughout his entire face like fireworks on the fourth of July.

Margaret had poked him in a tender area, but he forced a smile through the obvious anger.

"I'll tell you what, twat," he began and at the sound of that word, Margaret began her own flurry of red fireworks. "Meet me after school by the big boulder on Creek's Path.

"I wouldn't meet with you if you had a scholarship to the ivy league of my choice."

Brian's eyebrows furrowed as if he was confused. "I don't give a crap what plants you like, freak, but meet me and I'll tell you my secret."

He had to be lying. He probably wanted to make her wait for him while he and his moronic friends watched and laughed at her, then tease her about it the next day.

"No," Margaret said.

"I'm not lying and I'll come alone. My friends won't tease you." Brian turned the exam back towards him so that it was now upside down to her.

Margaret felt as if a ghost had walked through her mind. Did Brian just answer her thoughts? No, her face had said it all. Angered, Margaret was easy to read, like the children books Brian struggled with after school.

"Look," he said. "It's a secret, no one can know, not even my friends, but I'll tell you," he said, pointing at her. "If you do one thing for me, just one, itsy bitsy thing," he said while holding his forefinger and thumb a few inches apart.

"And that is?"

"Make out with me."

Again she felt the need to hurl to such an extent that Brian must have noticed it too as he was reddening again.

"Fine, twat, meet me at the boulder and I'll tell you how I got the A."

"Did your loser drunk for a father teach you that word or is it just his pet name for your mom?"

Brian's pigmentation turned candy apple red, his nostrils pulsated like an angry bull readying to charge, and his jaw muscles flexed, making him look as if he wanted to bash Margaret's head. She would love it if Brian hauled off and hit her; the result would yield a definite expulsion and a possible lawsuit.

"Like I said, meet me there."

"Yeah, right," Margaret said and rolled her eyes incredulity.

Brian clasped his hands together as if a meeting of the mind was about to take place. "I'll be there. This is a one time offer. Miss out and I promise you'll regret it forever. I'll get the same grades as you for the rest of the school year and it'll drive you mad."

There. He admitted it, the dumb shit. He said he'd get the same grades as her. The moron had figured out a way to cheat off of her, making him a little—forefinger and thumb distance apart—smarter than she had given him credit for.

Later that day after the final bell, Margaret stood at her locker debating on whether or not to meet Brian. She grew furious at herself for having to waste her thoughts on such a loser. Despite her knowing better, she decided she couldn't risk not knowing why Brian, if it was to be true, would continue receiving A's. Was she deluding herself? Could he really keep up the honorary marks? Something in his words rang true earlier.

The boy was not just overly confident, but certain he would keep getting A's. It had to be some device he purchased or he had a friend that could access Mrs. Morgan's computer files. Deep down, Margaret didn't believe any of the ridiculous ideas her brain concocted, but even more unbelievable was the fact that Brian could achieve A-plus status.

She went to the library and spent the next hour studying while she waited for the clock to hit 3:25 p.m. She left the library and headed to the trail. The moron had to stay after school for tutoring, like it would help. But he wasn't staying after for help, was he? No, he was using it to cover his ass and make people think he was trying harder so when the good grades began pouring in, he'd be covered.

The teachers would pat him on the back and congratulate him on the fine grades. He'd become the poster boy for losers that could change and that the public school system was working. Margaret wasn't sure what was happening, but she was certain she'd show the liar for who he truly was, a no good cheating waste of brain matter.

Margaret arrived at the boulder on time. The monstrous mass sat alone, the ground around it worn and littered with cigarette butts.

The vicinity surrounding the small clearing consisted of dense forest. Many of the immediate tree branches had been broken, the trunks scarred with numerous carvings.

The huge rock was once a true emblem of nature's beauty, but the vagrants that traipsed the area had covered it with markings. Graffiti, mostly curses, names of lovers and drawings of youth at its wildest, made the stone a hideous clown.

She despised her peers and felt privileged that none were her friends. Everyone was an opponent, at least until after she was established in life after which she'd settle down, marry and make babies. It was what a good woman was supposed to do, after all.

She sat on a dried, mossy log lying near the treeline. She wasn't afraid to get dirty or have an insect crawl on her. She glanced at her watch; Brian was late and it was coming upon 3:45 p.m. Losers were late, punctual was proper.

She was about to leave when she heard the irritating sound of Brian's voice. "Hey, Atwood," he yelled. "You came."

The delight in Brian's voice angered her and a spider scurrying across the ground took the brunt of her rage as her heal squished it into the dirt.

"Better," she whispered and turned her head in Brian's direction. "I just couldn't pass up not knowing how you managed to cheat off me."

Brian stopped a few feet from Margaret. He took long deep breaths, as if he had sprinted the entire way, only slowing when he approached, not wanting to seem eager.

"Good, you came alone," he said.

"Of course I came alone. Who was I supposed to bring?" She cringed at the invitation she awarded Brian by her comment.

"I forgot, you don't have any friends," he said and snorted. A tiny amount of spit flew from his mouth. Margaret would have to add 'doofus' to the list of adjectives she used when describing Brian, she thought.

"I may be a doofus, but you're still a stupid twat."

Margaret began grinding her teeth before briefly shutting her eyes. She'd have to endure Brian's antics if she wanted to find out the truth, at least for now.

"I have to get home, so could you get on with it," she said, her left foot tapping impatiently.

Brian's face relaxed and a seriousness overcame him. "What are you going to do at home?" he asked.

"Pretend I never met you." A cool breeze swept through, pushing her hair into her face; it tickled. She swiped it aside with an annoyed haste.

"No, you aren't," he said.

"What the hell are you talking about, you loser?"

"You're going to go home, do your homework, then touch yourself and dream about Bobby Mildrum."

Margaret tried standing up too fast and instead flew off the log. She landed on her side, her cheek hitting the ground where some leaves were piled. She lay still for a few moments, not knowing what to believe.

Opening her eyes, she saw a millipede a few inches from her nose. The insect's many legs were working furiously to get away from her, not wanting to wind up like its friend, Mr. Spider.

Margaret sat up and wanted to refute her liking of Bobby, but that would only feed Brian's fire.

"Don't try to deny it. I read you like a book, even though I don't read them." Brian laughed at his own attempt to be humorous. "You like him. You want to make out with him, make babies with him." He was snorting now, loudly.

Margaret got up, dusted herself off and said, "I don't know who told you that, but it's not true." She stomped her foot like an angry child. "I'm leaving."

Brian reached out and grabbed her by the arm. His grip was strong, sending a tinge of pain into her forearm.

"Ouch," she yelled. "Let go of me, you toad."

"Don't you want to know my secret?" he asked, and let go of her.

"I don't give a crap about your secret," she said and turned to leave.

"I read minds," he blurted.

She froze, as if turned to stone like a Greek adventurer caught in Medusa's stare. What she heard was so ridiculously preposterous she wanted to giggle, but it was the only—as impossible as it was—reason for his A on the test.

"You're right, twat, it would explain my A."

Margaret spun around and met his stare. Her face was drawn and angry. She couldn't believe she'd actually fallen for such a tale.

"What am I thinking now, asshole?" she asked.

"How much you despise me," he said, before crossing his arms over his chest.

"That hardly requires telepathy," she said hotly, but felt weak inside. Her skin was warming, sweat was beginning to build around her hairline, and each gulp of air seemed more and more difficult to grasp. Reality was fading. She had to prove Brian wasn't telepathic. "What number am I thinking of?" she asked.

"Seven," he said with no hesitation. A smirk began to form on his chubby face.

Margaret was angry at herself for thinking of such a common number. Seven was usually the number people picked. She quietly changed it and was about to ask him again when he said, "Negative nine," his smirk becoming a huge grin.

Margaret's safe and predictable world was over. Everything would have to be different now. How could she compete against someone who knew people's thoughts? If mind readers were real, where were they? How many of them were out there? Was Brian some kind of a freak?

"I'm no freak," he answered her. "I'm important."

"You're weak!" she screamed as tears began to flow down her cheeks. "You're nothing but a cheater, a no-good-for-nothing-cheater!"

"You're the weak one, you're 'Ordinary.' That's what we call your kind because that's what you are, weak and ordinary. You're no match for my kind. I own you, Margaret Atwood." He beat his chest proudly like a gorilla. "I have a better question for you, Margaret. What color undies are you wearing or aren't you wearing any?"

She immediately thought of her underwear, the color and design. She flashed back to the morning when she picked them out. All Brian had to do was ask a question to get what he needed. It would be almost impossible not to think—at least for a second—about the answer to a question.

Mind readers would always know. She felt her body begin to weigh down under the emotional pressure that soared throughout her. Her mind would always betray her. She needed to act without thinking, keeping her mind on false images. She unzipped her purse, thinking the whole time she needed to keep talking. It was hard to think when talking aloud.

"Pink, with hearts, how cute," he said.

On top of all of her emotions, she now added embarrassment to the list. Brian had intruded in her mind, violated her inner sanctuary and all without laying a hand on her. She had to stop him.

"You shaved or natural?" he asked.

He was a pig. Worse than a peeping tom because at least they hid and tried not to be seen. He would keep on violating her, over and over. Margaret had to keep talking and keep her mind from thinking.

"Where did you get the ability to read minds?" she asked, after which she thought of a black ball suspended in space and hummed to herself.

"Passed down from my parents," he said.

"Couldn't have been long ago or you'd of been an A student all along," she said before returning to the black ball.

"My ability was recently grown into, as my parents like to put it. The same thing happened to them after they turned nine."

Margaret had her right hand in her purse. She found it difficult not to think of the task at hand, but kept concentrating on the black ball.

Flashes of her purse and some of its contents popped into her mind, but she managed to keep the ball focused almost all of the time. She had to keep him talking and let her fingers meander around the contents of her purse.

"Hey, what's with the ball?"

"What ball?"

"Oh, I get it. You're trying not to think of something so I can't read you." He took a step forward and was almost nose to nose with her. His breath stank of shit and cherries.

"I won't let you cheat anymore," she said angrily. "I work too hard for someone like you to come along and take it away. I'm the best, not some cheat like you. I was given a gift, too, the gift of brilliance. You're nothing but an abomination."

"Face it, Margaret. I'll be getting the good grades, going to the good schools, working my way to being president someday, and then eventually take over the world."

Margaret found the razor. Relief fell over her like a cooling wind on a scorching beach. Glimpses may have gotten through, but she kept focused on the ball.

She wrapped her little hand around the hilt. Her thumb slid along the cold steel, sending a shiver to the back of her head. She took the razor out of her purse and held it hidden at her side. Brian was too busy blabbing about his superiority to notice.

With the blade extended, she found its pleasurable vibe too strong to hide and let it out.

"You want to cut my throat with a razor?" He began to chuckle. It was an irritating laugh that turned into a snort, dislodging a loose booger, launching it at her. She watched as it sailed towards her, never taking her eyes off him. She ducked her left shoulder and narrowly missed getting hit by the projectile.

Brian's snorting chuckle slowed enough for him to add, "If only you really had one."

Margaret had been staring at Brian's sneakers. She looked up, her face taut and filled with death. She focused on her right hand, the one holding the weapon and smiled as she saw his face falter into a panic as he realized what was about to happen.

He tried backing away, but she was too quick. She slashed forward with the blade, striking him in the side of his neck. The blade's thirst was evident as it sliced its way into his jugular.

Margaret forced the blade down and across Brian's neck, where the blade slowed as it cut into his Adam's apple. It popped through as she added the required pressure, then continued on across his neck.

She managed to sever both the carotid artery and jugular vein on Brian's left side before pulling the razor free. Blood splashed her entire frontal region, but her face was caked, and she found it hard to see through the mess. She began wiping away his warm fluids.

Brian was grabbing at his mortal wound. He gurgled as he tried to breathe or speak, Margaret wasn't sure which. Blood spewed from the sides of his neck, but the middle of it was like an overflowing sink as the red liquid poured from the gaping slit.

Brian reached forward to grab her, but she backed away and slashed wildly at his hands. Most of his fingers lost the battle with the blade and went plopping to the ground.

Amazingly enough, his fingers had plenty of blood in them as they mimicked his neck, but in a far cuter fashion as the spewing was to a much smaller degree.

Margaret was in control finally. She had her place back, and rightfully so. She watched Brian fall to the ground, where he held his neck in a futile attempt at saving himself.

Margaret glanced around, making sure no one was watching.

She bent down and leaned close to his left ear. "There's no place for cheaters, but you go far beyond the norm, mister. The world will be safer without you in it, Brian Avine...and without your parents, too."

THE RIDERS

ERIC S. BROWN

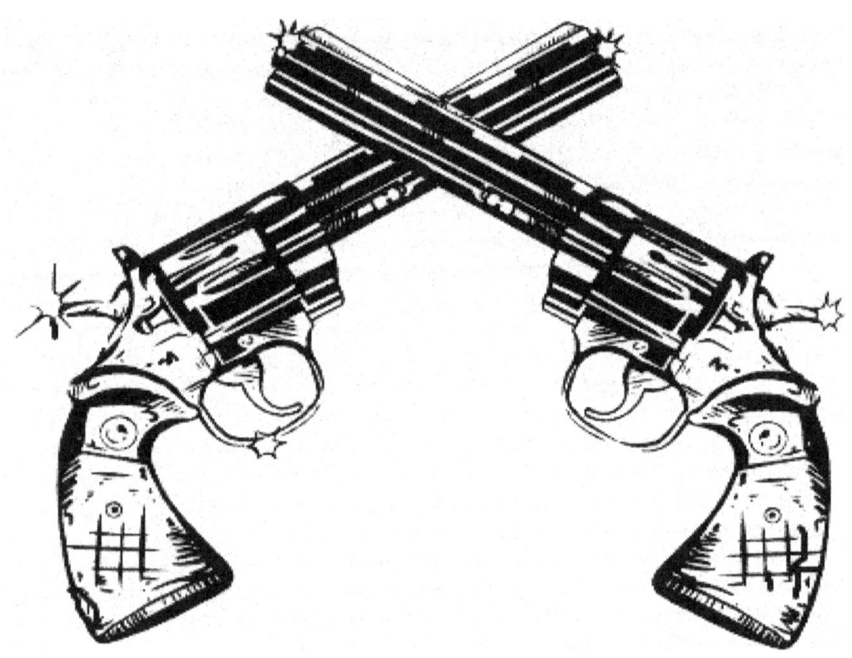

Buck sat on the porch. The heat of the day was harsh and he couldn't remember when the last rain had fallen. His eyes were red from tears and his breath stunk of moonshine. Three years had passed since the world was lost to the dead. Everyday was a struggle to get by. Even with the rationing of the first years, the supplies the city of Hyattsburg had started with were long gone. Everyone was relearning life. There were no longer things like the internet, corner coffee shops, or bookstores. Kristen was all Buck had now. Her love kept him strong and gave him the will to go on.

He could hear his wife coughing all the way from the porch as another spell hit her, and he knew there would be blood on the sheets and pillows when he went to check on her. A fresh wetness filled his eyes and he rubbed at them, then helped himself to another swig from the jar beside his chair.

"Hold on, honey! I'm coming!" he shouted, getting to his feet.

That was when he saw them. At first they were nothing more than a glimmer of movement on the horizon, but he soon recognized the tiny shapes as two riders galloping for his farm at a frantic pace.

Poking his head into the house, Buck called out, "Kristen, there's folks coming. Will you be all right for a minute?"

He heard her weakly croak the word, "Yes," followed by another bout of fierce coughing that must have shaken her entire body. Buck adjusted his gun belt and drew his revolver, checking the weapon's chamber. He slid the gun back into the holster on his hip. Trouble wasn't something he wanted, but he figured it was coming one way or the other. Closing the door tight, he turned and watched the riders as they approached.

The sheriff and Dr. Hall, one of the few military personal who'd traveled to Hyattsburg with the civilians when the town was being built, slowed their horses as they neared the house and came to a stop below the porch.

"Afternoon, Buck," the sheriff nodded at him, tipping his hat in his customary way. Dr. Hall sat silently and solemnly in his saddle, not meeting Buck's eyes.

Buck reached into the pocket of his shirt for his cigarette case and began rolling a smoke as he spoke to the two of them. "What brings you boys by, Sheriff? I know food is pretty scarce, but I can't make the crops grow any faster." Buck nodded at the sky. "With this weather, it'll be a miracle if we get anything out of them."

"We're not here about the crops," the sheriff informed him. "Come on, Buck, please don't make this any harder than it has to be for all our sakes."

Buck's hardness cracked for a brief second and the pain he felt was clear on his face. He stared at Dr. Hall. "If you can help her, do it, but I ain't about to let you murder her and toss her body on a pyre."

"Buck, I..." Dr. Hall started but Buck cut him off.

"You go check on her, Doc. The sheriff and I will wait right here."

The sheriff and Dr. Hall swung themselves from their horses and tied them up. Dr. Hall walked by Buck and into the house without saying a word. The sheriff stomped up the steps to where he stood and Buck saw him spot the jar beside his chair. "Mind if I have some of that? Been a tough day and a hard ride."

"Help yourself, Sheriff," Buck told him but kept his guard up. "She's all I have, ya know?"

"I know," the sheriff said sadly, taking a gulp of the shine. "I hope you understand this isn't personal, Buck. It's the law."

"Still don't make it any easier," Buck pointed out.

"No...no, it doesn't," the sheriff agreed, placing the jar back where he'd gotten it. "Look, Buck..."

"I don't want your pity, Sheriff. I just want Kristen well again. Ain't none of this stuff that's happened to the world fair. I reckon' everyone's lost their share, but there comes a point where a man has to stand his ground and just say he ain't losin' anymore."

The sheriff cleared his throat as Buck lit up the cigarette he'd been rolling and puffed on it, flipping the ashes into the dirt of the yard as they waited in silence for Dr. Hall to return. The minutes ticked by like hours until the doctor emerged from the house. Buck could see from his expression that the news wasn't good.

"How is she?" the sheriff asked.

"Bad," Dr. Hall informed them. "I can stabilize her for now, maybe do something for her pain, but that's it. At best, she's got days. She could pass on at any time."

Buck flicked the remains of his cigarette off the porch. "Stabilize her then. I'll take all the time I can get."

"That's not your decision to make, Buck. We can't risk you falling asleep and her getting up in the middle of the night. You know what has to be done."

"Reckon I do," Buck said. His hand moved like lightning, going for the gun on his hip. The sheriff was faster though. His Colt cleared its holster first and thundered. Buck felt the bullet slam into his shoulder, knocking his gun from his grasp, as the sheriff's Colt boomed again.

Blinding pain tore through Buck. A growing spot of red formed on his shirt just below his heart. He slumped forward to his knees with his hands clasped over the wound, trying to stop the blood from flowing out of him. Smoke drifted from the barrel of the sheriff's weapon as he kept it trained on him.

"I'm sorry, Buck. I really am," he said. "Kristen was a good woman. She truly was, but you and I both know it don't mean spit. If you die, you get back up as one of them. I have to think about Hyattsburg first. One of those things on the loose can become a dozen before you even know what's happening. You've seen it with your own eyes. That's how they won the war and we ended up here."

Buck grunted and tasted the salty bitterness of blood in his mouth. "At least you have to kill me now," he rasped.

"I know," the sheriff said, "and I'm sorry for that, too."

Buck smiled as he felt the cold metal of the sheriff's Colt touch the warm skin of his forehead. He looked up and the sheriff slowly pulled the weapon's hammer into place, chambering another round. "God be with you, Sheriff. You're gonna need him."

Buck saw Dr. Hall turn away, before his life ended with a flash and a clap of thunder.

THE EYES OF CORA VARS

JESUS "DARK RIDDLE" MORALES

THE DAY I MET HER

"No-o-o-! Damn it, no more autographs! I'm just trying to get some work done here," the ex-magician yelled.

Several teenagers turned their heads in disappointment and walked off angrily. Seeing a nurse coming his way, the TV star decided to take a more polite approach, feeling his needs might be met with more success if he were to act nicer.

"Sandi? The Amazing Sandi? That is you, right?" an orderly at the hospital asked.

Sandi, an elder Jewish man, took a look at the somewhat star-struck orderly and answered the black woman with his usual courtesy.

"That is I, little lady. What can I do for you?"

"Uhm, well, are you here to see someone? I know you're not a patient here, so if you're here to visit, you have to sign in."

"Yes, I'm here to see someone. A child, a girl they call Cora Vars."

"Cora Vars? The girl fortune teller?"

"Non other. Is there a problem?"

"I'm afraid I can't allow that. She's in a coma. The car accident she was in last night was a bit worst than they expected, the doctors I mean."

Sandi was a millionaire who gained his popularity and wealth by debunking people that claimed to be paranormal. He had successfully debunked a myriad of conmen: from magicians, ghost whisperers, escape artists, and zombie makers.

But there was a specific interest in his fascination for Cora Vars. The eight-year-old girl was practically worshipped in the small farm community where she came from. There, the nymph's supernatural influence was so prevalent that the townsfolk dared not look directly into her eyes for fear of seeing their future.

On the child's birthday, to commemorate their odd faith, they all wore blindfolds. For The Amazing Sandi, this oddity of small-town mass hysteria was one he couldn't ignore. So, he set forth to debunk yet another modem mythmaker.

Even so, he didn't expect the girl to be unconscious, let alone in a coma.

"Mr. Sandi? I'm afraid you'll have to leave if you don't have any further business here," the orderly said.

"Business? Oh, yes, business. Well, I can't very well break the law, can I? I mean, if I were to ask for just a glimpse of the girl, would that be so bad? Especially, if I were to *compensate* your efforts for my, uhm, unscheduled visit," he explained in a sly gesture.

Seeing that the popular man was handing over two one hundred dollar bills, the orderly hesitated before taking the money.

"Look, Mr. Sandi, I'll give you ten minutes with her. After that, whatever happens is on you, understand?" she said.

"Of course, my friend, all I want is a peek at her. I'm very curious about such people, as you may very well know."

The Amazing Sandi entered the hospital room and saw that the girl was alone and tethered to a host of small machines. Frail, with long blond hair and striking blue eyes, she seemed to be at peace.

As he drew closer to her, he felt a queer sensation in his gut, something he'd never felt before. The infamous skeptic was soon at Cora's bedside, where he looked at her face.

The girl's porcelain features seemed to reach out to him, and even though she didn't move her mouth, he could swear he heard a faint voice. It was then that he fell, while staring into the wild blue eyes of Cora Vars.

QUATRAIN #1
EUROPA, KANSAS

When Sandi rose, he wasn't himself. He could feel the reality around him, but somehow felt as if he were in a dream. He brushed dust from his clothes and took a look around.

He appeared to be in a rundown town, perhaps a rural region far from city adornments. Passing by a hardware store, he read the sign and dropped his jaw in shock. It read, **Lenny's Hardware. Open Since 2117.**

How could this be? Was he somehow kidnapped into the far future? He seemed to be the victim of an elaborate joke, but he wasn't thwarted. He enjoyed a challenge and this was a trick he would get to the bottom of yet.

"What the hell are you doing here? Are you crazy?" an old woman asked.

"Where am I?"

"Where are you? You're in Europa, Kansas, you dimwit! And you best be on your way, lest you wanna be lunch for the 9's!"

Sandi laughed, amused at such a wonderful hoax and illusion. "The 9's? What's that mean?"

"The devil dogs, man. The canines, the K-9's! Get it?" the rude woman said.

"Really, I'm a good sport, how did you come up with all this?"

"Dagnabit, you must be a real kook, I just told you the 9's are coming, fool. I'm heading off to sector 17, I suggest you do the same, you nut ball!"

Sandi watched the woman run to a beaten down vehicle, but gasped when he suddenly saw the scratched-up machine rise on an invisible rift of air.

It was clearly some kind of hovercraft. From that point on, the debunker of the paranormal was beginning to feel very afraid.

Suppose this really wasn't a hoax after all?

In the distance, he could see a wide dust cloud of red mist quickly blowing in from the south. It was very similar to the dirt tornados of the 1920's dustbowl, yet something ominous laced its approached.

Perhaps it was the bizarre hissing that seemed to grow louder as the dust cloud came closer.

"Hey!"

Sandi was startled by a weak tug on his arm. He turned around to see little Cora Vars, dressed in a weird red jumpsuit of some kind. She peered directly at him, but didn't seem to recognize him.

"Come on, come on, they come out of the dust! We need to get to Pegasus, fast!"

By now, the dust was upon them, yet its thin texture was so silken and powdery that he could still see fairly well through it. Cora pulled hard on his sleeves, as Sandi followed her past odd-looking barns and fields of tall corn stalks.

Reaching a rounded grain hut, Cora opened the door and pointed at a very strange vehicle. It was about fifteen feet long and segmented in parts.

The front consisted of a glass bubble cockpit with copper sides and what appeared to be bicycle handlebars.

"Can you ride a hover bike? My legs are too small to reach the pedals," she explained.

"Well, I can ride a bicycle."

"Good, then let's get in before."

R o-oo-agh!

A wide arch of blood flew past them and spattered across an adjacent barn. Sandi dropped to the ground, looking past the dust to see a mob of dark red creatures.

Some stood up in bipedal fashion, while others trotted around on all fours, savagely munching on human limbs. The wan sunlight passing through the dust clouds gave these creatures a truly hellish appearance.

"Good lord, what are those things?"

"They're the 9's! Now come on, we have to get into the Pegasus!" Cora cried.

The little girl pressed her hand on an oval slot and the door to the Pegasus opened. Both of them got into the hover bike as fast as they could, but they were unable to stop one of the wolves from latching on to the door. It stuck its gory head inside and grinned with a blood-ripping maw.

Black eyes and red fur rippled in evil delight. Sandi acted in pure instinct, kicking the creature in the head, sending the odd beast to the ground. It got up quickly, growling like a mad dog, but the Pegasus' door slid closed before it could get its claws on them.

Nevertheless, several of the creatures leaped upon the copper hover bike, viciously digging into the thin metal with their thick, sharp claws.

"Go, go!" Cora shouted.

Sandi crammed into the front of the vehicle, as he flinched at every ripping sound he heard on top of the bike's copper canopy. He sat on a comfortable seat and adjusted his feet to the pedals. Indeed, there was a bicycle somehow merged within the technology of the hovercraft.

While the demon wolves began to cause small cracks in the glass windshield, Sandi began peddling as fast as he could. In unison, the coppertop bicycle rose several inches from the ground and took off at surprising speed.

Obviously boosted by some other power source, Sandi's rampant peddling sent them rushing through the sinister dust cloud, while Cora kept her wide eyes glued on the window ports behind them.

"Hurry, hurry! They're gaining on us!"

But Sandi's panicked determination gave him the strength to pedal hard and fast, and soon, the vast mob of ghoulish wolves were slowly growing smaller in the distance.

Cora jumped up from the back seat and gave him a childish peck on the cheek.

"We made it, we really made it!"

Sandi sighed in relief. "Yes, we made it. We really made it!"

INTERLUDE #1

"We made it, we really made it!" Sandi mumbled as he squirmed on the hospital floor.

"Excuse me, sir, but you're not supposed to be in here!" a male doctor warned as he leaned over him.

Sandi awoke with tears in his eyes. "What happened? Where am I?"

"You're in Mount Sinai Hospital, in Cora Vars' room. I don't know who you are, but you need to leave, now!"

Sandi calmed himself, adjusting to the reality of his own world once more.

"Of course I'll leave."

"Wait," the doctor said. "Are you an epileptic? Perhaps you need help?"

"No. Thank you. I was just dreaming." He stood up.

The doctor gave Sandi an odd look and folded his arms as if waiting for some kind of more honest response.

"Well then, I'll be leaving now," Sandi replied casually. As he reached the door, he was urged to turn back, as if something wasn't yet finished. "I *am* leaving, Doctor."

"Really, what makes you think you can?" the doctor asked mysteriously.

"What's that supposed to mean? Of course I can leave. You're not going to stop me, are you?"

The doctor said nothing, then, after a long moment, he uttered one single phrase.

"Stop you. No, not me. Not *me*."

The doctor practically tiptoed out of the room, making sure not to disturb the strange girl.

"Doctor, wait! I *can* leave. Can't I?"

"I'm not sure, sir. You're the one who keeps staring into her eyes. Good luck, whoever you *were*."

At that, the doctor left the room, leaving Sandi and Cora alone once more. Sandi scoffed at the doctor's emphasis on *were*. It was a past tense word.

What could he have meant by that? Whatever the case, Sandi thought he had enough chills for one day and began to leave the room, but once again, a voice rang in his ears, and it pleaded with him to stay.

Spooked by his first experience, he tried forcing his will to leave, but the compassionate voice of a child stifled him. Now wasn't the time to leave it said.

He sucked in a brave gulp of air and moved back to Cora's bedside. A slight smile grew on the tiny girl's visage as he felt the shock again.

QUATRAIN #2
BOOMERS

"Let it be known, my faithful sheep, that God himself has cursed us all!" the moon man yelled.

"I, Pastor Kent Vars, have decreed that we will face the hordes and we will not flinch!"

Sandi found himself seated in the front row of a church of some kind. Far above the high, transparent ceiling, he could see the Earth, bright blue and white.

Along the side of the church, a gigantic maze of corridors, complete with a grand utopian look, careened from every which way.

Where am I now, Sandi wondered? He didn't know, but from his past experience, he knew to play along.

"We live on the killing moon now. But we will learn to hope again."

"Amen!" the hundreds gathered around him replied.

Sandi figured the church was being used as a sanctuary of sorts; but from what? As if his question were answered by evil itself, a ball of gray fur rolled into the hall. It was huge, ten feet in diameter, and rolled around like a rabid hedgehog. The tall preacher instantly gestured for his young daughter to take cover. Sandi recognized the youth easily—it was Cora Vars.

"Damn you to Hell, demon!" the angry preacher shouted as he pointed accusingly at the weird ball of gray fur.

To Sandi's shock, the fur ball stopped rolling about and unfolded, straightening out to form the shape of a six-legged wolf with a very scary, skeletal head. It blurted out a queer array of sounds, to which Sandi took as some kind of alien language.

"Blurgotta mo-butava!"

The pastor's eyes widened in shock, then, before he could run away, the werewolf exploded. People screamed in terror, as the wolf's eruption had caused a breach in the lunar skycap.

Sandi keenly observed the back of the ceiling slowly mending itself through some newfound technology, but not in time. The preacher, already bloodied and partially limbless from the werewolf's bang, was pulled out into the vacuum of space.

Cora cried out to her floating father, "Dad, Dad! Don't leave me!"

Blood was still dripping from the closing hole in the ceiling's skycap, when another four fur balls came rolling through the panicked aisles.

"Hit the deck, the Boomers are here!" an old man cried.

Sandi got up and ran toward Cora, frantically pulling the girl to the safety of a serving hall. As a series of loud bangs were heard, he realized he'd done so just in time.

Turning to peek across the curved bend of the white halls, he saw dozens of people blown to pieces...quite literally. The church hall was a grim mess of crimson gore and bloodstains. He and Cora watched, while the last few survivors slipped about clumsily on the guts and blood spatter of their church peers.

"Hey you, over here. More are coming. I know a spot where we can ditch these monsters," a heavyset woman said.

Little Cora and Sandi followed the woman, and ran though the illuminated aisles of the lunar mall. Minutes later, the three of them taking cover in a sports store.

"I'm Lana Mills," the woman introduced herself. "I own this store. Don't worry, those creatures can't see us through the flexi-steel. I had the cover shields dyed in one-sided stain."

"Can the Boomers break the glass?" Cora asked nervously.

"Only if they find us, but like I said, they can't see us through the door's shielding."

Lana noticed how distraught Cora was over losing her father. To distract the girl, she asked her to wait in the viewing room of the store's window front, where she could gaze at the stars above. While Cora did this, Lana focused her attention on Sandi.

"You're not from these parts are you, sir?" she asked.

Sandi answered carefully. "You can say that again."

Taking notice of his behavior, Lana watched him, while he picked up a long golf club. "Well, I'm waiting," he said, taking in a few deep breaths.

"Waiting for what, sir?"

"I noticed the blood and gray fur on your sleeve just after you locked us in here."

"Really, what are you implying?"

He didn't fall for Lana's puzzled look of innocence.

"This!" he yelled while slamming the golf club on her head.

The hit didn't do any damage to Lana other than making her angry. Sandi ran to collect Cora, but Lana took after him, strangely rolling after him in a ball, yet still in human form.

When she caught up to the two terrified humans, she straightened up and her skin began to peel from her face and body. First her clothes seemed to burn off, while steam and a dripping liquid slime covered her.

Within minutes, her face grew outwards and a deep skeletal appearance came into being. Fur sprouted from her body and two extra appendages budded from her ribs.

"Leave us alone, monster!" Cora cried, hiding behind Sandi.

"What do you want from us?" Sandi demanded.

"Just the sound that makes us."

The creature crouched in a tight stance, and let go with explosive results.

B-o-o-o-o-om!

INTERLUDE #2

Sandi flung back from the premonition dream so hard he nearly broke the window behind him. He opened his eyes to see Cora still lying in the bed in front of him.

"What do you want from me, girl?"

Cora said nothing, merely stared at the ceiling in a comatose look of inflection.

"What? You think I can't leave this room, little girl?" he retorted in salty anger.

He took a long gaze at Cora Vars, and then began to storm out of the room, but in doing so, he didn't pay attention to the many wires and tubes that fed into Cora's bedside. Tripping over an IV tube, he suddenly fell flat on her unmoving body. Now, involuntary face-to-face with Cora, his unintended gaze wrapped his soul into the future once more, despite his hardy refute.

"No. Not again!" he yelled, but alas, it was too late.

QUATRAIN#3
LIL' RED RIDING HOOD

Sandi awoke in the streets of some truly downtrodden ghetto. The new age buildings around him were tall and flickered against the sunset like beacons of a once great society. This new world was already a visage of tragedy.

Hundreds of windows were broken and stains of rancid rust and neglect were clear evidence that the city surrounding him hadn't been kept up in many, many years.

After walking the weed-infested streets, he came to a slanted road sign over a highway, indicating where he now resided. Sandi giggled frivolously in a slight sense of madness, while reading the sign aloud.

"Welcome to Detroit. Detroit?"

Reaching the curb of the debris filled street, he peered over Lake Michigan, which was covered with a barrage of rust-colored garbage and filth. It came to his mind that mankind had suffered some type of vast apocalypse, but one he could not yet recognize.

Even so, his observations of this future world were cut short when he heard the growling—lots and lots of growling.

"Oh, no you don't. You bastards aren't going to catch me unprepared this time!" he spat as he turned around in mad circles, trying to figure out where the growling was coming from.

But as he feared, the growling was coming from everywhere, from every stained concrete building, from every black alleyway, from the lichen covered rocks near the darkening lake side.

He was afraid, very afraid. The moon above him seemed giant, like an evil cosmic eye, staring into the depths of his soul.

Then he saw them, hundreds of unfathomable black shadows. They were tall and grisly looking with the pointed ears of furry devils' cowls. Indeed, the wolves were here again.

"Ha, what manner of werewolves are you godforsaken beasts this time!" Sandi shouted in a suicidal rant.

The creatures around him paused for only a second before they lunged forward. Like sharks about to embark in a feeding frenzy, a mob of seventy-four were-ghouls came ravaging toward him. Sandi paced about in circles, waiting for the inevitable tearing of flesh, but the ear pounding screeching of tires diverted the wolves' attention.

In an instant, half of the were-pack ran off for the cover of the lake side rocks and the darkness of the adjacent buildings beyond.

"What? Who the hell are you?" Sandi asked while looking at a slim-hooded figure on a bizarre motorcycle of futuristic design.

The rider didn't speak. A strange gun, adorned with odd graffiti runes, arose from the long sleeves of the mysterious person and fired. Wildly loud gunshots of burning buckshot raced past Sandi, tearing into the remaining werewolves surrounding him.

Sandi flinched as brain matter and rotting flesh splashed about him like some nightmare food fight.

The werewolves of this particular dimension were of a disgusting nature. They stood over ten feet tall and sported round heads and very zombie-like faces. Each had a pair of shark-like teeth that appeared to consist of several gory rolls.

"Hey, you moron, get your ass on the ground!" the dark red figure with a raspy female voice shouted.

In another moment of ear-popping gunfire, liquefied guts and hot cinders of powdery ash filled the air. Smoking corpses of irradiated zombie-werewolves littered the street with buckshot-puckered limbs torn every which way.

Yet even this macabre scene didn't deter some of the bigger wolf-ghouls, who were now collecting themselves for another lunging attack.

"Well, you idiot, are you gonna jump on or do I have to shoot you, too?" the slinky woman asked while driving her motorcycle toward Sandi.

He wasted no time. He leapt upon the vibrating back seat of the hooded woman's motorbike. The vehicle was long and black, and was striped in blood red swirls of spray-painted stencils.

Along its sides, glowing dark letters of some styled oddity shined like iridescent lamps. The bike was in chopper style, but had a weird biomechanical look about it. Quite simply, it was the coolest thing Sandi had ever seen.

"Hold on, and don't touch anything, old man!" the red rider yelled.

Sandi held on to the woman's waist as the heaving pull of gravity was thrust upon him, and the motorbike hurled forward, directly over the savagely mangled bodies of the zomboid werewolves just slain.

When Sandi accidentally flicked a lever on the bike's side with his leg, a pumping loud song from ages past suddenly saturated the air.

"Son-of-a-bitch! I told you not to touch anything!" the rider reprimanded. "Hell, leave it on, I love this song."

Sandi held tightly as his eyebrows narrowed. He knew the old song. It was from the band U2 and one that seemed to fit their circumstances in more than mere irony.

"*Where the streets have no name!*" shouted Sandi over the motorcycle's roaring engine.

"What?"

"I said I know this song: *Where the streets have no name!*"

"No, shit, old man. I know, I downloaded it with my Z-pod."

For fifteen minutes, they raced over desecrated roads of an apocalyptic city, racing past torn and tattered habitations long left abandoned by the world.

Every so often, Sandi could see a gathering of werewolves mounted on building roofs, and some that seemed determined to ambush them from the dark side streets, but the red rider's motorbike was a lightning fast, mean machine.

It sped up at intervals so fast, that he could feel his face reeling back from the G-force. Speeding away to the U2 song, they covered miles of terrain, until finally reaching some type of eerie fort.

With a wild turn of the brake, the motorcycle spun into a reverse parking position, and its momentum sent Sandi flying off. He hit the dirt and rolled several feet before stopping near the iron barred entrance to the dark fort.

"Oh yeah, I forgot to tell you I was gonna stop," the female rider said while her slim form leapt off the humming motorbike.

Sandi stood up slowly, brushing off dirt from his aching arms. "Yeah, you could have told me that."

"Sure, I could have, but then I would've missed you falling on your ass!" the hooded figure joked brazenly.

After letting her giggle fall silent, Sandi began his questions, as he still couldn't see the woman's face under the dark red hood. "Who are you?"

"Who am I? Who are you?"

"I'm The Amazing Sandi! I'm not from around here."

"Yeah, I figured as much, and amazing at what? Getting mauled to scraps by Muck-Puppies?"

"What are Muck-Puppies?"

"The damn zombie-dogs that were going to gulp you down like a paralyzed fish!"

Pulling her hood back, she revealed a beautiful face with familiar features, but Sandi's attention was drawn to her left eye, which consisted of nothing but a glossy ball of blue swirled glass.

"Your eye..."

"Shut up! It's a marble."

"A what?"

"I said, it's a damn marble. Nothing but a regular ole big blue marble. The real one got eaten by a Muck-Puppy."

"Oh, I'm sorry. And thanks, thanks for saving me back there."

"Thanks for what? You're human, right?"

"Yes, I mean, of course I'm human."

"Then that's reason enough. Every one of us matters now."

"How many of us are left anyway?" he asked.

"Oh, there are a whole lot of us, probably over a thousand."

Sandi felt a relief fill him. "Good, then this fort must be filled with soldiers. I suppose we can run those...Muck-Puppies as you call them, out of town in a few years."

"Nope."

"What do you mean?"

"It's just us here. Detroit is a No Man's land. That fort behind us is abandoned; been like that for years. No one lives in America anymore—well, no humans anyway."

"Then what the hell are *you* doing here?"

"Getting to Grandma's house, of course. You are slow, aren't you?" She chuckled. "After all, I am Little Red Riding Hood, or just a little red, riding in the hood, to be more precise."

"That's just great, a wolf hunter with cynicism," Sandi cursed.

"What's cynicism?"

"Oh, forget it. So where's this so-called Grandma's house you're talking about?"

The rider simply pointed her thumb casually at the rusty old fort.

"It's filled with all sorts of cool ammo. Hardcore techno type stuff, too. Come on, I figured a way to *jimmy* the porthole two days ago. We can rest in safety in there until I rustle up all the ammo I need to beat back the Muck-Puppies in this area. I always wanted a little place of my own, you know."

The red rider took off her robe, revealing an athletic body and sensuous shape that drew Sandi's attention. She fidgeted at a square lock on the small door of the fort, and soon they were both in a wide lounge, decorated with an assortment of dilapidated furniture.

"Hey, you, sit down!" the rider ordered.

Sandi smirked and sat down on a dusty couch, while the rider woman lit up a makeshift fireplace. Still, something didn't seem right to him. As he began to stand up, she leapt on top of him like a stalking panther.

Within seconds, he was pinned back on the old couch, while the rider held him in place with a very predatory smile on her face.

"No, don't eat me!" he begged.

"Eat you? Well, that's not exactly what I had in mind. Though I wouldn't mind it the other way around!"

"Then what? Hey, I know you!" Sandi exclaimed as the red rider began to undress.

"No, I can't! We can't do this!"

"Why not? You're still a man, aren't you?"

"But I know you, you're just a kid, you're Cora Vars!"

"I'm twenty-two, and no one calls me that anymore. Now shut up and take off your clothes!"

Safe in the deserted compound, the sounds of distant howling rang through the night as a predatory action of another sort was taking place. Even so, Sandi still felt the part of the victim, for the rider was wild indeed.

THE LAST INTERLUDE

Sandi woke up, throwing himself off the girl's body with a sense of shameful humiliation, though the face of Cora Vars, the child, had a very snarky smirk on it.

"That does it. I'm leaving here—for real this time. You're a witch, a futuristic witch!" Sandi shouted.

To his surprise, little Cora began to wake from her deep slumber.

"Puh—puh—p—please, don't leave, Sandi."

Surprised at the child's rapid recovery and supernatural prowess, Sandi stumbled backward in fear. What did this little monster want from him? Would she keep him in her spell forever? No. He would not—could not let that happen.

Without another second passing, he ran to the door, kicking it open and rushed out into the hospital hallway. There, things seemed ever so normal.

Doctors and patients alike did their ordinary things, cluttering around paperwork, or seeing to the ill. All appeared typical. Was everything he'd seen a mere dream? A trick of a child's very witty and keen manipulations? Was The Amazing Sandi finally fooled?

"What was that crazy kid trying to do?" he mumbled as he rapidly paced toward the exit.

Then suddenly it hit him. At first, he thought it was the sound of the roaring ambulance just outside the door. But no, he knew what it was when he heard it, the unmistakable sound, the unmistakable growling.

"Oh, my God. No!"

He finally realized what Cora Vars was doing and why she wanted him to stay with her so badly.

"She was protecting me. She was protecting me!"

As the background sounds of panicked people and wild screaming began, Sandi grimaced in sad tragedy. It had finally started and the world pandemic was about to take its first victim.

That's when he screamed.

LITTLE RED

JOE MCKINNEY

Vicki Sanchez and I sat in one of our agency's cars, watching the house from the street. It had rained earlier that evening and the air was thick and sweet with the smell of summer honeysuckle, and pulsating with the dull droning of crickets.

The house was a derelict set far back from the road, waist deep in weeds and partially obscured behind a screen of chinaberry bushes and huisache that had gone to seed. Dead, soggy leaves covered the roof. The front porch sagged from rot.

Vicki turned from the house with a sigh. "Well, I don't hear anything. Do you?"

I didn't answer.

"Alicia? Hello?"

Vicki had our case file open in her lap. It contained a week's worth of police reports and some photographs taken inside the house. During the previous week, the San Antonio Police Department had responded to nearly forty calls at this little abandoned house on Ashley Lane. Neighbors had reported hearing horrible wailing noises coming from inside the house. Some of them said it sounded like a child.

And that kicked the SAPD into high gear.

They searched the area, and they did find evidence a child had been living inside the house. Fairly recently, too. The floor was littered with pieces of rotten fruit, orange rinds and apple cores. There were toys. A rubber ball. A Tonka truck with the wheels chewed off. Part of the rubber seat from a playground swing. A grimy, mud-caked mattress.

But it wasn't the food or the toys or even the mattress that piqued my curiosity. It was what they found on the mattress that got to me. It was a filthy green tablecloth scrunched into a long, snakelike shape, one end curled back over itself like the head of a shepherd's crook. I'd been with the Texas Department of Child Protective Services for three years at the time. I'd seen a lot of blankets just like that in a lot of beds, and I knew exactly what it was.

A security blanket.

"Alicia?" Vicki asked. "Are you okay, sweetie?"

"Yeah," I said, and nodded.

"Are you sure? Because from here it looks like you're holding that steering wheel like it's the edge of a cliff."

I looked at my fingers. My knuckles had turned white.

"You're thinking about Janet again, aren't you?"

I started to lie, tell her no, I was fine, but there were tears coming down my cheeks. I wiped them away with the back of my hand and tried to laugh. "I guess I'm pretty transparent, huh?"

"Alicia, sweetie, you're not being fair to yourself. There's no way you could have known."

I'd been hearing that a lot lately. Five, six times a day, in fact. A few months earlier, we'd learned that five-year-old Janet Hernandez, one of my cases, was dead, starved to death by the first-time foster family with whom I had placed her.

In the office, our boss, Dr. Philip O'Dell, gave me the pep talk. "You're not being fair to yourself," he said. "You couldn't have known what would happen."

It made me sick every time I thought of it.

There are twenty-one investigators in my office, and between us we handle eighteen thousand cases a year. You do the math. How much individual attention do you think those kids get? We try to console each other by saying that our job is like standing in the middle of a river and being told you have to drink every drop that comes by, because every drop is a child's life. But it just can't be done. Not with the resources at our disposal.

But as impossible as it is, you still have to work the problem. And about eighteen months before Janet's death, one of my problems was her alcoholic mother, who used to spend her nights driving from one south side bar to the next, leaving Janet to sleep in the car while she went in and drank.

Janet's mom got busted for her fourth DWI, and while she was doing six months in the Bexar County Jail, I found a family that seemed like a nice temporary home for Janet. They were willing to do a job that nobody else wanted. I did the requisite number of surprise home visits and ran background checks and credit reports. They seemed okay. They passed. I decided to trust my instincts. I delivered Janet into their hands, and I walked away to attend to all the other cases that were stacking up on my desk.

But ten months later, I was standing next to Janet's autopsy table. Most of her hair had fallen out. There were deep shadows beneath her eyes and even deeper hollows in her cheeks. They tried to tell me that I couldn't have known what would happen, but I looked into her dead eyes and all I could do was whither beneath the voice roaring in my head, screaming at me that I had failed her.

And so, months later, I was back in the car with Vicki, my hands shaking and stiff from gripping the steering wheel, and I said, "Why did they have to hurt her? I would have taken care of her. I would have loved her."

Vicki, who's been doing this job for thirty years, didn't say a word. She just let me cry it out. When I was done she handed me a flashlight and said, "Are you ready? We have a job to do."

We got out of the car and walked up the drive to the house. I was in cream-colored linen slacks, a green blouse, and open-toed pumps. It certainly wasn't the best choice for traipsing through all those weeds and bushes, but it wasn't any worse than Vicki's lavender pantsuit and white tennis shoes. We looked more like mother and daughter about to raid a yard sale than a pair of state investigators with the legal authority to arrest.

The screaming started just as we reached the front porch. I thought nothing would ever be able to stir the part of me that had gone numb after Janet, but the screaming went right through me. I heard that long, warbling note of confusion, fear and loneliness and I sprinted up the steps.

"Alicia!" Vicki hissed. "No, don't."

I mounted the three steps at the base of the porch in a single jump, landing on rotten boards that sagged beneath my weight. The wood groaned and popped, and the wailing stopped.

"Alicia," Vicki said.

She was standing at the foot of the stairs, breathing hard.

"I'm going in," I said.

"Alicia…"

I pulled the front door open and poked around with my flashlight beam. The floor was damp. Trash was scattered everywhere. I saw crumpled paper, sheets of dirty plastic and a syringe here and there. The place was thick with the smell of rot.

We moved inside. There was a bedroom off to the left. It was trashed like the living room, but empty. Straight ahead was the kitchen. Beyond that, a doorway that didn't have a door led into a tangle of densely overgrown huisache and guajillo. I could just see the dog park through the bushes.

The house was silent.

I went to the kitchen, where the cops had found the mattress, and there, in a gap between the countertops and the wall, in the spot where a refrigerator had once stood, was the child. He was naked, his skin a fiery red and covered with warts of all different sizes. His nose was skinny as my finger and just as long. It hooked down to a point that extended over his upper lip and looked far too fragile to be real. The ears reminded me of dried ancho chili peppers, but with thick tufts of hair growing out of the center. His eyes were large for his face and almost completely black, but they sparkled in the flashlight beam.

One look at me, and he began to hiss and spit. Like his eyes, his mouth was too big for his face, and when he drew back his lips I could see two enormous rows of sharp, yellow teeth.

I knew what he was. So did Vicki. Still, despite my training, I had never seen a real goblin before. Kneeling down in front of him, I said, "My name's Alicia Driscoll. Can you tell me your name?"

I held out my hand, palm up, trying not to convey a threat. His lip twitched at the corner of his mouth, and I caught a glimpse of his tongue, dark as a chow's. He snapped at my hand, and I barely pulled it back in time.

"Oh my," Vicki said from behind me.

"He's scared, Vicki."

"Hungry too, I'm sure."

"I bet you're right." Glancing around the floor, I saw the rotten pieces of fruit the cops had described. "I've got something he might be able to eat out in the car."

"No," she said, her hand on my shoulder. "You stay here. I'll get it. You're keeping him calm."

The little boy flinched when Vicki walked out of the room, and for a second I thought he might try to run for it.

"No!" I said. "No, no, no. It's okay. She'll be right back. Nobody's gonna hurt you."

His body was an improbable combination of squat legs, long arms and a thin, bony chest, and there was a furious electrical tension running through him that reminded me of a rattlesnake just before it strikes. I sensed the capacity for great strength in him.

"My name is Alicia. What's your name?"

I smiled at him. He tilted his head, as if he didn't know what to do with an expression like the one I was making. For a moment, the violence faded from his face. The muscles around his mouth relaxed.

Vicki surprised him when she reentered the room and the boy scrambled into his corner, lips pulled back from his teeth, eyes suddenly wide and feral. He made a hissing, popping noise, like an angry cat.

I took an orange from my lunch sack and showed it to him. "Let me peel it for you," I said. But before I got the chance, he snatched it from my hand and bit right through the peel. In seconds, there was nothing left but a bit of rind and a few wet ropes of orange spit hanging from the knobby point of his chin. That big dark-colored tongue of his licked the juice from his face, and he looked at me in surprise, the way a child tasting chocolate cake for the first time does.

"You like that, huh? Are you still hungry?"

He looked from the bag, to me, and back to the bag again.

"I guess so," I said. He leaned forward and tried to take the sack from me. "Easy. I've got more."

I took out some celery and some carrots. I put the carrots on the floor in front of him and he wolfed them down. Then I took a single celery stick and held it out for him.

"Go on," I said. "Take it. It's okay."

Once you've worked with abused children, you learn to recognize the look, the mistrust, the fear of an adult's hand—even one offered in kindness. That was the look I got from the little boy.

But hunger is a powerful motivator, and eventually he reached out and snatched the celery stick from my hand.

As he ate, Vicki said, "You know what he is, don't you?"

Our eyes locked on one another, that little boy's and mine, and I think it was at that moment when I named him, at least in my mind.

Little Red.

"Of course I do," I said. "He's a child."

"I can see that," Vicki said, and knelt down next to me. Her knees popped like pistol shots and she winced. Then she looked at me. "Alicia, what are you doing?"

"He's hungry, Vicki. I'm feeding him."

"Alicia, he's a goblin child. There are protocols for this sort of thing. People we have to notify. I don't need to remind you of that, do I?"

Red had started to coo softly. I reached out and touched his face, his left ear, his neck.

"I won't turn him over to those bastards from the federal government, Vicki. I won't. You know what'll happen to him if I do."

"Alicia, if they find out that..."

"If they find out they'll murder him. They'll come in here with their soldiers and they'll wipe the place clean. It'll be just like Evansville, Indiana in '96. You've read those reports. I know you have. I can't have that on my conscience, Vicki. I won't."

A long silence followed. I hadn't meant to snap at her.

"Alicia, I know why you're doing this. Believe me, I do. I understand the need, the guilt. But don't fool yourself. This won't change what happened to Janet."

I fed Red another piece of celery.

"What are you going to do, Alicia?"

"I'm going to take the rest of the week off," I said.

"And you're going to do what with your other cases?"

I just looked at her, my expression blank. Beside me, Red dabbled at the celery juice on his lips with a rust-colored fingernail.

"We're taking him with us, then?"

"Yes," I said. "To my house."

At my place, I put Red in a chair at the kitchen table and went to the refrigerator to find him something else to eat.

I didn't hear him get down.

I found some white flesh nectarines that looked good, but when I held them up to show him, he was gone.

"Red?"

From my study, I heard a loud, furious stuttering noise, like a cat working up a hairball.

"Red!" I shouted, and ran for the study. He was there, but he wasn't choking. He was barking at a painting I'd been working on, a still life of a fruit bowl. Heavy on the reds. Pomegranates and crabapples, mostly.

"Well, it's not great I know, but give me a break, would ya?"

Red waved his arms in the air and barked some more. Then he stuck his hands out at me, opening and closing them rapidly, like he was signing the word for milk.

"Okay," I said. "If you want to see it that badly."

I took the painting off the easel and lowered it down to his level. I was about to point at the fruit and tell him what everything was when he lunged at the picture and ripped the canvas to shreds with his fingernails. There was barely time to flinch, and before I could stop him, he had a big wad of it in his mouth.

"Spit that out!" I said, and snatched at a shred of canvas hanging from his lips. "That's bad. That's oil-based paint. That's yucky." I made a sour face. "Yucky."

Red just stared at me, confused and maybe even a little hurt.

"I'm sorry," I said. "Here, I'll tell you what. You want a pomegranate? Come on."

He let me lead him by the hand into the kitchen.

"Now you stay in that chair. You hear? This'll just take a second."

I got the bowl of pomegranates and crabapples from the fridge and set it on the table. Then I got a knife and a cutting board and put them on the table, too. "This is called a pomegranate," I said, holding it up for him to see. "Can you say pomegranate?"

He was making an odd noise, an impatient sort of deep breathing. His eyes never left the fruit in my hand.

"The good part is on the inside. The seeds are yummy." I rubbed my belly and made a happy face. "Yummy. Let me get a bowl of water."

He snaked the pomegranate from my hand. One moment it was there, the next I was blinking at my empty palm. While I watched, Red gripped the fruit like some kind of maniacal squirrel and tore into its nutlike rind with his teeth, shredding it to pieces. When he finished it, shell and all, he jumped up and down on the chair, motioning wildly for more.

"Okay, okay," I said. "Just go slow, okay? It's not healthy to eat big bites like that. You could choke."

He ate the last two pomegranates, then started on the crabapples.

"I've never seen anybody eat those things and actually enjoy them," I said. "But okay. If it makes you happy."

His face colored a vibrant red, bright as a holly berry, and his eyes almost rolled up into his head. He was in ecstasy.

"Yeah, your name is definitely Red. Is it okay if I call you that?"

He put another crabapple in his mouth, stem and all, and stared up at me with bright, shining eyes.

My heart went out to him.

He kept me up late that night. I couldn't get him to sleep. I made him a bed with fresh sheets and a big soft pillow, but he wouldn't have anything to do with it. Instead, he backed all the way into the farthest corner of my closet and stared at me from the dark. All I could see was a pair of pale yellow eyes and the faint outline of his face peeking out from behind an old shoe rack.

"It's okay," I tried telling him.

But I wasn't getting through to him.

I changed into my PJs, crawled into bed, and turned out the lights.

That's when the whimpering started. It was soft, sad, insistent, and there was no way in hell I was going to be able to sleep while he was doing it.

I turned on the lamp next to my bed, and the whimpering stopped.

"Are you okay?" I asked.

Nothing.

"I'm turning out the lights."

I waited. When he didn't answer, I turned off the lights again.

The whimpering started all over.

Finally, I just left the lamp on and fell asleep, too exhausted by the day and the stress of thinking about the cases waiting for me when I returned to work, to fight with Red about a nightlight.

I don't know how long I slept after that, but it had to be close to morning when I woke up again. I felt hot, stifled, and there was a strong musky odor in my nostrils that made my face crinkle up like I just licked the bottom of an old shoe.

Red was sleeping next to me. His eyes were closed, but there was a look of contentment and security on his face that quickened something inside me. I have heard people say—sometimes while flinching with embarrassment, like they're admitting something shameful—that watching their children sleep is the only time they truly feel like a good parent. I had always thought that was an odd statement for a parent to make, but as I put my arm over him and drifted off to sleep, I thought maybe I understood.

"So, where is he now?"
"At my place. Vicki's watching him."
Debbie Tibbits nodded. Debbie manages a used bookstore near my house. We met in grad school back when we were both in our mid-twenties and hell-bent to make the world a better place. Or maybe a best friend is too strong of a phrase for someone like me. Between my sixteen hour days and going three weeks at a time without a day off, best friends are kind of hard to come by.

But if anyone could understand where I was coming from, I figured it would be Debbie Tibbits. We worked together at Child Protective Services after grad school (Vicki had trained us both, in fact), but her term there didn't last long. She quit shortly after her version of Baby Janet. For her, it was a young boy named Juan Escarole, and he wasn't starved to death, but strangled with an electrical cord and thrown into a dumpster behind a furniture warehouse. The mother's boyfriend told Debbie Juan just ran away, and he went on denying it even after Debbie got a surveillance video from the store and a search warrant for the boyfriend's car.

She had her ghosts, same as me.

Her hand drifted to a weathered paperback copy of John Irving's *The Water-Method Man*. The cover looked like it had been chewed by a mouse. The spine was curved, cracked and peeling. She pushed the book around with her finger, "Do you want this? I can't sell it in this condition."

"Debbie, come on."
"Oh, all right. Yes, I think I know somebody I could call."
"Who?"

"A friend. She's in here all the time. Buys books on stuff like this."

I had shown her some printed photos I'd taken with my digital camera. Before and after shots involving the destruction of a head of iceberg lettuce that I thought were absolutely adorable, little shreds of greenery hanging off his nose.

"They write books about kids like Red?" I asked.

Debbie rolled her eyes. "You're trying to be obtuse," she said. "She buys books on, you know, strange creatures. Honestly, Alicia, I don't see why you don't just get a cat. It'd be a whole lot easier."

"You don't get it, do you?"

"Yes," she said, "I get it. I understand. Look, I'm your friend, okay? I mean that. But you've got a lot of weird shit going on. You know that, right? You're taking what happened to Janet and you're trying to fix it by adopting a child that isn't even human. You're stepping away from your humanity, Alicia. This...this isn't going to make things any better. You know what they'll do if they catch you? We're talking serious jail time here."

"Debbie," I said, "I know what I'm doing. I appreciate what you're saying, but that's not what's going on here."

She just stared at me.

"I promise," I said.

She wasn't convinced, and she didn't try to disguise it.

"You sure you don't want this?" she asked, and pushed the Irving book at me one more time.

"Debbie!"

"Okay, okay."

"Will you call your friend? Please?"

When I let myself in my front door Vicki was sitting on the couch, knitting a scarf. She glanced up at me and smiled. I listened for a second, then closed the door. The house looked to be in one piece.

"How'd it go?"

"Fine," she said.

"No problems?"

"Not a one. He was really sweet."

Wow, I thought. Truth be told, I kind of expected to find her clinging to the light fixtures when I came home, Red beneath her, snarling and yapping.

"Is he sleeping? I don't hear anything."

"Yeah. Poor little guy was tired. I put him in your guest room about an hour ago. He's been quiet as a mouse ever since. You know, I think a couple of good meals have really done him some good."

That made me smile. I put my purse down on the table in the entryway and kicked off my shoes.

"What'd you guys do?"

"Well, he ate. A lot, to tell you the truth. He must go through a lot of fruit."

"He does," I admitted.

"I've actually never seen any one eat crabapples like that before."

"Yeah. Cute, isn't it?"

She hesitated.

"After that I gave him some coloring books and he really went to town on those. You know, I think green is his favorite color."

"Green? Really?" I thought of what he'd done to my still life with pomegranates and crabapples, all those reds, and shrugged.

"I left some of his drawings on the table for you," she said. "He's a natural."

"Oh yeah?" I went into the kitchen, eager to see what Red had done, but the table was empty. "Vicki?" I said, looking back at her on the couch.

She put down her knitting and followed me into the kitchen. "What's wrong?" She stared at the table. "Oh. Uh, I don't understand. It was all right here. Alicia, I swear. It was all right here."

I ran to the guest room door and stopped, my hand on the doorknob, listening.

Nothing.

I looked back at Vicki, who had just trotted up behind me.

"Is he in there?" she asked.

"I don't know."

I took a deep breath and opened the door, terrified that he had managed to get out of the house and run off into the night. My neighbor, Mr. Everett, had this horrible pit bull named Elvis. The thing was a chainsaw with a tail. In my mind, I saw the dog getting a hold of Red and it nearly made me sick.

That is, until I saw Red standing—perched, really—on top of the wrought iron foot rail of the guest bed. It was a girly little twin-sized bed, painted white, and his toes were wrapped tightly around the iron rail, like a giant brooding bird on a wire.

I let out a heavy sigh of relief. Only then did I notice the room. Vicki wasn't kidding when she said green was his favorite color. Red had not only taken his artwork from the table, but his crayons as well—and he had gone crazy on my walls. The whole left side of the room was alive with the Crayola Company's world of green—Granny Smith Apple, Electric Lime, Sea Foam, Shamrock. Even a few swipes with a brownish-green that might have been Asparagus. I needed a long moment to take it all in.

"Alicia, I'm sorry," Vicki said. "He was so quiet. I thought...I really did think he was asleep."

How many times have I heard parents say the same thing? The only time you really need to worry is when they're quiet.

I turned my attention back to Red. He made that same soft cooing noise I'd heard the night we met, only this time it was punctuated with an odd, occasional clicking sound I could have sworn was him asking what I thought of his artwork.

Vicki started to apologize again, but I shushed her with a wave of my hand. She hadn't seen it yet, but I had. The eyes were all wrong, too big, too round, and I hoped my cheeks weren't that chubby in real life, but he had definitely caught the small upturn at the tip of my nose. The shape of my mouth.

"I love it," I said, and the clicking stopped, melting into a sort of contended hum.

I thanked Vicki and sent her home. It took me forever to convince her that it really was okay about the room, that I really wasn't angry. She apologized over and over as she packed her knitting stuff, then again on the doorstep, and yet again at her car when she turned to wave goodbye.

"Go home, Vicki," I called after her, and gave her a big smiling wave good night.

"Good night."

She got in her car and closed the door and I heard angry barking. Mr. Everett and Elvis the pit bull were turning up his driveway from their evening walk. Everett was dressed in striped linen shorts in green, yellow and tan, a threadbare t-shirt tucked into the shorts, black socks, and white tennis shoes. I could see the hairs on his enormous kettle belly through the thinness of his t-shirt. Elvis wore his collar and a red bandana.

He was straining at the leash, right at the edge of my yard, snarling and growling and flicking white foamy bits of spit all over the grass. I tried not to look scared, but I didn't do a very good job of it, and of course I couldn't hide it from Everett. I looked from his dog to him and saw him smile, obviously enjoying my discomfort. "Asshole," I muttered, and went inside and closed the door.

Red was at the living room window, watching Elvis through the blinds with great interest.

"Red," I said. "Come away from there."

He looked up at me with an expression that was pure disappointment—but he did as I asked.

"Don't make that face at me," I said. "You know as well as I do what would happen if that man saw you."

Red went into the kitchen and stopped in front of the refrigerator. But on the way, as he passed me, he gave me the strangest look. His skin grew intensely red, like a fresh chili pepper, and if I didn't know better, I'd have sworn the smile on his face was the beginning of some mischievous plan.

Of course, in light of what came later, I should have known that's exactly what it was.

He slept that night on a pile of my dirty laundry.

At first I tried to get him back into the little bed on the floor near my own bed, but he just sniffed at it and looked up at me as if to say, "*What do you expect me to do with that?*"

"It's for you," I said. "To go night-night."

He pulled himself into my bed.

"No," I said. "Red, I'm sorry, but you can't sleep in my bed. Not tonight. I couldn't sleep at all last night." I patted his bed. "Will you please sleep here tonight?"

He turned his nose up at the bed and then ran to the corner where I kept a laundry basket full of clothes waiting to be washed. He jumped into the basket and sat down, then he looked at me. His smile was ear to ear—which, considering the size of his mouth, was literally true.

"You're not sleeping in my dirty clothes either," I said.

He reached into the basket, took out one of my gym socks, and threw it at me.

I batted it away and tried to look serious. "No," I said. "You're not going to sleep in my laundry. Now come out of there."

Another sock flew at my head.

I picked him up and carried him back across the room, putting him in the bed I made for him.

He looked at me, pouting, then threw back his head and bayed like a coyote, a high, wailing sound that was enough to carry next door and get Elvis' attention. From the backyard, the dog began to bark furiously.

Red stopped baying and listened to Elvis carrying on.

"Yeah, you hear that? We have to be careful, baby. No loud noises like that, okay? You hear me?"

He jumped out of his bed, loped across the floor, and emptied my laundry into a pile. Then he jumped into the spilled clothes and snuggled down and sighed like a cat who's just found a shaft of afternoon sunlight in which to sleep.

It was a battle I wasn't going to win. In the end, I settled down into my bed and he in his, while Elvis went on barking his stupid head off.

I woke hours later. It was dark in my room and my feet were wet. Two thoughts went through my head at pretty much the same time. First, that Red had crawled back into bed with me, and second, that he peed on me.

Oh no, I thought.

I groped at the bedside table for the lamp switch.

Red was perched on the foot rail of my bed, staring at me. He smiled, and his teeth were wet with what looked like blood. On the bed, just beyond my feet, was the body of Elvis the pit bull. He was on his side, his belly and paws pointed towards me, his head cranked backwards and away from me at such a violent and improbable angle that he was obviously dead.

A scrap of his red bandana was hanging from one of Red's toenails.

Red leaned forward and nudged Elvis' body towards me. A gesture that said, *"Go ahead, it's for you."*

I tried to speak, but it felt like I had a softball jammed in my throat.

He stepped from the foot rail and waddled over to the dog's tail. I saw his hand come up, the nails dirty and pale yellow, despite the fact I'd scrubbed them with soap and lots of warm water earlier that day, and before I had a chance to look away, he had torn off one of Elvis' back legs.

Red held it out to me with one hand, while making the *yummy-yummy* sign over his little warted pot belly with the other.

I made it to the sink in time, but only just.

Elvis weighed, near as I could tell, about seventy pounds. I put him in a plastic garbage bag, tied off the ends, and hefted him out to my garage, where my car was waiting with the trunk open.

Turns out those garbage bags aren't as strong as they say they are.

I felt the bag sag, then it split open, and a mutilated Elvis oozed out onto my feet with a wet-sounding slop.

I groaned in between dry heaves.

Clean up was painful.

Debbie Tibbits called her friend, the self-proclaimed expert on cryptozoology, just as she promised, and the woman agreed to meet with us the following afternoon at Debbie's book shop. Her name was Jeanne Manchester.

She was in her early fifties, still pretty, like Jessica Lange, with a thick head of steel gray hair that went down to the middle of her back. She wore a dress made of layered silk in green, crimson and yellow. Over that she had a shawl that rattled with innumerable golden coins, like chain mail courtesy of Vera Wang. There were bangles on both her wrists, and large, cascading earrings. They looked like the cheap beaded curtains in the doorway of a Bowery whorehouse, hanging down to her shoulder.

Good God, I thought, *the gypsy queen.*

She frowned at Debbie and me and said, "You did a very stupid thing, Ms. Driscoll."

"I'm sorry," I replied. "What is it, exactly, that you think I've done?"

"You know perfectly well what I'm talking about. Why would you take that thing into your home? What were you thinking?"

Well, that pretty much floored me. If there had been any chance of feigning innocence, it was gone with the look of guilty surprise on my face. Up until that point, I hadn't really given much thought to what I was going to say at this meeting Debbie had set up. I did know I had no intention of telling anyone else about Red. I guess I figured I would pretend I'd snapped the pictures I showed Debbie while I was out on a call, and I was merely curious what it was I had captured on film. But I'd done a stupid thing, and I realized it now.

"Alicia," Debbie said, "I had to. She saw the pictures and knew what it was right away. She said your life was in danger. I'm sorry, Alicia. I had to."

I didn't say anything.

"If she hadn't told me everything," Jeanne Manchester said, "I would have gone to the police. I assure you, your friend did the only thing she could do."

I tried to speak but I couldn't. I was so mad. I was mad at Debbie for telling this woman my secret, and I was mad at myself for betraying Red. I wanted to tell Jeanne she was wrong, that I wasn't the one in danger, Red was. But I couldn't. The words caught in the back of my throat and choked me.

"This really is for the best," Jeanne Manchester said. "There are countless species of dangerous creatures in the world, Ms. Driscoll.

Our government won't admit they exist, but they're out there. Goblins are the worst of the worst. They're savages. Horrible, brutal creatures who rejoice in nothing but killing."

"Sounds like some people I know."

From the look she gave me, I guessed she already knew about Janet. "Tell me, has it started to hunt yet?"

That stopped me. I thought of Elvis at the foot of my bed, of running to the sink to vomit. But there was no point in lying. Once again my expression said it all for me.

"I was afraid of that," she said. "Ms. Driscoll—Alicia—this is important. You don't have much time. We have to get that thing back to its own kind immediately. The sooner the better. Goblins are fiercely protective of their young. If they find you keeping one of their own as a pet, they *will* kill you. They'll find their offspring and they won't stop to ask if you're protecting it or trying to harm it. They won't care. They'll simply rip you to pieces. You can be assured of it."

"But he's just a child," I said. My voice was shaking. Red would never hurt me. I felt that to the core of my being. I could picture his face, those round, yellow eyes of his, the way the color rose in his cheeks and forehead when he cooed at me, and I knew he would never hurt me.

Perhaps she could guess what I was thinking, because when she spoke again, her sarcasm was touched with an unmistakable note of tenderness.

"You wouldn't make a cobra a pet, would you? Well, that's what you've done. Worse than that, in fact. The cobra can't pretend to love you. But the goblin, it *can* fool you. Do the smart thing, Ms. Driscoll. Get rid of this thing before it kills you."

There was really nothing more to say, and our meeting broke up shortly after that. We made plans to meet at the little house on Ashley Lane later on that night and then Jeanne Manchester left, leaving Debbie and me alone.

"Alicia," Debbie said.

I wiped my eyes with the back of my hand and looked at her. She was staring back at me, eyes wide and shining, swallowing nervously. She was wondering, I'm sure, if our friendship would survive this.

"How could you do this to me, Debbie? I asked you for help." I pointed towards the front door, where Jeanne Manchester was walking across the parking lot to her car, her outfit a blaze of yellow and copper in the reflected sunlight. "I didn't ask for *that*."

"Alicia, please. I told her because I was trying to help you. I promise you. Alicia? Baby, this isn't a Christina Rosetti poem you've stumbled into. This isn't some fall from grace or a loss of innocence. This is way more. This is your life we're talking about. She's trying to save you."

"Debbie, imagine you have a hole inside you big enough to drive a truck through. Now imagine you've found someone who not only fills that hole up, but fills it to the point of overflowing. That's what you're asking me to give up. Do you know, I haven't cried for Janet in two days? That doesn't sound like much to you, I know, but it's my personal record."

Debbie waited a long time before answering. "Alicia, do you hear yourself? Do you really hear what you're saying?"

I knew a guy in college who liked to get stoned and listen to Pink Floyd for hours on end. His favorite album was *The Wall*, and as I stood there thinking about Red, I flashed back to listening to his music in a darkened room, pot smoke curling around my head like a thick wool scarf, and I wanted to build a wall of my own, one just big enough for Red and me.

"Alicia?"

"I hear you, Debbie."

"Baby, I don't think you do."

"I love him, Debbie. Don't you think that's enough?"

"No, I don't. I'm sorry, Alicia, but I don't. What you're doing here isn't right. You're taking your grief over Janet and you're calling it love, and you're giving it to a creature that can't possibly love you in return."

"You have no idea, Debbie. You don't know what this has been like for me."

That stopped her cold. She looked at me, mouth open, eyes shining with incipient tears. "You fucking bitch. How can you say that to me? Alicia, goddamn it, this is me you're talking to."

"Debbie, I...Debbie, I'm sorry. This is killing me. I can't do this."

She sniffled and wiped her nose with the back of her hand.

"It's not fair," I said.

"No," she said. "It's not."

Red and I spent our last few hours together on the couch, watching Scooby Doo on the Cartoon Network. He was absolutely crazy about that dog, and went nuts every time he was on the screen.

I knew we were going to take him back to the dog park, and there would be people there, so I dressed in a little t-shirt and jeans before I drove him to the house on Ashley Lane. We stopped in front of the house and he looked at me, and it took everything I had to keep from putting the car back in gear and blasting away from there.

"Don't look at me like that. You know we can't stay together. You've got to be with your own family."

He clicked his tongue a few times, but it wasn't like before. It was rapid fire, and there was a note of fear and loss to it that I felt as clearly as if he'd put it into words.

Debbie and Jeanne were waiting next to Debbie's minivan. Debbie was dressed in blue jeans, tennis shoes, and a beige t-shirt with the City Lights Bookstore logo on it, her hair tied back in a pony tail. She looked, clothing-wise at least, like she was ready for this.

Jeanne Manchester, on the other hand, was dressed like some kind of reject from a Johnny Weissmuller Tarzan film. Her outfit consisted of khaki cargo pants, a deep sapphire blue flannel shirt, a khaki safari vest that was covered with pockets, and to hold down the dense gray bulk of her hair, an Afrikaner campaign hat. The ancient pair of bifocals still hung from the beaded chain around her neck.

She said, "I brought a dog crate. I assumed you wouldn't bring anything to contain the, uh, creature."

"We're not putting Red in a dog crate," I said. I looked to Debbie for support. "Help me out here, Debbie."

No help there.

"We're not putting him inside a crate," I said.

"Alicia," Debbie said, "it's for his own good."

"There's that phrase again. Would you people please stop saying that? It's all I've heard for the last two days. Jesus!"

"You are impossible," Jeanne said.

Beside me, Red made a loud popping sound in his throat, like an overloaded electrical outlet about to short out.

Jeanne backed away from him, clearly alarmed, then she looked at me. "You still think that this is a child we're dealing with. It's not. It's a monster. You may be willing to risk your life on a delusion, but I won't do it. Cage that thing. It's in everybody's best interest."

That put me over the edge. I was tired. I was frustrated. I was mad at the world for being such a mean and nasty place, and I took it all out on Jeanne Manchester.

I lunged for her, missed, took a swipe at her with my fingernails, missed again.

She moved quickly for somebody in her fifties.

"Alicia!" Debbie yelled. She stepped between us and got an arm across my chest to hold me back.

"Alicia," she said. And again, "Alicia!" when I wouldn't look at her. "Alicia, please."

"Tell her to get away from me," I hissed.

"Alicia, stop. Look at me."

I did.

"Alicia, look, you're right. Okay? You're right. No dog crate. Fine. Just, please, no fighting. We're all way out in Weirdsville here. I mean, what the hell, right? We're about to release a goblin back into the wild." She waited for me to calm down, then said, "Let's just do this thing."

Reluctantly, I nodded.

"If you won't cage him," Jeanne said, and paused menacingly, "then I won't be responsible for what happens."

"Come a little closer and say that," I dared her.

"Jeanne, Jesus. Stop it, would you?" Debbie turned to me, took me by the arm. "Come on, Alicia. I'll help you get him out of the car, okay?"

Debbie and I got Red from the car and walked with him. Jeanne trailed behind us. We went around to the back of the house, pushed our way through the tangled underbrush, and came out on the immaculately manicured lawn of the Kingsbury Village Municipal Dog Park. The park had once been a nine hole golf course, and you could still see the ghosts of fairways and greens and improbable little ponds in the view that stretched out before us.

Though it was nine o'clock, there were still plenty of dogs and their owners walking the dirt trails, sitting on the benches that dotted the landscape. It was pleasant, peaceful.

Suddenly, I was aware of Red beside me. Something was wrong. His body was stiff with tension. He couldn't stand still. He was breathing funny.

"Easy, Red," I said.

He looked up at me and clicked his tongue. He was keenly interested in a golden retriever sitting in the grass next to two women on a park bench about fifty feet ahead of us.

I heard the beginning of that stuttering caw he'd made when he first saw my still life of the fruit bowl, and I got scared.

"Red, please don't," I said.

From behind us, I heard Jeanne Manchester say, "Don't let him stop. Come on, keep going."

Earlier, Jeanne and Debbie had shown me a map of the dog park, and Jeanne had pointed to a densely wooded area on the opposite side of the park from the abandoned house, and said that's where she thought Red had come from. Her reasoning was that Red's clan would be looking for him in that area. His cries that had prompted so many police reports were undoubtedly his attempt to make contact with the clan, and she seemed to think if we got him in the general area, Red would know what to do. It wasn't much of a plan, but it was the best we could think of.

So we headed across the park, the four of us, coming up on the bench where the golden retriever rested, its head on its paws. I knew we were in trouble as soon as the dog perked up its head. It sniffed the air in our direction, jumped to its feet, and a bristly line of fur spiked up along the top of its neck and back. Lupine instincts awakened; it watched Red's odd, loping gait, the almost simian movements of Red's long arms and short legs, and a furious tattoo of barks and snarls erupted from deep in its chest.

The two women on the bench flinched from their pet, then looked in our direction.

Red was watching the dog and breathing very fast.

"Red, don't," I said, but there was no stopping what the golden retriever had put in motion.

The dog sprinted at us, its leash streaming behind it. Red let out an ear-piercing wail and charged.

Red ducked under the dog's teeth at the last second and swept its front legs out from underneath it, sending the dog skidding along the grass on its chin. Before it could regain its feet, Red grabbed its leash and spun the dog in a wide rainbow arc over his head. The animal let out a strangled, startled yelp as its paws traded places with its head in the air above Red. Then, a horrible moment later, Red brought the animal down on the ground with a furious downward slap of the leash. The retriever hit the ground and crumpled, unable to move. But Red didn't relent, even at that point. He jumped onto the dog's back, dug into its hide, and ripped it in two.

Screams came from every direction at once. Dogs barked and howled. A woman off to my left gasped for air like she was in the middle of an asthma attack.

"Oh my God," I heard Debbie mutter.

Three dogs sprinted past us to get to Red. He threw back his head and out came a sound that was feral and bloodthirsty, full of the joy of battle.

He went on the attack. Red charged the dogs and gutted a black poodle without losing a step. A big shepherd got behind him and tried to go after his legs. Red grabbed it by the neck one-handed and snapped its spine with a flick of his wrist. All I could do was watch in horror as the furious barking, yelping and snarling of the dogs was drowned out by the triumphant screams of Red's war whoops.

Then, out of nowhere, Jeanne Manchester stepped forward with a nickel-plated, Clint Eastwood-sized revolver. She leveled the weapon, one-handed, squinting down the impossible length of the thing at Red, who was disemboweling a husky. She pulled the trigger.

The crack of the shot echoed across the park, and for a moment, as the enormous boom of the gun faded, everything stopped.

I could hear my heart beat in the silence, then the park erupted into complete chaos. People fled in panic, and all I could do was stand there, gaping at the screaming people and the sight of Red causing so much violence and pain. It wasn't right. It didn't fit.

Meanwhile, Jeanne Manchester, realizing she missed Red with the first shot, screamed at the top of her lungs for him to stand still. Red, of course, ignored her. He was running at top speed through the grass, slashing and biting at every terrified dog he saw. I stared after him, and I couldn't believe how savagely he fought. It was almost beautiful.

A bullet whizzed by my right ear and Debbie shouted, "Alicia! Get down! Alicia!"

From where I stood, I could see a gentle slope of grass that rose up to a dense treeline of cedar and scrub oak, where we had planned to take Red. People and dogs alike were running down that slope, trailed by at least a dozen full-grown goblins. The goblin troop moved towards us with a speed that left me breathless. I caught sight of Red through the crowd of screaming people and dying dogs. He was looking toward the advancing goblins, and the joy on his face was unmistakable. He began to caw. The goblins veered towards him without slowing, like a school of fish or a flock of birds on the wing, and a moment later they had swarmed over Red and scooped him up, carrying him off into the trees. We never made eye contact, and I never got to say goodbye.

After they were gone, a quiet settled over the park. People stared around at the carnage. There were dogs everywhere, most of them dead. Others limped away with shock in their eyes. Jeanne Manchester was furious. I saw her pointing toward the trees with her enormous pistol, but no one would get near her.

Off in the distance, I could hear the approaching warble of police sirens.

I've never seen so many cops in one place before. At first it was just cops in uniforms, lots and lots of them, and then later, the detectives showed up in their suits. The funny thing was, nobody would acknowledge what they saw. Everyone told more or less the same story. Some kind of horrible animal—possibly some kind of monkey—had gotten loose and killed a bunch of dogs before running off into the trees. I saw people pointing at Jeanne Manchester. They were distraught. They made their hands into the shapes of guns and pantomimed Jeanne shooting up the park, then the detectives would ask them something else, and they would frown and shrug.

A pair of policemen arrested Jeanne Manchester. She put up a pretty good fight when they cuffed her, and the fight continued all the way to the backseat of the patrol car. I heard her shouting, "But I saved us all! I saved us all!" but of course no one listened. I saw the face of the young officer who put her in the car. He closed the door on her, then looked at his partner as if to say, "Jesus, you believe that one? What a nut."

They took her away and that pretty much ended the official version of Red's story. No one ever followed up on Jeanne Manchester's assertions that I was responsible for bringing a goblin baby to the dog park, and eventually, after a few nights of gory footage on the news, the incident played itself out. Like everything else, people just forgot about it.

After I left the dog park that night, I went home and sat at my breakfast table, opening a bottle of white wine. I drank most of it, though I never did manage to get drunk. I was crying too hard over Red's crayon drawings for that.

Depressed as I was, it would have been a fairly easy matter to sink into soul-sucking despair. That was what Debbie feared most, I think. She was convinced I would completely withdraw from the human race, that whatever psychological process of escape had been set in motion by my failure with Janet, would turn me into the mental health equivalent of a shipwreck.

But she was wrong.

I returned to work later that week, put my shoulder to the stone, and like every other tormented Sisyphus in civil service, went right back to rolling it uphill.

For two years I worked my cases. Most of the time I hated my job. Sometimes I loved it. I had a few failures; won a few victories. I thought about Red every day for a long time, and there were days during the first year that my dreams of Red were all that got me up in the morning.

Then, as the pain softened and he became a bittersweet memory, I thought about him less often.

But tonight he's been on my mind a lot. You see, earlier this evening, just after nightfall, I heard my neighbor, Mr. Everett, out on his back porch, calling for the pit bull he bought last year to replace Elvis. Hearing him brought back all the memories of Red, and I poured myself a glass of white wine and went out my back door to feel the night air on my face.

That's where I found the drawing. It was propped up in a corner next to yet another potted plant I'd managed to kill.

I recognized Red's generous use of green right away. He had improved some. He still had trouble capturing my eyes, but the cheeks were thinner, more realistic, more human. I smiled at the paper and ran my fingers over it. My Red. I heard a rustling in the trees beyond my back fence, and I turned, hoping to catch a glimpse of him. Nothing. Just weeds and scrub brush, but I knew he was there.

I waved and went inside.

And so I came in here to my study to write this out. I can type about fifty words a minute when I'm on a roll, but I've handwritten this. I wanted to be as close to the story as I could, and though my hand is killing me right now, I don't want to stop. We take our penance any way we can get it.

So this is where I end this little story, I guess, with the decision I made about my life. We tend to think of decisions as singular events, as a choice.

Two roads diverged in a wood, and I...
I took the one less traveled by.

But you know that one. You've heard it a million times. The words have been so overused by self help gurus and inspirational posters that we've stopped thinking of them as something power-ful. They've become cliché. And that's a shame, because they're powerful words, no matter how many times they've been quoted.

The image Frost captured with those lines is timeless and beau-tiful, but it is also misleading. For a decision, especially one that concerns the shape of a life, is rarely so simple as a choice between two options—chocolate or vanilla, left or right. A decision about one's life is not a singular event.

We become who we are by degrees, and in that sense, decisions are more like road maps of one's past, suggestions for the future. I look back over the journey I've taken these past two years, over the high points and the low, and I find myself wondering why I keep coming back for more of this torture. The job is killing me, aging me, making me angry at the world and mute with frustration, yet I keep coming back. Why?

The answer, I think, is that after Janet, I turned my back on myself, and Red helped me to see that. It was never a question of me turning my back on humanity, as Debbie believed. The problem went deeper than that. I hated myself for what happened to Janet, and I think I always will, on some level at least.

But these days, I've come to the decision there is no accounting for the evil that men do. The world sucks most of the time. It's a brutal place filled with horrors too inhumane to be believed, and the injustice of it will devour you whole if you don't know why you're fighting. I had lost sight of that for a while.

I had lost sight of myself. But Red got me back on the path. He loved me, and his love both validated and recharged me, and for showing me why the good fight is worth fighting, Red, I thank you, and I love you.

SHERI AND NATHAN

MARK RIVETT

Nathan tried to shield his head from the downpour as he slid his key into the lock on his apartment door. Sheri laughed—they were already completely soaked, the rain so heavy even an umbrella wouldn't have kept them dry.

Having just returned from dinner, the couple was helpless to avoid the downpour and the cold, fall evening was very dark. The yellow streetlights flickered with the crash of thunder and the downpour drowned out the traffic on the street.

"You think I'm funny, Sheri?" Stepping inside Nathan began to slowly peal off his drenched shirt and shoes, but positioned himself to block his girlfriend from entering the apartment, leaving her outside beneath the relentless rainfall.

"Come on, Nathan! I'm cold." Sheri whined with a smile "The longer you stand there the longer it'll take me to get undressed."

Nathan's playful grin changed into a smile and he moved to allow her inside. Approvingly, he kept his eyes on her as he pulled off his pants and underwear. Sheri, smiling back at him, slid her shirt and braw off, followed by her shoes and pants. "Go get us towels so we can warm up, jerk."

"What if I want to warm you up?" Nathan moved in to grip her waste and pull her close.

Sheri, pants around her ankles, stumbled into him to retain her balance and gripped him by the shoulder. Her beautiful naked body pressed up against his, and she grinned and craned her head for a kiss. As he leaned in to kiss her, she pulled back. "Towels, now."

Sighing, Nathan released her and disappeared down the hallway to retrieve some towels.

He returned a moment later to see his beautiful girlfriend posing seductively by the couch. While the rain and thunder punished the world outside, she had gotten blankets and candles, turning the dark living room into a romantic candle-lit sanctuary.

"Come here, Nathan, I need your help drying off."

"I love you." Sheri was lying with her body wrapped around Nathan's, her head resting on his shoulder as she gazed up to look up at him.

"I love you." He wrapped his arm around her as he pulled a second blanket up to cover their exposed bodies. They quietly enjoyed each other in the afterglow of passion.

A few moments passed, the thunder died into a gentle rumble, and the rain became a light drizzle. Reaching over, Nathan gripped the remote and turned on the television.

Sheri smiled. "See if there's something on Comedy Central. I'm in the mood to laugh."

A few button presses on the remote and Nathan found the channel. They laid in each others arms, laughing when the comedy on the television struck a cord.

Suddenly, the familiar sound of a key entering the apartment door lock alerted them that Nathan's room mate was returning home. There was no time to get dressed and Nathan and Sheri glanced about quickly to make sure they were both completely covered by the blankets.

With his usual dour demeanor, Aaron lazily opened the door and walked into the apartment, flicking on the overhead light. Glancing around, he muttered, "Are you kidding me? The whole building could burn down!"

Aaron worked nights and always returned home in a sour mood. Nathan and Sheri were used to him entering the apartment and stomping off down the hall, then closing his bedroom door for the rest of the evening. He was the type of personality that was just never happy, and they were both glad he chose to isolate himself most of the time. To their surprise, he walked into the living room and blew out each candle.

"It's okay, man. We're watching the candles. It's no big deal," Nathan protested as Aaron reached down and snatched the television remote from the arm of the couch, turning off the TV before placing the remote well out of reach.

Sheri looked at Nathan, a questioning expression on her face. Nathan watched Aaron in disbelief.

"We were watching that. What's your problem?" Nathan wanted to stand up to confront Aaron but glanced down at the blanket concealing his body and thought better of it.

Ignoring him, Aaron turned off the living room light and sluggishly wandered down the hall, slamming his bedroom door a moment later.

"He must have had one hell of a bad day." Nathan glanced down at Sheri. His eyes took a moment to adjust to the darkness before he caught the gentile light in her eyes reflecting back at him. "Let's get dressed. I'm not tired. We'll give him a few minutes to fall asleep and we'll turn the TV on again with the volume down."

"We could just run around naked. It doesn't really matter now." Sheri sat up and glanced around the dark room.

"I know, but I'd like to feel like I don't have to dive for a blanket every time I hear a thump or thud in Aaron's room." Nathan stood up and turned on the light. Sheri kept a change of clothes at his place for the nights she spent there. "I'll get us some dry clothes," he said.

A few moments later, he returned, clothes in hand, just in time to see the flashing lights of several emergency vehicles fly past the front windows. The blinds were almost always closed but the bright light of police cars shined through as they went by.

The lights got Sheri's attention and she frowned. "Wow, that looked like a fleet of cops and fire trucks. Something really bad must have happened."

Nathan handed Sheri her clothes as he slid his underwear and trousers on.

"Yeah," he said. Sheri seemed somewhat affected by the emergency vehicles and Nathan glanced down the hallway toward Aaron's room. "The weather was terrible. I'm sure they're heading to the scene of an accident."

Nathan walked over to the front door of the apartment and opened it. The night was still—without wind—and the only sound remaining was the drip of rainwater off the trees and onto the sidewalk. The cold air drew around him like ice as he peered out to see the emergency lights vanish behind a bend in the road.

"What the hell!?" Aaron's bedroom door flew open and he angrily stomped down the hallway in his boxers toward Nathan, who stepped inside the apartment, shocked at Aaron's attitude.

"What?" Nathan asked.

Gripping the door handle in his right hand, Aaron slammed it shut and turned the lock with the other. In a second smooth motion, he turned the overhead light off and stormed back down the hallway toward his bedroom, slamming his door again.

"What the fuck, man?" Nathan protested. He stood there for a moment in the darkness of the living room in shock.

"He's just trying to get some sleep, Nathan. He probably has class tomorrow and we're not helping him recover from his day." Sheri stopped Nathan's intentions to march down the hall and erupt into a screaming match with Aaron.

The two roommates had had arguments before but Aaron was being blatantly rude and Nathan had little tolerance for that behavior.

Nathan turned the overhead light back on. "I'm not tired. If I want to stay awake all night I don't see a problem with it as long as I'm not disturbing him. He and I are gonna have a talk about this tomorrow."

"Come lay with me. We'll watch TV with the volume down." Sheri had finished getting dressed but the cold night air Nathan had let in forced her to curl up beneath the blankets. She patted the area on the couch generally reserved for her boyfriend and smiled.

Nathan, still irritated from the way his roommate was behaving, reluctantly sat next to her and drew the blanket over him to keep warm. He turned the television back on and reduced the volume. They sat in silence for a long while, forgetting about Aaron and allowing the television to put them back into a light-hearted mood.

Hours passed before someone spoke.

"What are we gonna do?" Sheri was the first to break the silence between them. She looked over to him with eyes that appeared to be welling up with tears.

"What do you mean?" Nathan asked with a confused expression on his face.

Sheri took her gaze off him and stared at the TV as she wiped the tears from her eyes.

"What's wrong?" Are you okay?" He was at a loss. He edged closer to her and put his hand on her knee. He looked at her with concern.

"I'm gonna see what you have in your fridge." She stood up abruptly and disappeared around the corner into the kitchen.

Nathan knew better than to follow. Sheri was upset and she'd talk about what was bothering her when she returned, but now she needed a moment to collect her thoughts. He leaned back in the couch, wondering what could be bothering her so much. Aaron's behavior was rude but nothing to get overly upset about.

His thoughts were interrupted by the house phone ringing. He glanced at the digital clock on the cable box and saw that it was after three. Normally people called his cellular phone and he only had the house phone as a package from his cable and internet provider. He didn't have time to wonder, as the instinct to avoid a confrontation with Aaron overrode his confusion at someone calling him at three in the morning on a telephone line he hardly used.

Before the phone could ring a second time, he jumped up, swiped the phone in one hand, and put it to his ear. "Hello?"

"Nathan! Oh, Nathan... this is Sheri's mom... hold on one second." The unmistakable voice of Sheri's mother came through the phone. Nathan listened for a moment and could make out the sounds of crying.

"Nathan..." Sheri's mother paused for a long moment and he could tell she was choking back tears. "There's been an accident."

A shot of terror rose up his spine. The tone in Sheri's mother's voice conveyed something serious. "What happened?" He tried to focus.

"They...they found...they found Sheri's car. She went over the side of a bridge." She spoke through powerful sobs.

Sheri, upon hearing the tone in Nathan's voice, peered around the corner. She stood in silence, watching him talk on the phone with her mother.

"Oh my God? Who was driving?" Nathan asked. It could only be Sheri's father or brother, Mike, and Nathan's heart jumped into his throat.

Sheri's mother paused for a moment, choking back tears. "Nathan, they found Sheri's car. She lost control and she went off a bridge." She sniffed, trying to hold herself together to communicate properly with him.

Sheri bit her bottom lip and her eyes turned sad as she watched Nathan. She walked back over to the couch and sat down next to him, putting her arm around his midsection.

"I don't understand. Who was driving? How did her car end up in the river?" Nathan couldn't grasp what Sheri's mother was trying to tell him.

"It's Sheri! Sheri's gone, Nathan...Sheri's..." Sheri's mother broke down into tears and Nathan couldn't make out anything else.

"That's impossible. Sheri's right here. Do you want to talk to her?" he asked, hoping to relive Sheri's mother's anguish.

"What!?" Sheri's mother stopped sobbing instantly. Her voice took on a tone of hope. "Put her on!"

Nathan handed the phone to Sheri.

"Hello?" Sheri frowned.

"No."

"No, Mom. ...I'm sorry, Mom. ...I know, Mom. I'm sorry." A tear fell down Sheri's cheek. "...I gotta go, Mom. I love you. Tell dad and Mike I love them, too." She hung up the phone and kept her eyes, wet with tears, closed for a few moments before opening them to Nathan's confused expression.

"What happened?" he asked, unable to wait any longer for an explanation.

"Exactly what she said happened. I lost control of my car and went over the side of a bridge on my way here." Sheri couldn't look Nathan in the eyes as she spoke. "They found me. Pulled me out."

"What? Why didn't you tell me? When did this happen?" Nathan was shocked. He couldn't believe what he was hearing.

"Tonight. On the way here, to see you," Sheri answered.

"This isn't funny, Sheri. I thought your mom was really upset. I thought I was gonna have to take you to your dad's or brothers funeral." He was angry. The sound of Aaron's bedroom door swinging open grabbed his attention for a split second before he refocused on Sheri.

"It's not a joke, Nathan. She was upset. I'm dead." She looked at him, not a drop of dishonesty behind her tearing eyes.

Aaron sluggishly walked down the hall and into the living room, where he seemed to glance around in surprise.

"But we just had a fantastic night! We went to dinner, we came home, hung out. Sheri, what the hell are you talking about?" Nathan ignored Aaron and stayed focused on Sheri. Aaron reached over the back of the couch, gripped the television remote, and turned off the TV.

"No, Nathan," Sheri tried to get through to him to what had happened. Aaron, half asleep, hit the living room light switch, casting everything in darkness.

"It happened on the way back here from the restaurant, Nathan. They must not have told my mother...I thought you knew...you...you were with me."

REVENGE

ANTHONY GIANGREGORIO

The small house in the Midwest sat nestled within the confines of modern day suburbia, but unknown to its occupants, Death was about to collect a debt far past due.

Jacob Masters snapped awake, his tired gaze trying to penetrate the darkness. His eyes were crusty from sleep and drool coated his bottom lip. The left side of his face had wrinkles pressed into his flesh from the sheet, attesting to how deep his slumber truly was.

He sucked in a breath, the sound loud to his ears, and he could feel his heart beating quicker, as if he was a wild animal sensing something was amiss.

His left hand slowly reached out to feel for his wife beside him, but he found the bed empty.

He was about to call out to her when a voice—one he knew well—spoke up from the corner of the room.

"She's in the living room," the voice hissed. "Don't worry, you'll be seeing her soon."

"What the fuck are you doing here? How'd you find me?" Jacob asked, his heart beating faster, if it was possible. His body filled with adrenalin and he unconsciously gripped the sheets, pulling the ends from the sides of the bed.

"How'd I find you? Well, that's easy, the internet is a magical thing, isn't it? The same thing you used to hurt me is now you're undoing. And I think we both know what I'm doing here. I owe you for all the shit you did to me for the past few years."

A small flashlight snapped on and Jacob blinked, trying to see through the glare.

"Do you mind?" he said, trying to sound confident, but deep inside he was terrified. If this man was here, and had come all the way across the United States to find him, to then break into his home in the middle of the night…well, it wasn't because he wanted to have coffee and catch up.

Jacob sat up straighter, painfully aware all he had on was his underwear. He felt exposed, even in the gloom of the room. The flashlight never wavered, his eyes blinded by the glare. "You need to leave now," Jacob said in as calm a voice as he could muster. "This is breaking and entering. This is some serious shit you've done. Before, it was all talk, but now…this is serious," he said again.

The man chuckled low in his throat, the noise more feral than human. "Serious? Oh, my friend, you don't know how fucking serious this is. You think what you did to me was nothing, just a bunch of words, shit said randomly, but I'm here to tell you that's the farthest thing from the truth." He took a step forward, his breathing now heavier as anger filled him. "Some things can't be taken back, some things can cut so deep, can scar someone so much, that they never, and I mean fucking *never*, let it go!"

"So what now? Are you gonna yell at me? Tell me how mad you are?" Jacob was feeling braver now, more confident. He knew the man was a blowhard, would rant on and on about how he was unhappy, how Jacob had wronged him, but in the end it would come to nothing. Right then, Jacob knew whatever was going on, whatever twisted ideas the man had for actually breaking into his home, would be for nothing.

In the end, Jacob would call the police and the man would pay for this intrusion. And the next day, when the world found out about what the man did, his reputation would be ruined, and he would go to prison for home invasion on top of it. Just as Jacob had hoped to ruin him, this would be even sweeter.

The man walked over to the bedroom door leading to the hall and flicked on the light. White light filled the bedroom and Jacob blinked, surprised that after being exposed to the glare of the flashlight, his eyes still needed to adjust.

Jacob was about to say something when he saw two things at the same time. The first was the man's right hand held a revolver and the second was the knife on his hip, the blood dripping from the bottom of the sheathe, a hole in the leather letting it free. There had to be a lot of blood in that sheathe, on that blade, for blood to drip out of it like that.

"Get up," the man said. "I want to show you something. You want to know how far I took this? How far I was willing to go to make sure you paid for your crimes against me?" He gestured with the gun. "One wrong move, one twitch I don't like, and I promise you I will fucking kill you." The man leaned forward slightly. "Look into my eyes, Jacob, and tell me you don't believe me."

Jacob did as the man said and his heart stopped for a moment. All he saw there was hatred, and as he looked at the man's face, he saw small red spots covering it, then he saw more on his neck and shirt. His gaze went down to the man's shoes and he saw splatter there as well; dark globules still congealing, stating they were relatively fresh.

"Get up and go into the living room. Move!"

Jacob did as he was told, the chill air caressing his exposed skin. As goosebumps appeared on his arms, he began to walk through his house. The man followed behind, his footsteps silent. Jacob let his eyes play over the photos on the wall of the hallway. There was one with his wife and their two children. They had been lucky, having a boy and a girl, so had stopped at two. Now their children were three and five years old, perfect ages for his perfect family.

As he walked into the living room, he saw the lights were on. All seemed as it should be until he walked around the couch and looked down. The instant his eyes saw her, he knew she was dead. There was no way she could be alive. He gasped and spun to face his intruder, at the same time knowing he was going to turn and run to his fallen wife.

"I wouldn't, asshole. I can squeeze this trigger long before you can reach me." The man gestured to the body on the floor. "Go, see to her."

"Bastard, you fucking bastard!" Jacob yelled as he turned and went to his wife. "She did nothing to you!"

She was dead, her throat slashed from ear to ear. Her eyes were still open, glazed over in death, her tongue protruding from her mouth. It had been bitten in half when she died. Her hands were curled into fists, each an inch deep in the blood-soaked carpet.

The once tan shag was now almost black with spilled blood. Jacob cradled his wife in his arms and cried, the loss, anger and fear welling up inside him. He wanted to kill the man, wanted to shove his gun down his throat and pull the trigger. He knew he would, too, if given the chance.

The feud between the two of them had been going on for years, a back and forth that seemed to never end. Though Jacob had never thought it would become physical, perhaps that was why he'd instigated it for so long, feeling safe with only words. But now, with his slain wife in his arms, he realized that what was said could have a deadly impact on his reality.

The man stood silent in the corner of the room, making sure he was far enough away from Jacob in case he tried anything. Jacob wanted to jump up and run at the man, but knew it would be futile, and besides, he had his children to think about, sleeping in their rooms, not knowing their mother was now dead, slain by a mad-man out for revenge.

The man waited a full ten minutes as he watched Jacob suffering on the floor, crying over his dead wife.

"Just so you know, I raped her before I killed her."

Jacob's eyes went wide at that. She was in her nightgown still, the lace see-thru, and underneath she wore nothing.

"I fucked her in the ass, and you know what? I think she liked it."

Jacob couldn't stand it any more and he jumped up, ignoring his wife's head falling from his lap. "You motherfucker, I'll kill you!" He began crossing the room.

The gun clicked in the man's hand as it was cocked. "One more step and you're dead." The voice was calm, in control. Something in its tone caused Jacob to stop walking, something said if he *did* take another step, he would be killed.

He stopped, trembling with rage.

"Good, that's very good. I wouldn't want the fun to end so quickly. I want you to suffer, like you made me suffer. It's payback time, pally boy and I'm gonna make sure you get everything you have comin' to you."

Jacob was still shaking in anger, the rage, loss, grief, all fighting for dominance of his soul. If only he could reach the man and kill him.

The man gestured to the hallway again. "Go check on your kids, after all, shouldn't they had woken up with all this yelling going on?"

A light went off over Jacob's head upon realizing the man was correct.

He'd been screaming at the top of his lungs, surely his children should have been woken by the noise. With panic filling his chest, he turned and ran to the children's bedroom, the man following close behind.

All thoughts of dashing into one of the adjacent rooms and slamming the door closed went out the window as Jacob thought of his offspring. His safety was forgotten, his dead wife was forgotten, only his children mattered.

The door was partially ajar and he pushed it open, turning on the light as he entered the bedroom. The room was large with a bed on each side. The children were young and for now were sharing a room.

When he stepped inside, he slipped on something and fell heavily, the light coming on at the exact same moment. As he fell to the floor, his eyes took in the Rorschach splashed walls, crimson still dripping in dark rivulets.

He landed hard, the breath leaving his chest as he grunted. He was up an instant later, rolling onto his side as he crawled to his little girl's bed.

He screamed.

She was dead, there was no question about it. Her arms and legs had been cut off, as if she'd been drawn and quartered. Her tiny organs had been scattered across the bed as if for inventory, and her face and hair—all covered in blood—was propped in the middle, set up like a dime store statue.

"Oh God, oh my God!" Jacob screamed, as he called out his child's name.

"Don't forget the boy," the man said from the doorway.

Jacob spun and gasped again, feeling as if he was going to faint. His son's bed was awash in dark plasma as well, his small frame gutted from groin to neck. The ribcage had been cracked and the heart was cut out, where it had been shoved into the boy's mouth. The small blue eyes were glazed over in death and Jacob fell to the floor, the unbearable loss simply too much to handle.

How does a man handle his entire family being slaughtered like so much cattle? How does a man handle retribution being delivered to his family, when deep down, he knew it was all on him? His crimes were the result of this, his actions, and though he hated the man before him for all he was worth, deep down, where no man wants to delve, he knew this was all his fault, he'd pushed the man too far.

"Why?" Jacob cried? "Why would you do this? How could you do this? You're a fucking monster, you hear me, a fucking monster!"

The man chuckled, as if Jacob's pain was nothing, as if instead of standing in the middle of a charnel house, he was leaning against an oak tree in the public park.

"A monster you say? Perhaps, but you made me this way, Jacob. You couldn't let things go, could you? You had to keep on going, adding fuel to the fire. And the funny part was there was no way to stop you. All you had to do was keep talking, to keep creating lies, and as far as you were concerned, it could go on forever.

Well, guess what, pally boy. What you do and say matters in the real world, and I've decided not to take any more of your shit." He gestured to the mangled little girl and licked his lips. "By the way, your wife was sweet, but I have to say, your daughter was even sweeter. She died a woman, you know."

There was a small wooden baseball bat near his son's bed and Jacob didn't let on that he'd spotted it. He remembered clearly when he'd bought it for his son. His boy was only two at the time but the bat was on sale, and he knew his son would be ballplayer one day.

He'd taken it home after paying with his credit card and his wife had shaken her head, wondering what her husband's obsession with baseball really was all about.

As the man talked, Jacob saw the gun being waved around. The man liked to talk with his hands and the gun barrel waved up and down, side to side, as if it was an extension of his arm.

At the right moment, Jacob went into action, reaching for the wooden bat, jumping up, and preparing to charge the man, to get revenge for his family, to kill the man who had taken everything he held dear, leaving him with nothing to live for.

Jacob barely made it to his feet when the gun went off, the bullet crossing the distance between him and the man in less than a second. As the bullet struck Jacob's heart and pulverized it, the man shook his head, mumbling about how he had wanted Jacob to suffer more before killing him.

The man was already unbuckling his belt and unzipping his pants before the report of the gun faded. Dead or alive, he would have his final revenge.

There were no last thoughts for Jacob, there was no life flashing before his eyes, only darkness.

A GENTLEMAN'S PRIVILEGE

DANE T. HATCHELL

There were few areas in the main house of Arbroth Plantation that allowed unrefined slaves. Recent arrivals brought with them a rebellious spirit that had to be *encouraged* out of them. That encouragement was given to them one lash at a time, and as often as necessary.

The kitchen, though, was one of those areas that Captain Hampton permitted some of the new younger slaves to work. Only those of the female persuasion, and just those carrying a certain amount of potential.

Mr. John Hampton built the plantation not far from the Mississippi River to take advantage of the waterway, to transport his cash crop of sugarcane. As a shrewd lawyer, he amassed a huge fortune that allowed him to retire in south Louisiana, to pursue other business ventures less demanding and more personally rewarding than defending unscrupulous corporations.

He went by the name of Captain to his friends and close associates. It was not a carryover from military service, but a label that stuck, having been the captain of his debating team at Columbian College in Washington, D.C.

A confirmed bachelor, and a man from the north unwilling to adjust to southern protocol, he did not fraternize in Louisiana societal circles, believing that supporting the local law enforcement with large cash donations did more to further his personal interest than rubbing elbows with gauche southern *aristocracy.*

Captain Hampton sat on his front porch, sipping on a whiskey. A thin slice of lemon sat saturated in the bottom of the glass. Growing sugarcane was quite profitable, but the business was becoming more difficult now that the South was at war with the North.

Slaves were more expensive and problematical to come by. In fact, the last batch was purchased from a trader through illegal channels. He'd contracted a sordid man of vile reputation to bring them direct from Haiti. The slaves were unloaded from the boat in the cover of darkness straight off the Mississippi River.

The lemon sat withered in the bottom of his empty glass. He walked from the porch, through the main dining area, and past twelve foot tall double doors leading to the kitchen. An old black woman and two teenage girls froze at their workstations as he entered.

"Good afternoon, Captain Hampton, sir," the old woman said, holding a mixing bowl and a large wooden spoon.

"Why good afternoon Lucy, I trust these lovely new girls are minding you in the kitchen." He opened a cabinet to retrieve a bottle of liquor, and poured himself a tall drink. He took a sip, and made a grimace as he looked at the ceiling.

The women stood still, waiting for his instruction, or waiting for his permission, not wanting to make a wrong move for him to punish them later.

He turned to them, stared with half open eyes, and took another sip of his drink. "You there," he finally said to the younger of the two girls. "What name did the Boss-man give you when he took you off the boat?"

The girl was only fourteen, and unsure of her place in her new environment. "Betty. Boss-man said I was Betty. He told me not to forget. He told me not to forget, or he would make me remember."

Captain Hampton wasn't sure why the young slave bothered to tell him more than just her name. Did she think he didn't know how Reeves, his lead Overseer, treated them? Did she think he cared?

"Well, I see you remembered your name," he said almost to himself. "Betty, that's a pretty name. I knew a lovely lady by that name long ago. Yes, she sure was..." he took another sip of whiskey, "like you."

Betty lowered her eyes to the floor, as if she'd done something wrong and was ashamed for it. The captain sensed her discomfort, and could feel Lucy staring at him with judging eyes.

He walked over to the other girl; it was obvious she was several years older than Betty. Their eyes met as he moved closer until he stood inches away from her. Captain Hampton was not a small man, standing two inches over six feet. The girl was nearly as tall as he was.

"And what name did the Boss-man give you?"

"My name is Darque, Darque Wight," she said.

He narrowed his eyes. "Darque? Why, I don't believe that's one of the names I would give my slaves. And I know the Boss-man didn't give you that last name."

"My father is French, it is his name. He was stranded in Haiti after a shipwreck. My mother's family found him on the beach. My mother nursed him back to life. They fell in love and married. He was away on a sea trip when my mother and I were kidnapped from our home. When he finds out, nothing will stop him from rescuing us," she said.

The captain held back his anger. She was a feisty one and would have to pay for the outburst of disrespect later.

He turned and walked over to Betty, pulled a peppermint from his coat pocket, and gave it to her. Leaning over, he whispered something in her ear.

Arbroth Plantation sat on over four hundred acres of rich soil nurtured by the Mississippi River. It was a living, breathing entity that required constant care in order for it to thrive and bear fruit.

The main house was built in a pecan orchard amidst sixty-year-old beautiful trees.

The road leading up to the house was lined with twenty mighty oaks to either side, an adornment left from the original house on the property that burned some thirty years before.

The slaves were the main caretakers, and the plantation as a whole was like a village unto itself. A large workshop teamed with those skilled in blacksmithing and woodworking, busy with projects needed for the day.

Several barns dotted the property that housed horses and milking cows. There was even a butcher shop to provide meat for the main house, as well as for the slaves.

The house slaves lived separately from the field slaves. Their quarters were near the main house, built by the captain for them.

The field slaves lived in sixteen cabins, each housing ten to twelve people, that they themselves built with a combination of discarded lumber and hand planed wood from fallen trees. Some of the roofs were made of thatch, a skill brought from their native countries.

Old rags plugged the holes in the walls to keep the drafts to a minimum. The communal bed was nothing more than a pile of straw. Blankets were the most prized possession, most being thin and not large enough to adequately cover the cluster of people huddling underneath.

Darque Wight and her mother shared a cabin with two other families from their village in Haiti. Little time was spent in the cramped quarters due to the long work hours required by the Overseers, and the time spent working for their own survival.

It was up to them to prepare and cook their own food—food mostly grown by the slaves, in small garden plots not far from the cabins.

The blast from an Overseer's horn at dawn had everyone awake and scurrying about, dressing for the day, and walking sleepy-eyed to the slave's kitchen for breakfast.

When Darque and her mother arrived, their fellow captives were in a state of unrest.

Darque stopped at a whispering group of people, her mother a step behind. "What's everyone upset about?" she asked.

"Puri didn't come home from working at the big house last night." The man used her Haitian name and not her slave name of Betty. "You were working in the kitchen with her. Why didn't she come back with you?"

"Miss Lucy told her to stay and help with preparing food for breakfast. She told me to leave. I didn't know Puri didn't come back," Darque said.

The scream of a frantic woman pierced the thick humid air. Four men walked down the road towards the slave quarters. One was leading his horse by the bridle, the body of a young girl draped over the saddle.

An old woman ran to the side of the horse, saying something in desperation in her native Creole. She looked for signs of life in the eyes of the girl. There were none.

Puri's face was battered and bruised, a gash across her lip where knuckles had met teeth. The body was wet, the clothing torn and ripped. Blood stained the back of her work dress.

The slaves gathered in the middle of the road, blocking it. Standing silent, they waited for the Overseer's explanation.

Reeves and his company stopped a few feet from the slaves. There was a stern look on Reeve's face as he passed his eyes over the crowd. "This is what happens when a slave tries to escape," he said.

The crowd sent jeers and raised fists in the air. Reeves put his hand on the butt of his revolver, and the other three men stepped to his side.

One carried a musket held across his chest, one started unfurling a bullwhip, and one had a machete gripped in his right hand, rotating it slowly in small circles by his side.

Darque pushed her way to the front of the crowd and faced Reeves. "What did you do to her?" she demanded.

Reeves spit, then scratched the side of his face. "I didn't *do* anything to her. She was found by the side of the river. Must have fallen down the levy, torn up her clothes, hit her head, and drowned."

Darque took another step forward, her nose almost touching his. "That's a lie," she said.

The murmurs from the crowed hushed. The only noise slicing through the silence was that of flies buzzing around the dead body on the horse. Darque made herself as large and intimidating as she could, daring Reeves to make a move.

It was rare that any slave would have the courage to stand up to him face to face, and even rarer for one to do so and live.

Reeves pulled the revolver from his right hip. Darque reached across with her right hand and grabbed the gun and the back of his thumb, twisting it to the outside. The gun fell to the ground as she overextended his wrist. A distinctive snap of bone breaking went before Reeve's startled cry.

Darque continued her assault by spinning her body around, catching Reeves to the left side of his jaw with the backside of her left arm. He went to his knees, clutching his right wrist with his left hand, writhing in pain.

The man with the musket raised it to his shoulder just as Darque grabbed the barrel and pulled it to her left side, away from her body. She pivoted back on her left heel and brought her right foot up, smashing the man in the nose and sending him backwards into the other two men.

She ran to a pile of wood used for cooking that was just a few feet away, and chose two moderately straight branches two inches thick and nearly three feet in length. Much to everyone's surprise, she ran back to the two remaining adversaries.

The man with the bullwhip had an evil grin cut across his face. The whip snaked out along the ground, ready for a target. The man with the machete stood several feet to his left. She would have to face them both at the same time.

Without hesitation, she ran full speed at the man with the whip. He tossed back the eight foot long weave of cowhide, and with the flick of his wrist, sent the stinging tip at her. At the last second, Darque ducked and slid towards him, just as the whip's tip *cracked* the empty air where she'd been.

She brought one stick crashing into the side of his left knee, and the other a full upper cut to his groin. The man went down before he could defend himself.

Darque tumbled forward and sprang up, ready to face the man with the machete, holding the sticks in front of her, crossing them in an **X**, a defensive ready position.

The man rushed her, the machete grasped tightly in both hands, the blade high above his head. Instead of slamming it straight down, he maneuvered the blade over his right shoulder and went down to one knee, bringing the blade around from his right to his left, aiming to cut Darque in half.

Fearing she couldn't move into him and past the blade, she was forced to retreat and step back. The blade sliced into her midsection, just enough to cut through her dress and leave a slight wound on her dark skin. A trail of blood marked the blade's path.

The man recovered from his swing and brought the blade back around from his left to his right. She brought one of the sticks hard across the back of his right elbow, stopping his arm cold. She raised the stick in her left hand and whacked it against the man's skull.

The next thing Darque felt was a numbing chill from the back of her skull, then down her spine. A massive pain filled her head as she succumbed to the uncertain fate of unconsciousness.

Captain Hampton stood over her crumpled body, an oak cane with a brass lion's head handle clutched tightly in his hand. Reeves appeared at his side. He spit and half the spittle dribbled down his chin. He removed the revolver from his left side, cocked the hammer, and pointed it to the back of Darque's head.

The captain reached out, put his hand over the revolver, and slowly pushed it down. "Not here. I'll take care of this my way."

The drums beat low in the background. Two men sat on opposite sides of the cabin, facing the wall. Their eyes were closed, each man pounding in rhythm with his bare hands.

Their backs were to the dead body of Puri, lying in the middle of the room. Her eyes were closed, and despite her ravaged face, it reflected the peace of death.

An old man walked through the door. Held tightly in his arms, were small burlap bags dirty from the earth. With reverence, he approached the old woman kneeling by Puri's side. The old woman's face was void of emotion, her spirit no longer in the world where her body existed.

He waited until her head jerked back and her eyes opened, before he spoke. "I have them for you, Alma. All of them."

She went to speak but her mouth would not move, and she waited until control returned. "I must hurry," she whispered. "Her spirit has not yet moved to the next world. There is still time."

The old man set the bags down and Alma hurriedly untied the thin cords, freeing the contents. She unrolled a soft leaf from one and pinched four different powders from the others onto the first leaf. She formed lines next to each other, powders of red, green, black, and white.

When she was finished, her wrinkled, gnarled fingers carefully rolled the leaf, encasing the powders. "Did you find what they have done with my daughter?"

"She is in irons, in the slave's prison cell by the barn," the old man said with reservation. All knew that the cell by the barn housed instruments of torture.

Alma held the rolled leaf in one hand, and waved a black feather from a crow in the air above Puri's body with the other. Her lips moved without letting any sound escape. The drums continued to beat, and the old man said a silent prayer. Not for Puri, but for himself.

Alma dragged the end of a match across the floor, a small flame bursting into orange and yellow, sending the smell of sulfur into the air. She put the rolled leaf between her lips and inhaled as she lit it like a cigarette. It burned with an acrid odor and gave off thick black smoke.

Alma inhaled deeply, filling her lungs with the mystic amalgam of burning powders. She placed her lips on Puri's, and exhaled.

Puri's chest rose from her expanding lungs. Alma moved away as the old man placed his hands on her chest and pushed down. Alma inhaled from the rolled leaf again, and filled Puri's lungs twice more, the old man pushing down on Puri's chest each time.

One last time Alma breathed into Puri.

When the old man pushed down, a blast of black smoke exited the corpse's nostrils...and Puri's eyes opened.

When Darque came to consciousness, she wasn't sure where she was or how she ended up there. Shackles bound both of her wrists, with six feet of chain connected to the wall on each of them.

She reached behind her head and felt gently, finding a large knot where the cane had struck her. Part of her hair was stuck together with matted blood. Her head still throbbed with pain.

Through the window, moonlight cast eerie shadows on her cell walls. The floor was covered in a mixture of hay and grime. She groped blindly hoping to find a pitcher of water, but found nothing.

Darque knew how she came to be in her present predicament, but didn't know how she was going to get out of it. Her father had taught her the art of *savate*, French foot fighting.

She had learned to defend herself while growing up, which may have been partly responsible for her rebellious nature. Growing up in Haiti, other girls were forced to do things against their will.

She was trained not to be forced to do anything.

Her uncle aided in her training by teaching her the art of *mati*, and she could defend herself with sticks against any assailant short of those with a firearm.

This wasn't the first time she'd gotten herself in trouble for standing up to others, but she felt it could be very well her last. Her heart longed for her father and her twin brother, both away on a South American trading ship.

She knew that nothing could stop them from finding her and her mother, but unless they were already near, it would be too late for her. Darque wondered if her mother could survive the shock of her death.

She heard a sound from outside, and then the fumbling of keys at the prison door. She'd looked death in the eye before, but the odds were never this great against her. She was alone, chained and shackled, and eventually, she would be overwhelmed.

As always, she turned her focus on her objective, and determined there were things worse than death.

She resolved to fight using every remaining ounce of energy left in her body, and to kill or maim any who walked through the door.

The door slowly creaked open.

She crouched against the wall, waiting for the final conflict.

The captain came down hard on the slaves for Darque's display of defiance. He was determined to make them all suffer even though it was the action of one.

Next week the slaves were going to have to survive on half the meat rations he normally supplied. He wanted to discourage any other would be martyrs.

As for Darque, he had special plans for her. She was going to feed every need of his perverted pleasure before he would use his bare hands to strangle the life out of her.

He loved strong-willed women. He loved to bend and break them, treating them like the black-hearted animals he believed them to be.

He walked through the sultry night air to the door of the prisoner's cell. He moved the four foot slave whip from his right hand to his left, retrieved the key, and opened the door.

The door creaked open and the stale air of the cell left a bitter taste in his mouth. It was dark, but he could make out the silhouette of the girl chained to the wall.

"Your time has come, you pathetic ungrateful savage. I pulled you from a world where you lived like a beast and brought you to civilization." He paused, seething with anger. "How dare you defy me!" His words reverberated off the walls.

"I'm not going to be as kind to you as I was to Betty, oh no. I offered her opportunity." He walked towards her with the whip grasped firmly in his hand. "She'd be alive today if she would have learned her place. But you, you have no option of opportunity. I'm going to beat you to within an inch of your life, and then I'm going to take delight in all my manly pleasures in your young, beautiful, battered body."

The whip snapped forward and struck her across the chest. The captain waited for a scream, a cry for mercy, but there was only silence. He raised it again and brought it against her three times in rapid succession.

The whip whistled through the air and snapped loudly against her body. Still, she spoke not a word, nor moved from the wall.

Repeatedly, he brought the whip against her. His breathing became heavy from exerting his full strength into every lash. Still nothing changed; she stood silently by the wall.

In a fit of rage, he reversed his hold on the wooden grip of the whip and beat her in the head. "Scream, damn you! Beg for mercy! Beg me for your life!"

The girl reached up and grabbed both of his wrists, pulling him to her. She twisted him around and slammed him into the wall. The moonlight through the window illuminated her face, and he gasped in horror.

The dead eyes of Puri glared at him, her split lip curled up, revealing her teeth and black tongue. She bit down hard on his neck as he franticly tried to squirm out of her grip.

Numbing fear washed over him as Puri bit out chunks of flesh; he was held captive in her grip. He watched the torn portions of himself hang from her teeth, blood dripping from her chin to splatter the floor.

That was when he screamed.

The slaves gathered in an empty field reserved for their dead, but they were not too far from the prison to hear the dying screams of Captain Hampton. The drums beat loudly, as Darque danced naked, the ceremonial fires burning high to light the way of the departed spirits.

Alma repeated her final chant. The air was charged with electricity, causing the hairs on her arms to stand on end. Slowly, the dead buried in the shallow, unmarked graves began to move, the less rotted being the first to emerge.

Darque ran to her mother's side and held her tightly. Never had she witnessed the power of voodoo in this magnitude. "How are you able to do this?" she asked in amazement.

"I channeled the power of the great evil released at the death of the captain. I have brought back the spirit's of the *just* for their revenge."

The dead now walked and waited for instruction. Alma pointed to the Overseer's barracks in the distance, for the time had come for the abused souls to reap the fruits of their final harvest.

"How's that wrist?" Zeke asked Reeves.

"Time heals all wounds—that and revenge," Reeves said, looking at the cards Zeke had just dealt him. A bandage was wrapped around his right wrist. "I tried to get the captain to let me take care of that slave bitch, but he insisted on handling it himself." Reeves laid his cards down to take a swig of whiskey straight from the bottle. "I didn't put up too much of a fight with him, though. From what I've heard, he'll do a much better job with her than I would've."

"She was one hell-cat all right. She broke your wrist and took your gun, gave Jed a blow to the balls, Henry took a punch in the nose that broke it, and Bob a cracked *noggin*."

Reeves grunted and said, "Give me three," and threw his discards to the table.

"She was a looker, too. Young, tall, nice legs and perky tits, her dark skin all smooth. Why, I even heard she was educated and could speak three or four languages. They say her daddy's French, and you know what they say about French women."

"No, what do they say?" Reeves showed his hand. Zeke shook his head and put his cards face down. Reeves raked in the pot.

"Well, I hear they can suck the life out of you. In a good way, if you know what I mean." Zeke showed his yellowing teeth in a smirk. "Darque Wight, that there's a queer name for a slave. I'd like to put me some white meat in that."

Sounds of scraping on the outside walls cut Zeke's words short. It was dark outside, but light enough to see silhouettes of bodies moving slowly past the windows.

"What the hell? Have them slaves lost their minds?" Reeves asked rhetorically. Ten Overseers were housed in the barracks. Five sat at the table playing cards and the other five had retired to their bunks. The activity outside had everyone up and scrambling for weapons in no time.

Reeves used his left hand to open the door, and immediately pulled the revolver from his left side, as he came face to face with a ghastly-looking zombie standing in the doorway.

What scared Reeves even more than the looks of the creature was that he recognized it. It was one of the slaves that died under his whip just two months before. The decrepit creature was naked from the waist up. The only clothing was a simple pair of trousers with a rope tied at the waist. Maggots writhed on the outside of its skin, and its eyes were darker than the night had ever been.

With shaking hands, Reeves pulled the trigger on his revolver, the round punching a hole in the zombie's chest. It staggered back at the impact, then fell forward on top of him.

From the door, more members of the walking dead entered, as the sounds of deafening gun blasts filled the air. The pungent odor of gunpowder stung the eyes of the terrified men, and mixed with the stench of rotting meat from the walking dead.

Reeves screamed in terror until the last spark of life exited his body, the zombie feeding ravenously on his tender flesh.

The others fell to the onslaught of the hungry horde, as revolvers snapped against empty shell casings. The final yells of the cruel Overseers replaced the sound of gunfire.

In the fray, oil-filled lanterns crashed to the floor, the pools of burning oil spreading quickly, creeping up the walls, and lapping across the ceiling in minutes.

Darque, her mother, and the rest of the slaves watched as their undead brothers and sisters sacrificed their lives once again for the survival of the village.

The dying screams of the slave masters faded into the snap and crackle of the fire.

"What now, Mother?" Darque asked.

Mambo Alma closed her eyes and looked inside her mind.

"Now our journey begins."

THE DEVIL'S PUNCH BOWL

DAVID H. DONAGHE

Lightning flashed, thunder rolled, and I materialized on a lonely desert highway, along with six of my bros. Our motorcycles faded from their majestic dazzling colors and chrome, to ordinary, older looking Harley Davidsons, as we touched down on the highway.

My name is John Brown, but my bros call me Cave Man. Back in '68, I rode with the Old Dogs, but the world went through a change and I wound up hitting an oak tree at 110 mph. That sent me to Biker Heaven, along with my bro, Old School. Now we ride with a band of troubleshooters and wear the halo patch. Whenever there's trouble in the biker world and the bros need a little help from the other side, they send us. Some people might call us angels, but don't get confused. We're not Hell's Angels; we ride for the other side.

It felt good to be mortal once more and feel the wind in my face, even though it was only temporary. We rolled down the highway with Little Danny Boy, our road captain, leading the pack. Hector, Hondo, Iron Man, Thumper and Old School formed up behind Little Danny Boy, riding in staggered formation with me riding Tail Gunner at the rear. We rolled around a bend, 150 miles out of Harlem Springs, Arizona under a full moon on a warm summer night, when Little Danny Boy pulled over to the side of the road next to a battered old oak tree.

He parked his bike, swaggered over to the tree, and the rest of us pulled over behind him. Old School and I sauntered up next to Little Danny Boy and I felt a cold chill run down my spine.

"You remember this place?" Little Danny Boy asked, but I just shrugged. Pulling a bottle of Old Number Seven from my vest pocket, I downed a shot. A cold wind caused a chill to run down my spine so I zipped up my leather jacket.

"How could I forget? This is where I died," I said and then Old School and I knelt down to examine the tree.

"Look, you can still see the scars. There's a dent where my head smashed against the trunk," Old School said.

"Are we going to stop at the cabin?" I asked, but Little Danny boy shook his head.

"No. They're back in town now. It's been thirty-two years. The worlds moved on. Things are back to normal now. The government finally got a handle on the flesh eaters in the late eighties. The one's we'll be fighting now will be much harder to kill than those zombie sons-of-bitches."

"What about Teddy Bear and Chops? I thought maybe they'd want in on this deal," I asked.

"They'll come if we need them. Even your dad said something about joining us if things got hairy," Little Danny Boy replied. That brought a smile to my face.

"It'll feel good to ride with the old man again," I said. "I've only see him at church. The rest of the time he's busy going hog wild in Biker Heaven."

Little Danny Boy walked over to his old Pan Head and said, "Let's ride. There's a storm coming, and it's coming straight from Hell. If we don't do something, the Road Dogs won't stand a chance."

We fired up our bikes, pulled onto the highway, and rolled on through the night toward Harlem Springs.

On another lonely desert highway, this one near the outskirts of Tortilla Flats, a desolate town on the California side of the Arizona border, Joker and Cowboy, members of the local Road Dogs chapter, had their fists on the throttle, heading toward town. A full moon looked down from above, a cool breeze tickled their face, and Cowboy felt a chill shoot down his spine when he heard a rumble of motorcycles coming up behind them. Glancing in his rearview mirror, Cowboy's eyes widened when he saw the headlights of over thirty motorcycles coming up on their tail at a high rate of speed. It looked as if they had a pickup truck traveling behind the pack as a chase vehicle.

Behind the motorcycle riders, unseen by human eye, an evil multitude of demonic entities riding on vile creature from the pits of Hell thundered forward just above the ground. The leader, riding a two-headed beast that looked somewhat like a cross between a rhinoceros and an elephant, wore a golden spiked helmet and carried a flaming sword forged by the Devil himself. The evil beast snorted fire, let out an evil hiss, and they thundered down the road following their human disciples.

When they passed by a ranch house off the road, the man of the house woke up in a cold sweat, feeling an urgency to pray. He fell to his knees at his bedside. Down the hallway, his six-year-old daughter screamed in the night in the thralls of a nightmare, and outside their German Sheppard howled, cowering in its doghouse.

Thunder cracked and lightning pierced the night when the leader of the evil host blew his horn. On the ground, the Hell Raisers, the motorcycle gang in pursuit of Cowboy and Joker, pulled up next to them. Their leader, known as Hellboy, lowered a double-barreled, sawed-off shotgun and let go with both barrels, blowing Cowboy out of the saddle. Cowboy's bike swerved sideways, high sided, and tumbled down the road. Joker locked up his brakes and went down near the centerline; when he stopped sliding, coming to rest on his back, Hellboy parked his custom chopper on the side of the road and strolled over to where Joker lay.

"Please. Mercy," Joker pleaded as he raised a bloody hand.

Hellboy laughed and said, "Sorry. I'm fresh out." The rest of the pack parked their motorcycles on the edge of the road. Grim Reaper, their Road Captain, walked up to Hellboy.

"You want me to do it?" Grim Reaper asked, shaking a one gallon gas can.

"No. This one's mine."

"Please no. Just shoot me, man," Joker said, trying to stand on his busted leg.

Hellboy laughed, and kicked him back to the pavement. He poured gasoline over Joker's body and smiled. "I'll see ya in Hell," he said while pulling a Zippo from his pocket. Making a flame, he set off the gasoline, and while Joker screamed in agony, Hellboy whistled a tune and ambled over to Cowboy's body. After pouring gasoline on Cowboy's remains, he lit the body up and turned to his club brothers. "That's two. We'll hit their clubhouse in Tortilla Flats and go east."

"We might need a little help with those old boys," Grim Reaper said.

"Our bros from up north are supposed to meet us across the boarder at Parker. When we hit those woods in Harlem Springs, we'll be over a hundred strong. Let's ride."

While the Hell Raisers roared down the highway, the moon reflected off the black and white patches on their backs, revealing the Hell Raiser Rocker, along with the patch depicting the evil-looking skeletal demon riding a chrome horse. The stench of burning flesh wafted on the wind, and behind them, unseen, the leader of the demonic crew let out a war cry, urging on his fiends from Hell.

He'd just collected two more souls.

* * *

The Hell Raisers hit the Road Dog clubhouse in Tortilla Flats hard and fast. They rolled up on the Thunder Dome, the combination bar and clubhouse, and gunned down the two prospects guarding the bikes in the gravel parking lot. When the bros inside the clubhouse heard gunfire, they rushed outside straight into a wall of automatic weapons fire. The survivors of the initial onslaught retreated into the clubhouse and returned fire after breaking a few windows at the front of the building.

Hellboy motioned to Grim Reaper and said, "Send half the boys to the rear to make sure they don't come out the back. Send Bone Crusher to get a crowbar to bar the front doors, then get the gas cans."

Dodging bullets coming from the clubhouse, Grim Reaper ran with the crowbar, as Bone Crusher followed along behind carrying two five gallon gas cans. While Grim Reaper barred the front door, Bone Crusher poured gasoline on the boardwalk and the front of the building. The tempo of the gunfire increased when the Road Dogs trapped inside the building realized what was happening. Ignoring the gunfire, Hellboy walked up to the boardwalk with a cocky grin on his face. He pulled his Zippo from his pocket, lit a cigarette, then tossed the burning lighter onto the boardwalk. The Thunder Dome burst into flames, but Hellboy just laughed. Ignoring the blood-curdling screams of the bikers trapped inside the burning clubhouse, he turned to his motorcycle and said, "We'll leave five guys here. I'll call some of our chapters from up north and have them send some more down. Have the guys we leave here find another bar to establish our presence. Maybe that place on the other side of town we saw coming in here. Within a month, we'll own this town," Hellboy told the Road Captain.

While Grim Reaper picked out five men to stay behind, the rest fired up their motorcycles and headed for the Arizona boarder. Behind them, hovering above the ground, the leader of the demonic swarm opened up a ceramic urn. Moonlight flashed off the jewels and diamonds embedded in the urn while he collected the souls of the dying men in the clubhouse.

We rolled into Harlem Springs at six in the morning and stopped in at the diner. Being mortal again required food and sleep, so after breakfast we holed up in a motel to get some rest, and rolled out to the High Noon Saloon about six that evening. The High Noon Saloon was a bar five miles outside of town run by the Road Dogs motorcycle club. They used the back room of the bar to have club meetings, which most bikers called 'going to church.'

The combination bar and clubhouse had another large room with beds, showers and a card table for brothers who needed a place to stay. Down in a basement, they kept supplies such as extra food, booze, guns, ammunition, and anything else they thought might be needed.

Pulling up next to the boardwalk, we parked our bikes in the gravel parking lot and walked onto the boardwalk. The two prospects guarding the motorcycles out front gave us the once over. The Road Dogs ran an open clubhouse, meaning that anyone could come and drink at the bar, as long as they behaved, but if they caused trouble, the bros would toss them out on their ears. It was mostly club members that evening and the party was in full swing. The large speakers behind the bar blasted a ZZ Top track and two young ladies danced on top of the bar topless. They looked like hang-arounds, not old ladies. A wooly bear of a man danced with another, big breasted blonde on the dance floor, while several people sat at tables throughout the bar room, and bikers lined the bar.

We stood in the center of the room, taking in the scene. All eyes turned to us, acknowledging our presence and then the bar's patrons went about their business.

"There's a lot of new faces here," Little Danny Boy said.

"What do you expect? It's been over thirty years. The world's moved on," I said, noticing a familiar face sitting at the bar. His hair had gone gray, his beard had turned white, and his face looked more weather beaten, but I'd recognize Sonny anywhere.

"There's Sonny," I said, a smile crossing my face. I swaggered over to the bar while Little Danny Boy and the rest of our crew found a table. John Taylor was the president of the chapter and my best friend when I bought the farm back in '68, but everyone called him Sonny. Elbowing my way between Sonny and a young Road

Dog with curly blond hair, I pulled a copper coin, about the size of a silver dollar, out of my vest pocket. Engraved on one side of the coin was our club emblem and the words *Road Dogs*, and on the other side of the coin was my name: *Cave Man*. I slapped the coin down on the bar.

"I'm calling the coin," I said. It was a tradition that when someone called the coin, the club member unable to produce his coin bought the next round of beer. All eyes at the bar turned to me and Sonny's eyes widened.

"What chapter are you from, brother? I think I've seen your face somewhere, but I don't remember," the young curly blond-headed biker said.

"I'm from this chapter. The name's Cave Man," I said and turned the coin over, showing my name engraved on the back. Sonny's eyes widened and his jaw dropped.

"I knew Cave Man. You look a lot like him, or like he did before he died back in '68. Where'd you get that coin?" Sonny asked.

"You gave it to me, Sonny. At the ceremony when you patched me in."

"I'll be right back," the blond-headed biker said and disappeared into a back room.

"Who's the young blood?" I asked.

"That our president. We call him Chico."

"Why aren't you still president?" I asked.

Sonny pulled a pack of smokes from his vest pocket and lit one up. "I ran my course. It was time for the young folks to take over."

Chico returned carrying a leather-bound book and his face looked ashen.

"He's in the book," Chico whispered to Sonny. "I knew I'd seen his face somewhere. So are those dudes sitting over at that table with that halo patch on the back of their vests. They're all in the Book of the Dead," Chico said and handed the book to Sonny. The Book of the Dead was a leather bound photo album with pictures of all our fallen brothers, and you had to be dead to be in the book.

"So, if you're Cave Man, prove it. Show me the tat we gave you the day you patched in," Sonny said. I pulled up my shirt and showed him my tattoo.

"Anybody can get a tat. Tell me the last thing you said to me the day you died. Tell me how you went out."

I sighed. "The very last thing I said to you was that after we died for you guys, to have a party for Old School and me. Then I said good bye to that young girl Cynthia. Then I climbed on my bike, I looked at Old School and said, 'let's ride.'"

"Old School. Is he here too?" Sonny asked.

"He's right there at that table."

"Who's Old School?" Chico asked.

"He was before your time. Little Danny Boy was president before me. He died in Vietnam. How'd you guys go out?"

"Me and Old School both got bit by zombies. We plowed into that old oak tree down the road from the dirt road leading back to the cabin. We hit the tree at over 100 mph."

"Is he telling you the truth?" Chico asked.

"I know it sounds crazy, but yeah, he is. He's Cave Man. It happened just like he said," Sonny replied.

"So what's with these halo patches?" Chico asked.

"I'll let Little Danny Boy tell you about that, I said and motioned for him and the bros from the other side of the bar to come over. They walked up to the bar and a few nervous "hellos" came from the Road Dogs lining the bar. It's not every day that a band of bikers come back from the dead and walk into the bar.

"Meet Chico. He's the new president. He wants to know about the halo patch," I said. Chico and Little Danny Boy shook hands.

"He don't feel like no ghost," Chico said and let out a nervous laugh.

"The halos are a group of trouble shooters. We're an auxiliary branch of the Road Dogs," Little Danny Boy replied.

"Why ain't we heard of them?" Chico asked.

"Because you have to be dead to sign up. We started the group in a church meeting in Biker Heaven," Little Danny Boy said and you could have heard a pin drop or maybe a fly fart.

"Are you guys like angels?" Chico asked.

"Sort of, but not quite. They gave us certain powers we can use while we're here to accomplish our mission," Little Danny Boy said.

"Why are you here? Why'd you come back?" Sonny asked.

"Because there's a storm coming and they're called the Hell Raisers. They already wiped out the chapter in Tortilla Flats. They burned their clubhouse to the ground and they're coming here next. This is the mother chapter. If this chapter falls, the Road Dogs fall."

Chico franticly pulled something out of his pocket and put it up to his ear. It reminded me of Captain Kirk's communicator on Star Trek.

"What's that?" I asked.

"It's called a cell phone. It's a telephone, but there's no wires," Sonny said.

Chico held a brief conversation over the phone. Then his eyes widened, he cut the connection, and put the phone in his pocket.

"He's telling the truth. They hit the clubhouse in Tortilla Flats last night and burned everyone alive that was inside," Chico said.

"Why would the powers that be in Biker Heaven, if there is such a place, care about a biker war on Earth?" Sonny asked.

"Because there's more to it than just a couple of bike clubs going to war. It's a war over souls and they have help. Someone unleashed the Devil's imps, but we'll deal with them. You know, Harlem Springs used to be a nice place to live for the citizens as well as for us," Little Danny Boy said.

"It still is. We keep the drug dealers and scum out. Oh there's a few people who sell weed, but they don't cause any trouble," Chico said.

"If the Hell Raisers take over, that'll change. They'll bring in crystal meth, heroin, you name it. This town will be in a world of shit."

"What are we supposed to do? How much time do we have?" Chico asked.

"We'll get into that, but first I called the coin. Produce your coins, brothers," I said. Everyone lining the bar produced their coins, so I had to buy the next round. "Make mine a Jack and Coke," I said to the prospect working the bar and put my coin back in my pocket.

"So how much time do we have?" Chico asked.

Little Danny Boy shrugged, the prospect passed out the drinks and I took a drink from my Jack and Coke.

"Maybe a day or two. We need to be ready," Little Danny Boy said.

A couple of bros started a pool game, a prospect turned down the music, and we put our heads together to talk.

"We've got enough arms and ammunition to hold off a small army," Sonny stated.

"That won't work," I said and shook my head. "They'd just burn this place to the ground with you inside. That's what they did in California. We need to lure them away. We need to trap them in an ambush somewhere."

"Yeah, but where?" Chico asked.

A memory flashed through my brain, penetrating the Jack Daniel's fog. *That's another thing I'll have to get used to*, I thought. *Hangovers.*

"What about that place east of here where we used to party at, back in the day? I think we called it the Devil's Punch Bowl," I said.

"It's still there. The dirt road going in is a little rough, but it's still there. The lake's dried up though," Sonny said and Little Danny Boy grinned.

"That's perfect. This'll all go down at the Devil's Punch Bowl. This is what we'll do," Little Danny Boy said. I sat back, drank my Jack and Coke, and listened.

The Hell Raisers gathered in Parker, Arizona. For two days, they partied and planned their attack while their brothers road in from the north and northeast. Others came up from Mexico, converging on the small desert town on the bank of the Colorado River.

It seemed as if a dark cloud hung over the city. The animals howled at night, and the ministers in the local churches felt an unexpected urgency and called special prayer meetings. What the mortals of Parker, Arizona could somehow sense, but not see, was the evil demonic horde gathering over the landscape.

The Hell Raisers kept a low profile, not wanting to draw too much attention from the local law enforcement, but even so, the police had their hands full with the local criminal element, and by the time they rolled out on a Wednesday evening, they were over two hundred strong.

They took interstate 10 East to Apache Junction, heading East on Highway 60. From 60, they went south on Highway 177, across one of the more desolate sections of Arizona toward Harlem Springs. The night wore on, a full moon rose into the sky, and when the Hell Raisers rolled into the parking lot of the High Noon Saloon, they ran right into a wall of lead.

When the Hell Raisers pulled into the parking lot, the Road Dogs opened up on them from concealed positions. One group of Road Dogs fired from a clump of trees on the edge of the parking lot, while another group opened up from fortified positions using several parked cars and trucks lining the other side of the lot. Meanwhile, the bulk of the Road dogs fired at them from the clubhouse itself. Muzzle flashes lit up the night and the initial onslaught cut down a third of the Hell Raisers and put the rest of the outlaw bikers in a state of disarray.

"Regroup! Back to the highway!" Hellboy yelled trying to rally his forces.

With their enemy in a state of confusion, Chico gave the order to abandon the clubhouse. The group of Road Dogs firing from the treeline ran to their motorcycles, as did the ones firing at the Hell Raisers from behind the parked vehicles.

The Road Dogs in the clubhouse fired a few more rounds, giving their brothers a chance to get away before they made their escape. On the highway, three hundred yards up the road from where Hellboy struggled to regroup the Hell Raisers, the Road Dogs formed up with Chico and Little Danny Boy at the head of the pack.

"We'll meet you at the Punch Bowl," Little Danny Boy said.

"I'll stay with Cave Man," Old School said.

Chico and Little Danny Boy nodded and the Road Dogs roared down the highway. We sat parked in the middle of the highway facing west, watching Hell Raisers form up, and above them, clouds covered the sky as the demonic forces gathered.

"Just like old times, huh?" Old School said.

"Yeah. We died together the last time, so we might as well fight these evil bastards together, too. Road Dogs to the end," I said. I took a bottle of Jack from my vest pocket, took a pull, and handed the bottle to Old school. He took a drink and handed the bottle back to me.

"That's right. Road Dogs in life, Road Dogs in death," Old School said.

The Hell Raisers roared down the road toward us, and above them, hovering over the ground, the leader of the demonic crew blew his horn and followed.

Breathing in the smell of brimstone, I held up my hand and blue lightning fired from my fingertips. In the sky above the road, the blue light flashed, engulfing the imps from Hell. The impact sent them flying in all directions, and their leader pointed his sword, sending a bolt of fire onto the road. Sparks flew into the air, and Old School brought his hand over his shoulder, as if tossing a softball, and sent a ball of fire down the road at the approaching riders. Tires squealed, ten bikes went down, and metal scraped against asphalt.

"That...should hold them for a little while," I said to Old School, feeling breathless from the loss of energy.

"Yeah...let's get the hell out of here. That one took a lot out of me," Old School replied. We whirled around, our bikes changing into radiant steeds of light and chrome, and headed east, flying above the highway.

"These bikes sure are cool," I told Old School. He just nodded and a big grin crossed his face.

We came in low, flying over The Devil's Punch Bowl, and touched ground facing north. When we landed on the dry lake bed, our bikes changed, the radiance fading, and they turned back into older, worn out Harley Davidson motorcycles. I saw something shimmer in the air next to me and three more motorcycles, plus their riders, appeared out of thin air. Once they solidified, I recognized Chops, Teddy Bear and my father, George Taylor. He looked more alive and vibrant than he ever did in life.

My father gave me a cocky grin and said, "You didn't think I was gonna let you have all the fun?"

I let out a barrel laugh, handed him the bottle of Jack, and said, "No, Pops, I didn't figure you would."

Little Danny Boy and the rest of the halo crew nodded at the new arrivals while a line of Road Dogs, sitting on their motorcycle behind us, watched the dirt road leading into the small valley. The rest of the bros wearing the halo patch pulled their bikes up next to us and Chico walked up to where I sat talking to my father.

"If I didn't see that with my own eyes, I wouldn't have believed it. What kind of bikes are those anyway? I've never seen a motorcycle that can fly," Chico said.

"They're spirit bikes. You get them when you cross over," I said, grinning.

"Yeah, whatever," Chico said. "I've got some bros hiding in that big clump of rocks to our left, and another group up on that embankment to our right. When those sons-of-bitches cross the lake bed, we'll get them in a crossfire."

"You guys will have to deal with the ones on the ground. We'll take care of their demonic friends," Little Danny Boy said.

"Yeah, don't worry about what you see in the sky above you, it'll be like the fourth of July," I said.

"I still can't believe this angel and demon shit," Chico replied.

"Just worry about those assholes when they come across the lake bed. We'll take care of the rest," I told him.

"Yeah, right," Chico said and walked back to join the bros lining up behind us. I took the bottle of Old Number Seven from my father, tossed back a shot, and handed it to Old School. He took a shot, handed the bottle back to me, I handed it to Little Danny Boy, who killed the rest of the bottle, and tossed it to the ground. I saw lights coming down the dirt road approaching the lake bed, and above the ground, I saw what looked like a dark cloud covering the valley.

"It's a good thing you only have to die once," I said to Little Danny Boy.

"Yeah, but when them lightning bolts hit, it almost makes you feel like you're gonna die again."

"You know what they said before we left. If we take too many hits and lose our energy, we'll vanish from this plane of existence and wind up back home."

"I know, but we can't let these evil SOBs win. Let's do this thing," Little Danny Boy said, giving me a nod. I looked up, watching the Hell Raisers coming across the lake bed. I gazed above them, seeing the evil imps from Hell. Gunning the throttle on my Pan Head, I let out the clutch and we took flight. Light radiated from the bike and fire belched from its tailpipe as it changed and we gained altitude, advancing on the demonic horde. Old School and Iron Man rode to my left, Little Danny Boy and Thumper to my right, and my father, along with Chops and Teddy Bear, brought up the rear.

We slammed into the dark cloud of the Devil's imps at full speed, causing explosions of lustrous light while below us the Road Dogs opened up on the Hell Raisers. Muzzle flashes blossomed, and lightning bolts and balls of blue light filled the sky when we collided with the demonic host with such force that the impact sent us, along with the demons and their evil steeds, spinning across the valley.

Cranking my throttle, I spun around, and hovered over the valley, slashing with my blade and firing my .357 at the evil vermin when they flew by. Lightning bolts shot out of the barrel of my gun every time I fired it, and blue fire shot from the blade of my knife. An evil looking, two-headed demon came at me, and I sliced my blade through its skull, the demon exploding into a cloud of dust. Beside me, Old School took a lightning bolt in the chest that sent him spinning across the valley.

My father slammed into an evil creature trying to crawl on my back and knocked it to the ground where the demon exploded.

"I sent that one back to Hell where it belongs," Pops said and laughed.

We fought the fiends of Hell above the ground, while our brothers dealt with the Hell Raisers on the lake bed. Teddy Bear took a ball of red light to the chest, and dissipated, fading from this plane of existence. Thumper caught a lightning bolt in the center of his forehead and exploded into nothingness. Iron man went down in flames and disintegrated when three demons stabbed him with their swords, but then the battle turned, both on the ground and above it.

In the dry lake bed, the Road Dogs had the Hell Raisers in a deadly crossfire, cutting them down with a wall of lead.

In the air above them, the imps from Hell flew in disarray, fleeing over the hillside to the north, heading back to the pits of Hell from which they came. Noticing their leader on his two-headed beast, I gunned the throttle and caught up with him. Diving through the air, I slammed into him, grabbed the silver canister, and drove my blade through the top of his golden helmet. He disappeared in a blinding flash of light. My old Pan Head, now my spirit bike, came to me. I climbed into the saddle and floated back down to the ground.

The battle won, the Road Dogs gathered around five figures sitting on their knees in the middle of the lake bed. Hellboy and five other Hell Raisers, now beat up and bloody, looked into the hard face of Chico, the president of the Road Dogs. Several more Road Dogs gathered around them with guns to their heads.

"I ought to just kill you all, but we're not gonna," Chico said.

"What are we gonna do with them?" Sonny asked.

"Cut off their patches, and then let's brand them," Chico said. He glanced at a prospect and said, "Build a fire."

A half hour later, with the sky turning purple in the east, the five remaining Hell Raisers rode away, with the back of their vests bare and the letters RD branded on their biceps. They left in shame. A loud cheer rose up and several Road Dogs shouted curses, urging the remnants of the Hell Raisers on.

"We're not done yet. There's one more thing we need to do," I said to Chico.

"What's that?" he asked.

"We need to set the captives free," I said. Climbing off my bike, I opened the silver canister. We stood back in awe, watching soul after soul ascend to their heavenly reward.

"Like I said before, if I hadn't seen it with my own two eyes, I wouldn't believe it," Chico said, watching what looked like blue streaks of light shoot up into the sky.

"I guess we're done here," I said to Little Danny Boy.

He just shrugged. "No, we'll give it one more day and then head home."

We all climbed back onto our bikes, drove to the highway, and those of us with the halo patch took up the rear, following the Road Dogs back to Harlem Springs.

We partied hard at the clubhouse for the next three days, but all good things come to an end and we needed to get back. Gathering out by the road on a Saturday evening, we did some backslapping and the entire Harlem Springs chapter was there to see us off.

"I'm gonna miss you, bro," Sonny said, giving me a hug. He passed me a bottle of Jack, so I took a pull.

"We'll see each other again," I said.

"Thanks for your help," Chico smiled.

I put my arm around the young man's shoulder and said, "You're gonna make a good president. You'll take the Road Dogs to new heights. In fact, from what I hear, the folk's upstairs think you'll be the best one yet. Just keep the faith. Road Dogs forever, bro."

"Let's mount up!" Little Danny Boy yelled. Those of us with the halo patch on our back formed up on the road and my father pulled up next to me on his old Knuckle Head.

"It'll feel good to ride next to you for a while. It's been a long time," my dad said.

"I know. I talked Little Danny Boy into letting us do about a hundred miles or so before we head home," I replied.

"Yeah, Biker Heaven can wait for a while. I want to feel the wind in my face, but when we get home, I'll buy the first round," Pops said.

Little Danny Boy fired up his bike and we did the same. I took my bottle of Old Number Seven from my vest, took a pull from the bottle, and handed it to my dad. He took a swallow, handed it back, and I tucked it back into my vest pocket.

Little Danny Boy pulled away, the pack following, but for a moment my father and I just sat there.

He looked at me, a big grin on his face, and said, "I'll beat you to the top of the hill." With that, he smoked his tires and peeled out, burning rubber down the highway. I laughed, gunned the throttle, and spun my tires, taking off after him.

ABIGAIL SMYTHE AND THE DEMON

MATT NORD

"Mirror, Mirror in my hand," she said, pausing to lick her blood-red lips, "who's the hottest bitch in the entire fucking land?"

If the demon spirit residing in the mirror had eyes, they would have been rolling. Azazel didn't answer for a time, holding his proverbial tongue. Every time he let Abigail know what he thought about her, she ended up adding another seven years bad luck to her life. She was up to about, oh... five hundred and thirty-nine years by now. And it really sucked to have to transfer his soul into another receptacle!

"Motherfucker, I asked you a question!" The mirror fogged up as she screamed at it, her nose mere inches from the glass.

Thank God I don't have a fucking nose, either, he thought to himself. Unfortunately for Azazel, the stink of her breath seeped in through the pores of the human skin and bone that served as the backing and handle of his prison.

"I heard you," he mumbled.

It wasn't that she had rancid breath by human standards. In fact, if someone was to smell Abigail's breath, they might be reminded of roses and cherries... and they may... mmm...be tempted by that aroma... and those sweet, voluptuous lips. To taste them would be... dammit!

My apologies, dear reader. This is a story about a demonic dildo and the witch who rides it rather than a broom, so back to her and Azazel.

"So," she snapped, glaring at the mirror she held in her left hand. Her right hand rested on her hip, which stuck out at an incredibly sexy angle that would have put Betty Page to shame. The short, black skirt she wore road high up on her thigh, affording Azazel a clear view of Abigail's lace panties.

"Ugh..." the demon groaned. Abigail was not Azazel's type at all, and while lying normally came naturally to him, he preferred honesty, most often, when it concerned how attractive, or 'hot,' he thought she was.

The look on Abigail's face changed from sexy to pouty to annoyed to furious in the course of a few seconds. Her cheeks flushed a fiery red. She didn't have any patience, especially when fishing for compliments from someone or something that was supposed to be a slave to her every whim.

"Uh, you are?" Azazel finally said.

"You don't sound very sure," she growled. She held the mirror at odd angles, twirling it in her hand. The demon got dizzy and would have vomited up any souls he'd eaten in his lifetime if he still had a mouth.

"You are!" he shouted through the mirror. "I'm sure of it! You're the hottest piece of ass since Aphrodite!"

"You're goddamn right I am," she said, slamming the mirror face down on the dresser.

"Hey, be careful," Azazel muffled in complaint.

"Shut up, you ugly shit, or I'll toss you in the recycle bin," she said as she applied more lipstick. "Now, I've got a hot date with Big Red."

It was a jab at Azazel that found its mark. *Not only am I forced to be her quick ego boost, but the bitch uses my amputated dick to get her kicks.* Well, that and to replenish her power. It was also disgusting for him to know his member was being put inside of... a woman.

"Something the matter?" she asked, raising a perfectly manicured eyebrow. An evil smirk flashed over her lips as she turned and sauntered across the room toward the bed. She got halfway there when Azazel let out a deep growl.

She stopped and turned back around. "Really?"

She walked back over to the dresser and turned the mirror over, propping it on its side, giving the demon an unobstructed view of the bed.

"Enjoy the view, fucker," she chuckled, turning back to the bed. She shook her ass back and forth as she walked over to it. She opened the drawer of the nightstand and reached in. The item she pulled out was a nine inch long masterpiece. Deep maroon in color, the shaft had thick veins that seemed to actually pulsate as though they were still living. The head that topped the cock looked like a small fist. While usually petrified, the possessed penis now vibrated and with the power of Hell, no battery required.

He hated it when she befouled his cock with her womanhood, and cursed her all the more for making him watch. He felt every twitch and tremble of every muscle and every fold of flesh as she masturbated with his glory, and he despised every second of it. He could bear a hundred thousand lifetimes of servitude to the lowest of human dregs if he could break free of his glass prison and flay the skin from her flesh. Then he would douse her wriggling body with vinegar and salt.

Oh, her pain would be exquisite! And in the pain of others, Azazel derived true pleasure. He could nearly taste her suffering when...

"Oh fucking shit fuck, yes!" she moaned as she rubbed between the folds of her lips, massaging her ever swelling clitoris. "You piece of shit…uh…probably didn't even know…ah…what to do with this…oooh…"

Azazel endured the humiliation with gritted…well, if he had actual teeth, they definitely would have been gritted. Abigail groaned as the tip of Big Red's head entered her love tunnel. Her back arched as she slid the massive shaft in…out…in again and again.

The cock began to glow, first barely noticeably, but then brighter and brighter by the second. It began to tremble in her hand, half because of the shaking that wracked her body, half from its own power that was about to…

Abigail let out a load animal growl, her ecstasy reaching its crescendo. The demonic penis released its seed into her as both she and the now seemingly living member came together. She screamed as it filled her with what felt like molten lava, the heat spreading quickly from her groin to the extremities of her entire body. Every muscle in her body spasmed, and an inhuman scream erupted from her mouth before she collapsed into a pile of sweaty bed sheets.

Seven hours later.

Abigail stirred at the knocking on her front door. If her bed hadn't been on the first floor, she probably would have slept through to the next day. She glanced at the clock to see it was 4:13 p.m.

She got out of bed, stretching in a cat-like manner. The purr she let out completed the image. She walked over to the dresser and checked herself in the large mirror. Looking quickly down at the hand-held mirror, she smirked.

Primping herself in the mirror, she asked Azazel, "Was it good for you, baby?"

There was no answer from the demon. The knocking came again at the door.

"Fine," she pouted, turning away from the dresser, "be that way."

Abigail stormed across the room and headed down the hallway to the front door. She reached for the knob just as whoever was standing on the other side of the door knocked again… unfortunately for them.

Her hand stopped an inch from the doorknob, and she rolled her eyes. She clinched her jaw and her fist, and then released both.

She grabbed and twisted the knob viciously, nearly breaking it off the door, pulling the door open with such force that it almost came off its hinges. She flew through the opening and came face to face with a young man standing on the doorstep, his hand still raised in the act of knocking.

"You are fucking late," she growled, the heaving breaths she took steaming up his thick glasses.

"I-I-I'm s-sorry, mistress," he stammered, retracting his hand and placing it into his pocket, matching the other one. He stumbled back half a step and averted his eyes. She glared at him for several moments and he began to shuffle his feet.

"My classes ran la..."

She turned away, her hair smacking him in the face, and walked back into the house. The young man stood dumbfounded outside the door.

"Well," she called over her shoulder, "get your ass in here and shut the fucking door, Timothy."

"Yes, mistress," he said softly. He followed behind and closed the door quietly.

He followed her down the hall, into her combination bedroom/laboratory/sex cave. He shucked his backpack from his shoulders and set it down on a pile of panties in the far corner of the room. He shoved a pair into an open pocket of his backpack while Abigail's back was turned.

"All right, numb-nuts. Get to work," Abigail snapped. "I want this place spic-and-span when I get back."

She stripped down naked and walked into the bathroom. Timothy cast a longing stare after his would-be mistress and mentor as she donned a tight pink sweat suit.

"Where are you going, mistress?" he asked.

"Not that it's any of your business, but I'm going to the gym," she said, slipping on an obnoxiously pink tennis shoe.

"But..." Timothy began, and quickly shut his mouth. He feared Abigail's wrath more than any other thing in this world and many others.

"But what, maggot?" she snapped, pulling on the other shoe.

"It's just…" He took a deep breath. "You said you would teach me a spell today."

"Yeah, I say lots of things," she said. She stood up and snatched a gym bag off the back of the bathroom door and strode past him, bumping into his shoulder and nearly knocking him off his feet.

"Now, get to work." Abigail sped out the room and down the hallway. Timothy heard the front door open and then slam shut.

He sighed, looking around the mess of a room. For all the care she put into her physical appearance, her living conditions were one step above a pigsty, but not a pigsty in the sense that a mother tells her kid his room is a mess.

There was rotting food lying about, mountains of dirty clothes in nearly every corner of the room, mold growing from various spots on the walls, and a pile of… well, you get the idea.

"How can anybody live like this?" he asked himself, contemplating what the place might look like if he didn't clean it twice a week. *Especially someone who is so concerned with appearance,* he thought.

"You get used to it," he heard a voice say from behind him.

Timothy pulled on some rubber gloves taken from his pocket, grabbed a basket, and started tossing clothes into it, trying not to gag at the smell.

"I mean, she is a witch after all," came from the dresser. "Not the green-skinned, wart-faced old hag with the pointy black hat, but disgusting nonetheless…wouldn't you agree, Timothy?"

"I'm not supposed to talk to you," he said, trying not to breathe through his mouth. He continued picking up dirty clothes.

"Come on, Timothy," Azazel said. "Lighten up. She's not going to be home for hours. You know that."

Timothy didn't say anything. He continued to clean up in silence, regretting that he'd forgotten his IPod at home. After half an hour, he started to get bored. Abigail didn't have a radio or a television. This fact hadn't been lost on him. He often wondered what the point of becoming a witch was besides being able to accumulate power and wealth. If Abigail Smythe was any indication, being a mage wasn't very lucrative.

If he hadn't seen her wield magic the way she did, he wouldn't have bothered begging to become her apprentice. But after eight months of basically being her bitch, she hadn't taught him so much as a card trick.

Unbeknownst to Timothy, his thoughts weren't very difficult for the demon to read.

"What would you say if I told you..." Azazel began. "Oh, never mind. You're not ready."

Timothy tried not to allow his curiosity to get the better of him, but his current boredom, coupled with his bitterness towards Abigail, caused him to throw caution to the wind.

"Not ready for what?" he asked.

"Well," the demon said, with an ethereal smirk, "what if I said I could give you power like hers?"

Timothy mulled over what the demon said. "I'd say you were lying, because that's what demon's do," he replied.

"And if I wasn't lying?"

"Then I'd ask what was in it for you."

Azazel let out a raspy laugh. "One of us is here because he chooses to be," he said. "One of us is not. I'll tell you how to gain the power you so desperately seek if you promise to kill once you have it."

Timothy doubted every word the demon uttered, but he couldn't help it. While he knew the demon lied as easily as he spoke, the thought of Abigail dying at his hand, after the humiliation she'd heaped upon him, was very tempting, and temptation was Azazel's specialty.

"Tell me," Timothy said.

"Very well," the demon chuckled.

Abigail arrived home at a little after seven o'clock. She dropped her gym bag inside the door and walked straight to her room.

"What the hell?" she mumbled, looking at the mess still filling her room. "Timothy! What the fuck have you been doing?"

She saw no sign of him in the room, but she did notice Big Red lying on her bed.

"Why is this back here?" she shouted, picking it up. "And why is there..." She sniffed, "Ugh, shit and blood all over it?"

She heard laughter coming from the dresser.

"What did you do, you sick fuck?" She stalked over to the dresser and snatched up the demonic looking glass.

"Who, me?" Azazel asked innocently.

"Where is that little shit?" she snarled, pointing at the feces-covered phallus at the mirror.

She heard moaning coming from the bathroom. The door opened and Timothy crawled out, blood dripping from every orifice.

"Help me... please," he begged. "My insides are on fire."

Abigail gazed at him in disgust. She looked from him to the mirror and back again, then began to laugh, continuing to do so for several moments.

Timothy collapsed to the floor, gasping for breath.

"Stupid shit," Abigail hissed while shaking her head. "Azazel is bound to me. Only I can take in his power."

Timothy turned his head and looked up at the mirror. "But..."

"He knew what would happen, too," she said, laughing again.

"Hey, a guy has to have some fun," the demon said. "Maybe I won't mind fucking you if I can think about this tasty morsel for a while."

"Oh, you aren't getting away with this so easy," she said, letting the mirror slip from her hand.

"Wait!" he shouted a second before it shattered on the floor.

"Oops," she giggled. "Seven more years."

She stepped over Timothy's now still body and went into the bathroom to give Big Red a sorely needed washing.

LOST AND FOUND

MICHAEL D. GRIFFITHS

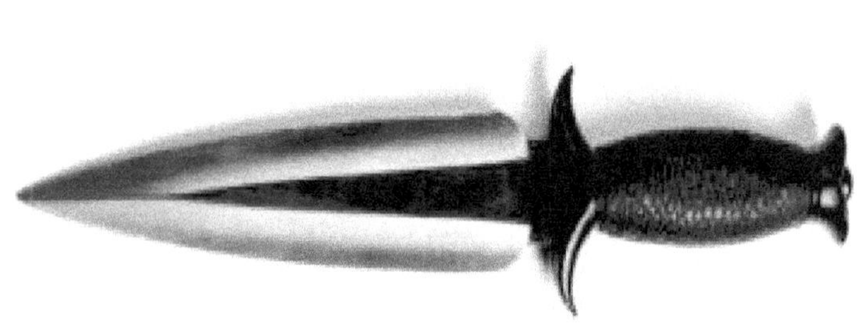

Sweat poured off Fritz's brow, his face feeling flushed all night from working. A well-deserved grunt was suppressed when Eden walked by. The long-legged brunette would probably rather shave her head than talk to him, but that was still no reason for her to think he was too wimpy to lift the box of meat without complaining.

After moving the last box into the freezer, he washed his hands, brushed them off on his pants, and headed to the front of the restaurant. Ginger was closing the register. She pushed a stray strand of her short amber bob back behind her ear and said, "You wrapping things up, Fritz?"

"Pretty much. You doing anything tonight? Feel like getting a..."

"Matt is picking me up. You could head over to The Joint with us if you wanted." She ended with a smile which just reminded him just how single he was.

"Maybe, I...uhm have to make a few calls first—see what my buddies are up to."

"Sounds good, just show up if you wanna. My friend's band, Slug Bacon, will be playing. They're pretty cool." She gave him a lackluster smile and fiddled with her purse.

He looked past her. "Hey, is that the lost and found box?"

"Yeah." She drew out the word, more focused on her reflection in the small mirror.

"I'm going to check for my missing zippo. I lost it here the other day." After crouching down near the box, he gazed in Ginger's direction. Her calf high boots were topped with a long expanse of midnight blue stockings before they reached her tight little mini. Despite her having a boyfriend, his eyes went from furtive glances to bold lingering, as she continued to apply her rosy lip gloss.

"Having fun down there?"

"I uh, hey, it's here." He sparked his lighter, then spied something under an old scarf. "Hey, what's this?" He pulled it out. "Holy crap, get a load of this."

The antique dagger filled his fist. A long twin-edged blade met an intricately carved brass handle with crossbeams shaped like curved talons.

"Wow, look at this thing. How intense!"

"I don't remember seeing that there," she said.

"Good, because I'm totally keeping it."

Standing up, he admired the dagger, turning it over in his hands as a wide grin spread across his face. Ginger was saying something, but he didn't hear her as he stabbed the dagger forward like a fencer, making several slashing motions.

A second later, he froze and his eyes bulged. "What the...?"

There before him—well, he wasn't sure what had happened. It was as if he'd sliced the air itself open, only it was more than that. The tear in the very air radiated colors liked a smeared oil painting. Looking closer, he saw the tear wasn't leaking colors as much as exposing them. He could see through the jagged hole into... something past it.

"No way..." he gasped.

Ginger had moved away and he called her over. "You have to see this."

"Put the knife away, first," she said.

He shoved it through his belt without taking his eyes off the glowing phenomenon. "It's like another world in there. A bright moving jungle." He stretched his hand towards the opening. "As insane as it sounds, I think the knife cut a portal between worlds."

She grabbed his arm. "Then don't touch it, you idiot!"

"Why not? Look at the stream and rolling hills full of fruit trees. And those animals, the place seems like a Disney movie. I…"

"What's all this shouting?" Max asked as he hurried into the main dining area. He was thirty pounds too stocky and had more hair on his face than his head. He was their boss, so they turned toward him. At once, Fritz realized there would be no way he could hide the vivid fissure hovering in the air behind him.

"What's that light? Did you break something?" Max demanded.

From behind Max another man called out. "Ginger, you in there?" The words were followed by a dark-haired pretty boy who looked like he'd spent more hours in the gym than Fritz worked in a week.

"Who is that?" Fritz demanded.

"Remember? It's Matt. My boyfriend."

"Oh great, just what we need, more witnesses," he groaned.

"Witnesses to what?" Max was shouting.

Fritz moved to the side while the other men stared. Max's jaw lingered half open, stuck in mid word. Matt's eyes grew large and he rushed over to Ginger. "What is that thing? Maybe you shouldn't get too close."

"Screw that," Fritz said. "I want to go in there and check it out!"

"Go in where?" Max asked. "What the hell are you talking about?"

"In through there," Fritz said, with a smile and a sweep of his arm.

"Are you sure about this, Fritz?"

He liked hearing the concern in her voice.

"You bet. This is the coolest thing to ever happen. It's like a wormhole or something. I stuck my hand through and nothing happened. How could we even think about turning down an opportunity to be the first to explore a new world?"

"Shouldn't we tell the police or something?" Max asked.

"Yeah, right." Fritz twisted his face in disproval. "They'd move us out for our protection and some astronauts or something would get to go in first. Then they'd never let us have a chance. This is it. We have to do it now. I don't care about anything else. I'm going."

"Should we tie ourselves together or something?" Matt suggested.

"It seems pretty safe to me and if there are any problems, the opening's right there. I already saw a butterfly come into our world. It didn't look any worse for the crossover." He looked over at Max. "You coming?"

"Yeah, I'll come just to make sure this isn't some trick. Who knows, maybe we can seat people in there." He grinned. "It could be quite a gimmick."

"Hold on. Should Ginger be going? It could be dangerous."

She crossed her arms. "I was here when he opened it. I want to go. I already changed back into my working shoes."

"I'm not sure..."

"Matt..." She was tapping her foot. "We've been on a few dates. We aren't married. I'm going to go."

"All right, just let me find some kind of weapon first—just in case." A second later, he came up with a two foot steel bar that the restaurant used for breaking up chunks of ice on the front walkway in the winter.

A smile crossed his face, as he said, "Okay, if we're all ready, let's go."

Getting through the tear itself was a little tricky, but Fritz used the dagger to slice and cut, until the opening was larger.

He walked inside.

The ground under his feet was grass on a warm summer day. Birds dived between the branches of trees. The very air reminded him of being a child, when the world was new and full of endless possibilities.

The others were at his back, so he cautiously moved forward. A wide winged insect floated before his face, its wings blazing with light. It was too much to take in. He moved a few more steps deeper into the vibrating jungle.

He was near a bush with pulsing violet leaves. He had never felt such peace.

Then something happened.

The color ran from the plants and flowers, like water tossed on a wet painting. Before he could finish his gasp of surprise, some of the plants faded out of existence. In there place were ragged, half-dead trees. The trunks were gray and faded, sky the color of wet cardboard.

Casting a glance behind him, Fritz saw that the four of them were in a graying world, and even as he looked, the tear through which he could see the dining room was closing.

"Max! The doorway is closing."

It was too late. Within seconds the passage had sealed. Before Fritz reached Max, he could no longer even tell where it had been.

Drawing the dagger in a panic, he slashed before him, but no doorways were opening this time.

A deep roar echoed through what was becoming a foul swamp. It was so loud he felt his teeth rattle.

To their left, a colossal footfall shook the ground.

They ran.

"What the hell are we going to do now, smart guy?" Matt badgered.

Fritz had done more than focus on his running. His mind was swarming with a dozen conflicting thoughts, and five times as many unanswered questions. During their reckless sprint, they found no signs of man or civilization—just more dead trees and gray swamp.

Before he could respond, Max was calling out. "Wait, wait. Come on, I need to catch my breath." Sweat dripped from the edges of his hair. "I doubt that thing's going to wait for us. All the money in the world won't help you here." He moved towards Fritz and thumped his fingers against the younger man's chest. "We aren't even in our world anymore, are we?"

"Why are you blaming me?" Fritz's face was red and he jerked his body into a fighting stance. "I only found the portal two minutes before you got there. No one made you go in with me. I'm as screwed as everyone else!"

"But you were..."

A titanic roar interrupted him.

"Keep going!" Max yelled and then sprinted away from them.

"You and I will finish this later, Max," Matt yelled and then, after grabbing Ginger's hand, he ran after Max.

Fritz cast a glance over his shoulder and wished he hadn't. Something huge was moving through the fog. A colossal dark beast. It slapped the earth with a long appendage the size of a train. The ground shook so badly he almost lost his footing.

Soon he was running so fast he passed them all.

Two hours had passed when they found a collection of boulders. There was a clearing in the center of the man-high, smoke colored stones, and they caught their breath inside the rough circle.

"It almost looks like this could have been man made, about a fucking million years ago," Matt said, running his hand across the stone's coarse surface.

"They won't protect us against that thing following us," Fritz said. "It was like half dinosaur and half Cthulhu."

"Don't you start up. It's your fault we're here in the first place!" Matt yelled.

"Quiet down," Max hissed. "Whatever that thing is, you're gonna attract it."

Stepping forward, Ginger said, "He's right. Whatever's going on, we need to be a team. Right now, we're all each other has." She paused and favored them with a joyless smile. "Please?"

"Okay," Matt said, moving in to hug her. "I thought I saw what might have been a mountain range in the direction we were going over the treetops. High ground is never a bad thing. I say we go in that direction." He turned to face Fritz. "Are you cool with that?"

"Yeah, I'm cool, let's go."

"Already?" Max complained.

"We can rest when we get to the mountains," Matt said, and led the way.

Fritz looked at the departing couple as he helped Max to his feet, then hurried after them before the fog swallowed them from view.

* * *

There must have been some sort of sun lingering above the clinging mists, because an even greater darkness was slowly claiming the harsh land. The frigid marshes were also being replaced by a rock filled terrain.

Fritz thought he heard something to his right, but when it didn't repeat, he let it go. His ears had been playing tricks on him all day, but then, he heard it again. He stopped to listen and heard something to his left.

He jogged a few yards forward until he was right beside Matt. The look on the man's face said everything. "I've been hearing it, too. Don't stare. Try not to let them know that we know they're out there."

Fritz caught a glimpse of Ginger's terrified face and set his jaw. "You still have a weapon?"

"It's never left my hand."

"I still have the dagger that got us into this mess so I guess it's better than nothing."

"Have you tried to make another doorway or whatever it was?" Ginger asked.

He sliced the air before him with the blade. "Only about a hundred times." His words came slower. "Hey, where's Max?"

Behind them there was nothing.

"He was only a few feet back, he should have..." Contorted laughter filled the night and drove shivers through his bones.

"Come on, keep moving!" Matt yelled. "We need to find some high ground or maybe a ledge."

Fritz didn't argue and they were soon running once more. Traveling proved harder in the twilight. Rocks loomed out of nowhere in the darkness and he could barely keep sight of the couple ahead of him.

The trio came to a stop at a rock wall.

"Oh shit," Fritz gasped. "Is this a dead end?"

"No, it's only about ten feet up. We need to climb. Ginger, you're first. Help me push her up there," Matt said.

She didn't argue and soon Fritz's hands were underneath her shoes and helping push her over the stony lip above. She screamed when two shapes crashed into the men below.

They were manish things. Both bodies were draped in torn and tattered gray rags. Like dirty beggars, they clutched and tore at the humans. Their eyes glowed like red death, twin coals from Hell.

A filthy hand found Fritz's throat before he could fend it off, as the other arm of his attacker raised a cold iron sickle. Without thinking, Fritz stabbed forward with the dagger. The creature screamed like the abyss had already claimed it, falling into a jerking seizure. Others of its kind, that were still racing in from out of the darkness, gave pause and held back beyond the dagger's reach. The one Fritz had stabbed continued to howl like its soul was being torn apart.

Fritz stared for a moment, amazed at what he'd done, then turned and drove his dagger into the back of the one Matt was wrestling with. Once again, it fell on the ground, uttering a horrid series of loud screams.

Matt's blood-streaked face was in shock for only a moment, before he yelled, "Go!"

Both men started up the rocky face. For Fritz, it was harder to scramble with only one free hand—the other holding the dagger—and before they made it over, the dirty half-men found their courage to follow. With twisted guttural cries, they charged the pair. Claw-like hands grasped the men's ankles and Fritz and Matt were pulled back into the masses of screeching fiends.

Their foul hands clutched at him and Fritz slashed again with the dagger. Each hit brought forth tortured screams and the creatures fell away, writhing in agony. Those that hadn't been struck moved away in fear.

Fritz rose to his feet. His body was battered and bleeding, but he managed to get his back against the stone. He held the dagger before him, keeping the fiends at bay. "Matt?"

"Here," came a gasp. Matt was trying to fight back with the metal pole, but it lacked the dagger's 'special' effect.

Suddenly, Matt's eyes grew wide as a sickle plunged deep into his chest. Through blood stained lips, he said, "Go! Keep Ginger safe. I'll try to slow them down."

The other creatures were forming a half circle around Fritz again, when Matt yelled and made one last attack with his iron club. Fritz didn't wait; he turned and leapt as high as he could. His fingers clutched a ridge and he was able to pull himself up just as the cold fingers of the creatures below sought to grab him.

He rolled away from the ledge, to find no sign of Ginger.

"What now?" he said. Picking a direction, he hurried along, hoping Ginger was somewhere ahead.

Ginger had cried long and hard when he finally caught up to her. Fritz couldn't get her to move for some time. They were crouched under a gnarled old tree set between two boulders. He figured she would move when they were attacked again, but that never happened.

They were several hours into the night and it had grown very cold. "We need to stay warm," he whispered, and when he put his arms around her narrow shoulders, she didn't resist.

Somehow, they made it through the night without being assaulted or freezing to death.

Ginger had remained still and silent for so long, and appeared completely traumatized, that he was shocked when she asked, "Why didn't those evil things attack us last night?"

"I'm not sure," he said, but he believed that the creatures were probably flesh eaters. That they had eaten enough for now and would be coming for them later, though he would never tell her that.

Despite everything, he still found her beautiful.

"Maybe they can't climb?" she asked hopefully.

"Perhaps they're afraid of what lives up here." As soon as he said it, the look of fear on her face made him wish he'd kept his thoughts to himself. "I'm going to go check where we fought them. I'll be real quick, I promise. You stay..."

"To hell with that! I'm not gonna be left alone."

"All right, but hang back, just in case."

She nodded.

He felt nervous, climbing back down from the plateau, but besides the swirling mists, nothing was there. If he had killed any of the things, it was impossible to tell. Besides a few patches of dark blood on the rock and ground, the area was as empty as they had found it. Then he saw something at his feet.

It was the steel bar.

When Ginger saw it, she began to cry.

After picking up the bar, Fritz hurried Ginger back up to the plateau. The rocks were sharp under his fingers and filth clung to his hands that he doubted he would ever be able to remove. They went back to where they had slept the night before and he didn't disturb her when she collapsed against one of the stones. Instead, he explored the area in ever-widening circles.

The first thing he found was a decent sized club, which he grabbed. There wasn't much else. Some damp twigs and a few logs he might be able to start a fire with later, but with all the creatures around, he wasn't even sure that would be a good idea. There was some type of gray moss clinging to the boulders. He wondered if it was edible, but wasn't desperate enough to try yet.

After checking on Ginger a few times, he found the edge of the plateau that was closest to their little camp. Looking out, he couldn't see much below him, due to the fog. A few dead trees poked out through the mists, a couple of rocky areas, but that was it.

"At least there won't be a shortage of fire wood here," he tried to joke, but couldn't pull it off.

More searching didn't lead to much. A maze of tangled trees and boulders was spread over an endless array of dull pewter peddles and splintered stones. He found a few more places where they could hide, but none were better to bother moving Ginger.

Looking over his shoulder, after hearing a rattling noise, revealed nothing. He had braced for an attack with the dagger and then remembered it was the dagger's fault that they were trapped in this strange land in the first place.

For over an hour, he slashed and fenced with the accursed thing, but unlike before, it never did anything different than what an old blade should. He thought back to how the creatures had reacted to the dagger. It had hurt them badly, far more than it should have. Even if he couldn't figure out how to make a gate with the blade, it was far from useless.

Before long, he returned to camp.

Ginger hadn't touched the steel bar he left near her. Nor did she address him or even look up when he returned. He set to carving the end of his makeshift club into a point. "Never can have too many weapons," he mumbled.

She didn't reply. He carved for a long time.

Later, the mists thickened and began to rise, threatening to saturate the plateau.

"It seems to be colder than last night." Her words startled him.

"Yeah, I guess so."

More carving.

"Should we make a fire, maybe?" Her hair hung in loose strings around her petite face.

He put down the knife and rubbed his tired hand. "I'm not sure. It could attract them."

Regaining some of her spunk, she said, "Don't you think they already know where we are?"

"Maybe, but even if they don't, there could be other things beside the ones we ran from."

"So, some might be afraid of fire. It could help. I'd rather not freeze and the light would make me feel safer. I have a lighter, if that's what you're worried about."

"Remember, it was me finding my Zippo that got us into this mess." He attempted a grin, while he fished the old lighter out of his pocket.

"I'll start gathering some twigs. I saw on a show that if the wood is damp you need to carve the branches to get shavings. I'll try to do that."

"Ah, genius," she said with a threat of a smile, "what do you call those at your feet?" He actually chuckled when he saw the pile of shavings from his carving lying between his feet.

The fire did help keep back the terror of the night. Fog had claimed the land. It was on every side of them, even above. The fire burned it away before it could touch them. If only just barely.

"I'm glad we have a fire," she said.

"I just wish we had something to cook."

She stared at him for a moment before saying, "I don't want to stay here. This is a horrible, horrible place."

"Do you think I do?"

"You brought us here." The smoke twisted in a slight breeze and he coughed when it moved his way.

"You can't blame me for that. I didn't mean to," he said.

"You used the knife, you led us here."

"It looked beautiful. Besides, the knife was in the lost and found box near you. Didn't you know where it came from?" His voice grew louder.

"Have you tried to use it again?"

"Of course I have, over and over."

"Maybe I should..." Her face lost all color when an all too human scream tore through the night.

"Oh no," her little hands covered her mouth.

"I'm sorry, Ginger."

Another scream echoed and Fritz hurried to throw a big log onto the already roaring blaze.

"That sounds like Max. Should we..."

He only nodded and she began to cry. Then she stood up and walked a few feet away.

Moving with slow steps, he joined her on the flat rock she had made her seat. He was trying to work up the courage to give her a hug when a horrid, hollow voice invaded their privacy.

"Far from home, are we?" Then, after a pause, the rasping voice continued, "Welcome to the Glooms."

"Who are you?" he called out. So far, the fog had hidden the speaker.

Ginger's face drew so close to his that he could feel the warmth of her breath. Then she whispered, "We shouldn't be able to understand him. There's no way whatever that is should be speaking English."

Then it loomed before them, parting the mists. The figure was tall and covered with torn and faded rags, save for its head, upon which a tattered animal skull rested. The figure was more goat than anything else Fritz could name, a horned monstrosity, almost two feet in length.

Ginger gasped and he stood. Drawing her back, he made sure the roaring fire remained between them and the ominous creature.

It was little more than a whisper, when Fritz said, "Who are you?"

"I am the king of the mound," its voice hissed. "This hillock was made from the corpses of thousands of bodies given over to me when your ancestors were still banging rocks together."

"Where are we? What is this place?"

A low diseased laughter echoed across the rocks. "You are in the Glooms, my lovely little fleshbags, the mists of the 666 have come to claim you."

"But how did we get here? It's…it's impossible." Fritz's knees were weak with horror and he could feel Ginger trembling against him. All around, the mists boiled and hovered as if they were living things ready to pounce.

The goat-man's voice was like an injured snake when he said, "I should be asking you that question."

"It was by a dagger we found," Ginger said. "We just want to go home. Can you make it work? You can have it as long as you just open a gate for us to go back!"

"Ginger, shhhh," Fritz said, but it was too late.

The goat-man took a step closer until the fire reflected off his greasy garments. "Let me see it." It was a demand, not a request.

Fritz had been holding his pointed club between him and the goat-man, and now, with a slow and deliberate movement, he took out the mysterious dagger.

"That blade is one of the Totems of Gray. Give it to me at once."

"No, not unless you agree to send us back to our own world!" Fritz yelled.

"Fool, at best you can bargain for a quick death," the goat-man laughed, but then wasted no further time on words as he rushed around the fire towards them, moving at impossible speed.

A hand clamped down on Fritz's wrist and he cried out. The cold was like nothing he had ever experienced. The iron grip felt like it was about to snap his bones.

He slammed his club into the side of the goat-man's skull, but this just brought forth waves of distorted laughter.

The pain Fritz felt was beyond what he could bear, and he knew he was about to lose consciousness, so he tried a different tactic.

He thrust the end of his club into the hot coals of the fire and then, moving quickly, flung them up into the goat-man's face. The figure shrieked and stumbled backward, forced to let go of Fritz's wrist in order to brush the coals from his face. That was when Fritz struck. Taking the dagger in both hands, he rushed forward and stabbed the goat-man in the chest.

The goat-man gasped, stumbling back, and that was when Ginger rushed forward and pushed the creature into the roaring blaze.

The screams lasted minutes.

Nothing changed with the dagger. Fritz still couldn't get it to work, but they both agreed it was a potent weapon.

Days passed, and Fritz explored the plateau while Ginger collected wood and tried to make a shelter for them. The evil creatures they had first fought upon arriving still lurked below, but some fear-driven dread or taboo kept them off the plateau.

Food wasn't impossible to find, though slugs and moss made for a poor diet. They were safe for now, but still trapped in multiple ways. They were trapped in a world of gloom and also trapped on the mesa, in the middle of the harsh fog that claimed the bleak landscape. They did still have each other and their morale was still high. Ginger was beyond melancholy and Fritz had not dared to do more than snuggle against her for warmth at night, but hoped one day she might come around.

One morning Fritz sat on the edge of the plateau and Ginger joined him.

"This place is like a living nightmare," she said as they each watched the dark fog boiling around them.

"No doubt, but where there's life, there's hope."

"Do you really think so?" she asked, while looking over at him.

"Yes I do, and I bet that one day we'll get out of here."

"I sure hope so."

He took her hand in his and she made no move to draw it away.

PAGE 89

TERRY ALEXANDER

Bob Simmons sat alone in his home on Ridgemont Street, shivering in the darkness. He'd checked the doors and windows several times, ensuring each was locked tight. He'd purchased the house many years ago. He knew every creak of the floor and every groan from the rafters. Only now things seemed different, changed. The familiar surroundings had taken on a sinister feel.

A muted television provided the only light, giving the room a surreal quality. "That's two." He stared at the dog-eared paperbacks on the coffee table. "Two dead."

He leaned forward. His hand lingered over the nearest paperback. He feared to touch the book. Dread circled in his belly like a living thing. Bob exhaled a deep breath. His whiskered jaw trembled slightly. He pushed the terror away to some dark place, and snatched the tome from the table. The colorful cover depicted a heavily muscled man in a blue, skintight uniform, battling a group of deformed wolf-like creatures.

The Samson Adventures, sprawled across the top in bold red letters, part one of an exciting new trilogy. ***Attack of the Unhumans,*** featuring the greatest hero of all time, Samson.

At first glance, it appeared to be a standard superhero novel, one of several hitting the racks lately, but this one was different. This paperback held death between its covers. He thumbed through the pages, stopping at page 89.

He turned his head quickly. Was that a noise? He froze, licking his lips nervously. Bob scanned the gloomy interior. That sounded like a voice. His lower jaw trembled. They're here. They're watching me. He concentrated, hoping to isolate the sounds. There it is again, footsteps, smooth soles sliding over polished floors.

He scanned the first paragraph.

The unhuman assassin crashed through the window, showering Professor Rory Kenspotter in shards of jagged glass. A scream of absolute terror burst from the scientist's lips. The short hairy bipedal monstrosity hopped around on stubby legs. Its obscenely long arms dragged the floor. A set of red, close-set eyes fastened on Kenspotter. His misshapen assailant plunged a massive fist through the professor's open mouth. His head exploded in a shower of the three B's, blood, brains and bone.

"Page 89," Bob mumbled. "Page 89, I read this book at the hospital when Uncle Rory passed." He tossed the book to the table; it slid across the slick Formica surface and fell to the floor. He ran a paw-like hand over his stubbly jaw, a bad habit he'd developed over time, one he subconsciously completed every time he was frightened. Uncle Rory seemed to be recovering from the knee surgery when an aneurysm burst in his brain. At first Bob refused to associate the death scene with his uncle's passing, thinking it a coincidence that his uncle carried the same first name as the professor.

He glanced at the garish cover on the second book. The hero Samson, his hands fisted, the right arm drawn back to strike the strange winged ape creature before him. The bold lettering proclaimed it as part two of the Samson trilogy. ***Samson battles the Mindrender in The Devil's Flame.***

He recalled the day he made the purchase at the local bookstore, some three months after Uncle Rory's death. The lurid cover caught his eye; Frank Frazetta himself couldn't have drawn a better one. He devoured the printed words with passion, savoring every one...until page 89.

He lifted the volume gingerly, afraid to touch it with more than his thumb and forefinger. "Lynn Daystrom is murdered on page 89." Tears filled his eyes, the most painful memory of his life happened on July fourteenth, the day he read those fateful words.

His fiancée Lynn Scott died in a car crash on July the fourteenth. A head on collision with a 4X4 pickup ended her promising young life. When the police, fire department and ambulance attendants finally succeeded in prying her limp body from the wreckage, they nearly gagged. The violent nature of the crash cut her in half at the waist, in the same fashion of the Black Dahlia. In the book, Miss Daystrom was murdered by a mad man copying the brutal nature of Elizabeth Short's death as a tribute to her unknown murderer. The local coroner placed her time of death at approximately 10:30 p.m., near the same time he read page 89.

"Lynn, I'm so sorry. I miss you so much." His hands covered his face, shoulders quivering. He tried not to sob. Grown men don't cry, he told himself. Grown men don't cry.

Bob never finished the second novel. He locked it in a desk drawer, vowing he'd never purchase another Samson novel or any book by the series writer, R.G. McShane, a pen name shared by a handful of authors trying to make a buck. He flipped the paperback at the table; it caught on the edge, dangling over the floor.

"I swore." His words became garbled, and he took a moment to wipe his eyes.

"I swore I'd never buy part three. I swore I'd never read another word of this crap."

He jumped, twisting his head, staring wide-eyed at the far wall, and the large window. There's that noise again, the soft squeal of a door opening and soft soled shoes shuffling on a tile floor. Voices, he heard the mumble of voices.

Bob's eyes panned across the room, certain in his mind that someone lurked in a shadowed corner. Unwilling to trust his eyes, he knew he wasn't alone.

The cold floor sent shivers up Bob's legs as he crossed the room to the television. His hand closed on the small package atop the set. The partially exposed cover showed Samson, battered and bruised, his colorful costume in tatters, on his knees staring toward the heavens. The raised lettering on the cover read, ***Samson battles his greatest foe in The Stars Against Us.***

"I didn't order this book." His voice cracked. "I know I didn't." He examined the spine. A lamp shade logo circled by the words, ***Black Light Books***, caught his eye.

I've never heard of this publishing company. The others aren't published by Black Light, he thought.

He tossed the book to the littered table; it slid from the packaging and fell to the floor in a tent-like fashion. He scratched his whiskered jaw. The sound reminded him of coarse sandpaper on wood. "I'll never read it." He spoke to the book as if it could hear him, his raised voice bouncing off the walls. "I'm not going to cause another death."

He grew silent. The creaking of the old house grew louder, as the house settled. He felt eyes watching him from the darkness. He glanced at the sprawled books, to see that volume one had landed face up. The eyes of Samson appeared to move, staring at him, watching his movements.

No more, no one else will die because of these things.

He gathered the books together, holding them at arm's length like a putrid dead animal. *No more death. It stops here.* Bob hurried to the kitchen, tossing them into the trash. The rotating lid circled furiously before losing momentum.

A sudden numbness began in his toes, spreading slowly to his ankle and up his leg. He clutched at the refrigerator for support, the metal surface vibrating under his fingers. "It's my imagination," he mumbled. "Only my imagination."

He reached inside the Kenmore for a cold beer.

The chilled can sent painful shivers up his arm to the elbow. A wave of dizziness ballooned in his head, growing at each breath. The can fell from his numb, unresponsive fingers. Beer splattered the floor. His extremities felt heavy. The numbness spread to his knees, up his thighs, to his waist. It radiated through his shoulders and down to his fingers.

"What's going on?" His speech became garbled. *What's happening to me?*

Bob walked on stiff legs, forcing his feet to slide across the linoleum's pastel patterns. He gritted his teeth together. Tears streamed down from the corners of his eyes, threading down his face.

The chair, I've got to make it to the chair. I can rest and catch my breath.

He fell to his knees. Each breath brought a new experience in agony. The fog slowly cleared in his mind, allowing a moment of clarity.

The books, it has to be the books. Page 89, I've got to look at page 89.

Agony wracked his body. His nerve endings burned inside his frame. He crawled toward the trash can, using his elbows to crawl forward. Sweat dripped from his nose. His skin burned against the linoleum. Slowly, ever so slowly, he wormed his way to the upright trash can.

The sound returned. The regular rhythmic beat of footsteps, only these were different, louder. They weren't soft soles. Hard heels smacked the floor. Bob felt the vibrations of each step through his prone body. The voices returned, low and mumbled bits of conversation drifting through the room.

What are they saying? Forget the voices, get to the trash can. Just get to the trash can.

His elbow slipped on the linoleum. He split his chin on the hard floor. His teeth sank into his tongue, and coppery blood filled his mouth.

Keep moving. Don't stop, keep moving.

Crimson leaked between his lips, dripping from his chin.

I'm nearly there.

He pawed at the trash can. It wobbled but didn't fall. He forced his unfeeling arms to move, striking the base of it harder. The top bounced against the wall. It turned a lazy half circle and tipped to the hard surface.

The lid bounced in the air, rolling to the cabinets and falling to the floor. The books tumbled to the floor, along with some empty chili and soda cans. Bob reached out. His fingers slowly closed on the third volume, pulling it to him.

The voices grew louder, and a single word came to his ears. *Dementia.*

He pawed at the book cover, his clumsy fingers struggling to turn the pages. After several attempts, he found it, page 89. He scanned the words, searching for a name, a name he didn't want to see.

He saw it midway down the page. *Bob Tuffield held his breath. The thick gas swirled around him. The locked door barred his escape. His lungs burned for air. Just a quick breath, one quick breath. The gas couldn't kill him that fast, Tuffield thought. Ducking his head to the floor, he filled his lungs. Fire blossomed in his chest, and a numbness spread to his extremities. A light headed, euphoric feeling centered in his head. Is this, what it's like to die?*

Bob closed the book, as reading further would be pointless. He had his answer; he knew he was the final victim of page 89. He rolled to his back, staring at the ceiling, listening to the buzz of whispered voices.

* * *

"Dr. Travers, what's your opinion?" a young doctor in a white lab coat watched Bob through a one-way mirror.

An older man removed his thick glasses. He popped the ear piece against his teeth. "I agree, Dr. Lenz, it's dementia. Do you have any theories as to its possible source? Has he suffered any traumatic experience?"

Lenz shook his head. "None that I'm aware of. His behavior is near normal during the day, however he has an odd fixation on his books, specifically page 89." The younger man ran a hand through his brown hair. "I don't understand how his behavior can change so radically in just a few hours."

"I wonder what he sees on page 89?" The older man replaced his glasses. "Very interesting case, keep me informed."

The pair turned to leave, Dr. Travers hard-soled shoes echoing on the tile floor, while the softer soles of Dr. Lenz's squeaked.

THE PATIENT'S NURSE

RICK MOORE

Emily attached the cuff to the patient's arm and pushed the green button on the blood pressure machine, the Velcro pulling tight as the cuff filled with air.

Beneath the ventilator mask, the patient's mouth moved continually, producing incoherent whispers.

A low draft of air as the door was silently pushed inward and the squeak of sneaker soles at her back told Emily she wasn't alone.

"Nurse Meadows," said her supervisor Marjorie Hunt, in greeting. "How fares Mrs. Thornberry today?"

Mrs. Thornberry was so wrinkled and frail that Emily had a hard time thinking of her as a woman at all. Only her hair, a curly mop the color of dishwater, that sat crooked on her head because it was a wig, hinted at gender. Emily looked into the patient's eyes and wished she had not. The woman knew death would soon claim her. Emily would have preferred not to share in her fear.

Emily averted her gaze, and busied herself by straightening the sheet and blanket she'd pulled back to take the patient's vitals. "As well as can be expected," she said.

"Still talking to herself, I see," Marjorie said. "Seems like she has a lot to say. Too bad none of it makes any sense."

Emily caught some of what Mrs. Thornberry was saying beneath the ventilator mask.

"Vita..." she muttered. "Vita..."

"Sounds like gibberish to me." Emily commented.

Marjorie cocked her head, listened. "Do you suppose it could be some other language?"

Emily shrugged. "Beats me."

Regardless of her labored breaths, the patient somehow found the will to keep up the ceaseless wittering. Emily did her best to ignore it and fix the bedding.

It was as she pulled the blanket up, covering the patient's chest, that it happened.

The old woman kicked out, sending the sheet and blanket back toward the bottom of the bed. Then her left hand shot up, tightening around Emily's wrist. Mrs. Thornberry's grip was stronger than Emily would have believed possible. Using her free hand, she tried to pry loose the patient's fingers.

Emily looked into her eyes, saw the fear replaced now with a wicked glint of hunger.

"Let go, you crazy old bitch!" Emily cried.

The patient's other hand reached beneath her arching back.

"Now, now, Nurse Meadows," Marjorie calmly admonished. "There's no call to speak to the patient in that tone of—Oh my God!"

The knife was small and sharp. Emily knew the latter for a fact. One swift swipe of the blade sliced open the back of her hand.

The old woman dropped the knife, reached up and pulled the ventilator mask over her head, dislodging the wig and revealing her baldness.

"Vita!" Mrs. Thornberry spat, sitting bolt upright. "Vita!"

The blood pattered down, and soaked through the old woman's nightgown, wetting her withered flesh. Emily still couldn't get free of the bony fingers digging into her wrist.

Mrs. Thornberry cackled. She wrenched Emily's arm down to her groin, parted her legs, and held Emily's bleeding flesh against her sex. Her legs clamped tightly shut, trapping Emily's hand.

"Vita…Vita…" the old woman said, softly now, her eyes rolling up, the whites glistening. "Operor retineo mihi intereo…"

She fell back coughing and rasping, drool and quiet laughter slowly escaping her mouth.

Emily pulled as hard as she could and the patient's legs parted, releasing her.

"My goodness," Marjorie said. "Where did she get that knife? She must have brought it with her from home."

Emily backed away from the bed, nursing her injured hand. She shot a look at her supervisor. "She should be moved to the psych ward."

"Absolutely," Marjorie agreed. "And if I thought she'd last more than twenty-four hours, I'd have her moved right away. But as it is, it hardly seems worth it. Better get that hand looked at, Nurse Meadows. And fill out a workers' comp form, too. Do you think you need to go home for the rest of the day?"

Emily shook her head. She was less than halfway through a twelve hour shift and had used what little sick time she'd accrued two months ago, when she came down with the flu.

"I'll be fine," Emily said.

"I'll get someone in to clean her up," Marjorie said. "And to check her bed for any other sharp objects she might be concealing."

When her supervisor was gone, Emily looked at Mrs. Thornberry, her eyes hardening. The old woman lay there smiling, like the cat that got the cream.

Die, you crazy bitch! Emily thought, using her good hand to give the old woman the finger.

"Vita," the old woman whispered. Her tongue flicked out, the mottled tip slowly tasting her inward sunken lips.

Emily held the old woman's gaze a moment longer, then had to look away. Leaving the room, she shuddered. In Mrs. Thornberry's eyes she'd seen a look of burning hunger. A look that made Emily think that given the chance, the old woman would eat her alive.

Before Emily could turn around and close the front door to her home, a figure—small and screeching—came hurtling at her legs, almost knocking her off balance. Its arms wrapped around her knees and held on tight. Then the arms reached up, outstretched, expectantly waiting.

"Hi, sweetie," Emily said, lifting the six-year-old into the air, a sloppy kiss and tickle of scraggly blonde hair against her face her reward.

"Mommy!" Holly cried. "I missed you, Mommy."

"I missed you too, sweetie," Emily said, her other hand closing the front door and locking it. "Where's Daddy?"

"Daddy's in the kitchen." Dave's voice called from that very location. "And if you don't want Daddy to screw up dinner, you better come rescue his ass, pronto."

Emily carried Holly through the house, circumnavigating a vast scattering of crayons which looked to have been employed in their entirety to eliminate the white from a sheet of construction paper. In the kitchen, she shrugged her bag off her shoulder, sliding it the length of her arm down onto the table.

Dave stood at the stove, absently scratching the quarter-sized bald spot at his crown, as he often did when he encountered information that refused to reveal its intention.

"Mommy, I drew you a new picture!" Holly yelled. "You wanna see it?"

"You bet I do," Emily said, and put her daughter on the floor. She watched her go running off—presumably to collect the crayon coated sheet of construction paper—then moved up on Dave, leaning against his back, her arms closing across his chest.

"Hi, babe," he said, turning his head and meeting her lips with his, but keeping his eyes on the box he held in his hands.

When the kiss broke, she placed her chin on his shoulder. "What's on the menu, big guy?"

"Lasagna," he said, studying the instructions.

"Great," she replied. "Looks like you've got it under control."

"You'd think," he said. "But look here..." He ran a fingertip across the cooking instructions. "It says cook for thirty to thirty-five minutes, or until it reaches an internal temp of one-sixty. But it's already been in for thirty-five minutes, and it still doesn't look nearly done, and when I tested it with the thermometer, the temp was nowhere close to one-sixty."

Right away Emily spotted his mistake.

"I think I see the problem here."

"You do?"

Dave sounded genuinely confounded. In his job as a landscaper, her husband wasn't required to do a lot of reading, and at home the only thing he read was the TV Guide. Still, it was hard to believe he couldn't see where he'd gone awry. Maybe his lack of confidence in the kitchen played a part, a condition born of never learning to cook and never being expected to—neither by his mother nor Emily.

Last year, after they watched *Super Size Me*, Dave decided to take a stand against the fast food industry, doing his best ever since to provide his family a halfway decent meal the three days Emily worked and wasn't home to make dinner. A lot of what he fixed were ready-to-eat meals, and Emily wasn't sure they were much better in the long run than fast food, but about this she kept quiet, appreciating his efforts.

"Look at the other set of instructions," she suggested.

"If cooking from frozen..." he read aloud. "Increase the cooking time by..."

He slapped his forehead with the palm of his hand, giving her his well-practiced 'what a dumb-ass' expression.

Looking at Emily for the first time since she'd arrived home, something in her husband's demeanor changed. There was a flash of confusion in his eyes, then fear, then a jolting flinch away from her.

"Dave? What is it?"

He stood frowning, the doubt in his eyes slowly lifting away. He shook his head and smiled. "Nothing. What happened to your hand?"

"Long story," she said. "You're sure nothing's wrong?"

He put an arm around her, pulling her close. The kiss to her lips felt awkward, uncertain. When he said, "Of course nothing's wrong," Emily knew he was lying. Because something was wrong, or had been—obviously, and Emily knew what. For a moment there, for one terrible moment, Dave had looked at her like he didn't know her at all.

Emily awoke in darkness. The rhythm of Dave's breathing was too heavy and rapid for sleep, more like the sound she associated with their lovemaking. She didn't turn, just laid there, listening. On Dave's side the bed rocked gently. The idea of him waiting until she was asleep, of not telling her what he wanted, felt like a betrayal. He didn't have to do that to himself, not with her beside him.

Maybe he was just being considerate, she reasoned, thinking she'd be too tired to want to fool around. Well, the situation was easily rectified. She turned toward him, her hand reaching under the covers.

What?

No. Impossible. Her eyes had to be deceiving her.

She blinked, watched. Waited for the illusion to disappear.

No illusion. Another woman was atop her husband, making love to him. The woman rode him steadily. Dave's hands moved from the woman's hips, roughly grabbing her breasts.

Emily's hand shot toward the light switch.

"You son-of-a..."

Light filled the room, and Emily's accusation caught in her throat before she finished it.

Sure enough, Dave was on his back. But there was no woman in the room with them. He was asleep, his nose making the whistling sound it sometimes did when he snored.

I must not be fully awake, she told herself, knowing this was the only explanation. She reached for the light switch with her injured hand, a steady pulsing thrum emanating from beneath its wrappings. The pain matched the one at her temples and the center of her forehead. She slipped out of bed, hoping there'd be something strong enough in the medicine cabinet to kill the pain—

with any luck something that would also knock her out. Otherwise, she knew, it would be a long time before she got back to sleep.

Yawning, Emily fastened her bra and slipped her scrub top over her head. She looked at her watch. Her mother was five minutes late and she had to stop herself from reaching for her cell phone. She attached her work ID badge to the front pocket of her top.

"Mommy!" Holly called from her bedroom. "I can't find my red shoes!"

"Look under the bed, baby," Emily called back. "I put them there last night so you wouldn't trip over them when you got up."

A few seconds later, Holly yelled. "Found them!"

Emily grabbed her purse, and checked herself in the closet mirror. Her hair was still damp, and until she had a few spare minutes to comb it out at work, she'd be wearing the tight and curly look, but that was the norm. Many of her co-workers somehow managed to start their shift looking like they'd just come from the salon, but for that Emily would have to get up the same time Dave rose for work.

Come on, Mom, she thought. *Where are you?*

It wasn't like her to be late. The three days Emily worked, her mother was there like clockwork, sitting with her until eight, then dropping her off by eight-thirty at school.

She turned off the lights in the bedroom and looked into Holly's room as she walked down the hallway. The child was intently focused on buckling up her favorite shoes, not even looking up as Emily passed. Crossing the living room, she decided on a quick extra half cup of coffee and glanced toward the front window on her way to the kitchen.

Her mother's car was parked outside. Emily went to open the front door, thinking she must have just arrived. Before she turned the lock, out of habit, she looked through the spy hole. Her mother stood outside, not moving, not using the key she'd given her, and not ringing the doorbell—just standing there looking at the door. Emily saw the confused look in her mother's eyes.

She unlocked the door and opened it.

"Mom?"

Her mother looked drugged.

"Mom?" Emily repeated, her voice edged with concern. "Are you okay?"

Her mother's eyes opened wide, like she'd snapped out of a trance.

She looked at Emily, frowned. "Okay?" she asked. "Of course I'm okay, Emily. Why wouldn't I be?"

"Grammy!" Holly hollered, speeding through the living room.

"Why were you standing outside?" Emily asked.

"Standing outside?" her mother repeated. She stepped past her into the house, sweeping the child into her arms. She turned to face Emily. "What do you mean, standing outside?"

"Just now," Emily said. "You were standing outside the house. You didn't use your key or ring the bell. You were just standing there."

A crease formed between her mother's eyes. "Me, dear? No, you must be mistaken."

Emily was already late for work and wasn't about to get into it with her mother about what she'd seen. A horrifying thought entered her mind. Emily's grandmother had fallen victim to Alzheimer's in her seventies and spent the last decade of her life a stranger to herself. Could her mother be suffering from the first signs of the same disease?

"You're gonna be late, honey," her mother said. "Better skedaddle."

Emily forced a smile. "Right." She kissed her mom on the cheek and gave Holly a kiss and a hug.

Walking the path to the driveway, Emily stopped, looked back, smiled and waved. All part of her daily routine. Her mother always stood there holding Holly, the two of them waving and calling goodbye.

But not today.

Today the front door was already closed.

The morning report was in progress when Emily slipped into the conference room, quietly closing the door behind her. The nightshift supervisor sat at the other end of a long table, reading aloud from the patient roster, the day shift nurses seated around the table making notes on their printouts.

A glacial, disapproving glare from the 'head of nursing' Sandra Gordon, was anticipated by any employee who dared arrive late for report, but somehow Emily made it to an empty chair without receiving one. Her supervisor, Marjorie, looked up, but not directly at her, then her attention returned to the printout on the table. Nobody else acknowledged Emily's arrival, not even her friend, Karen Boyd, who usually raised a hand and mouthed 'hi' or at least greeted her with a smile.

Emily just assumed the supervising night nurse, Phyllis Dunn, held everyone rapt with an unusual or interesting account of an admission from the previous night, but when she tuned in, it wasn't special—a standard cardiac.

When the report ended, the nurses pushed back in their chairs, some sipping coffee in paper cups, others swigging their first diet sodas of the day. The custom of greeting one another, at least in report, had long ago all but been dispensed with, but Emily couldn't help feeling slighted when none of her co-workers so much as looked at her as they left. There were none of the obligatory nods, silently registering her presence, none of the half-smiles, not even from Karen Boyd, who like everyone else, instead treated her as though the chair she occupied was empty.

"Hi, Karen," Emily called to her friend.

Karen kept walking, not turning around.

"Oh," her supervisor Marjorie said. "Emily, there you are. I'm going to need you in telemetry again today. Will that be okay?"

"Telemetry?" Emily said while standing, the strap of her bag falling over her shoulder. "Sure."

She hurried to catch up to Karen, but when she was in the corridor, her friend was already gone. Then Emily saw two visitors headed her way, two women, and all thoughts of her friend fled from her mind.

As the women drew closer, Emily's mouth dropped open. The woman on the left was her high school music teacher, Mrs. Penbury, not a day older than she'd been twenty years earlier. The one beside her was Emily's Aunt Gloria.

Of course that couldn't be. Gloria had died eight years ago.

Neither of the women's faces showed signs of recognition of Emily.

In fact, none of the faces showed any recognition, not those of the people passing by or in the waiting area. And they should have known her, because Emily knew them all. They were the people who had, in one way or another, touched her life deeply enough that they would always be a part of her.

Now, came Jack, her boyfriend in college until he dropped out. Jack still had the nose ring and barbell in his eyebrow, still had the skin head, cropped so close you could see the shine of his skull. Only now Jack was dressed as a doctor, and he hadn't aged, not a day.

A nurse walked on either side of him. One was Emily's sister, Julie—Julie who lived two hundred miles away. The other was her best friend in high school, Ellen Gans, looking not a day over eighteen.

"You're not real..." Emily groaned. "None of this is real..."

"Are you feeling all right, dear?" Aunt Gloria asked.

Now some of the people looked, responding to her outburst.

Shaking her head, Emily sobbed, "None of this is real."

Then she ran.

Breathless, her heart racing, Emily found herself at the door leading to the second floor patio. She shoved open the door and ran outside, gulping air as the wind blew over her.

Past the shrubs, potted plants, plastic tables and chairs, she saw the staff parking lot down below. She saw her car, a blue Lancer, parked in the spot where she'd left it. Three of the overnight nurses were walking together across the asphalt. One of them, Helen Porter, broke away from the other two, calling goodbye, saying she'd see them that night. Then she went to Emily's car, used the remote to deactivate the alarm and unlock the doors, and got in. She placed her bag on the passenger seat and started the engine.

Evidently, the other nurses saw nothing wrong about this. They waved as Helen Porter reversed out of the space, and Emily stood there, her hand searching her bag for her keys and not finding them, while the woman inside her Lancer honked the horn, rolled down the window to make some joke that got the other nurses laughing, then passed them and drove away.

Inside her bag, Emily's hand closed around her cell phone. Her husband's number was on speed-dial.

"Dave?" she said, when he answered.

"Hello?" Dave said.

"Dave it's me. Something's happening to me. I don't know what to do. I think I need you to come and get me."

"Hello?" Dave said again. "Who's there?"

Couldn't he hear her?

"Dave, it's Emily," she sobbed. "It's me."

To the men he worked with, she heard him say, "There's no one there."

The line went silent, disconnected. Looking at the parking space, her face screwed up in confusion. Did she see a transparent ghost of her car, still parked there?

A hand fell on her shoulder. Her eyes traveled past the naked wrist, up to the woman's face.

"Are you feeling all right, Nurse Meadows?"

Emily didn't nod, just looked into her supervisor's eyes. She saw concern within them, but also something else. It seemed to Emily, that Marjorie was acting, pretending. Mingled with the care expressed for Emily's well-being, wasn't there a touch of mockery?

When her eyes returned to Marjorie's wrist, Emily saw the woman's watch, the one Emily's mother had given her for a birthday present six years ago, 'a special present to her daughter,' she'd said.

"Your watch..."

"This old thing?" Marjorie asked, turning her wrist. "I've had it forever."

"Something's happening to me," Emily gasped. "I think I'm losing my mind."

"Well," Marjorie replied, only it wasn't Marjorie at all but Dave, holding Holly in his arms. "In a sense, you probably are, babe."

Holly, clinging to her father's neck, said, "Think of it as dirty water being poured out of a vase, Mommy. You wouldn't put fresh flowers in dirty old water, would you?"

"No of course not," Dave continued. "You'd want the water to be clean. Pure."

"I think I need to sit down," Emily said.

Dave said, "Please report to telemetry, Nurse Meadows. I need a full set of vitals on Margaret Thornberry."

Her legs felt weak, her mind clouded.

Who am I? What am I doing here?

"Do I know you?" Emily asked them.

The man and child were gone in the blink of an eye. It took Emily a few seconds to recognize the woman who appeared in their place.

"Mom?"

Her mother was gone as suddenly as she arrived, her face melting like hot plastic. When the features again took form, Emily no longer recognized the woman standing before her.

Emily's eyes became glazed. Her mouth dropped open, hung slack, the corners wet with drool.

"Your reality belongs to us now, Nurse Meadows," Marjorie said, her voice warm, reassuring. "Soon we'll finish bleeding it out of you and this will all be over."

She placed a hand on Emily's back, gently guiding her to the door.

Emily stood at the foot of the bed, facing the patient.

The ancient leathery strips of flesh that were the woman's lips parted. They turned up into a smile, the maw within empty and black.

Emily heard the door gently click shut behind her and the squeak of sneakers on tile.

A woman Emily vaguely recognized moved past her, going around to the far side of the bed. She folded back the blanket. Beneath it the old woman lay naked.

Marjorie moved to Emily's side. "Nothing against you personally, Nurse Meadows," she said. "You have a healthy body. That's the only reason."

"Enough prattle, Marjorie," the old woman hissed, her English heavily accented. "Let's get on with it."

The woman Emily couldn't quite place pushed against the back of her head. Emily had no reason to resist. She glimpsed a thatch of gray, a pale twist of gristle, then her nostrils filled with the unmistakable stink of stale sweat and piss. She tasted the old woman's sourness, and thought she would pass out, but then it became much worse. The skin on her face was pulled taut as she was sucked into the darkness, the hands forcing her deeper. The flesh folded around her, engulfed her, marrying with her eyes, nostrils and mouth.

Fear exploded in an adrenaline surge that enabled her escape. Wrenching her head free, Emily pushed back against the woman's hands, knocking them away. Emily felt as though saran wrap had been pulled tight across her face. She couldn't breathe, couldn't see. Her hands came up to her face but all she touched was smoothness. Her nose, her eyes, her mouth—all were gone. Her lungs tried to draw breath. Could not.

"Get her back, you idiot," she heard the old woman hiss. "Get her back before it's too late."

The hands pushed against her head a second time. If nothing else, Emily knew trying to fight was pointless.

She opened her eyes and saw them, the two nurses, standing at the foot of the bed. One had a face she couldn't quite place, the other had no face at all.

There was movement beneath the pink blank oval, grating and squelching as bone re-sculpted, muscle and sinew realigning. The mouth formed, the eyes took shape, the nose sprouted and grew to fullness. The lips parted, the nose drew breath, the eyes opened. The face was again complete.

Emily tried to cry out for help but all that came from her aged throat was a feeble whimper.

The nurse with the new face caressed her features, admiring her reflection in the hollow of a bedpan she held.

Too weak to move, Emily could only lay there, her wasted lungs fighting for breath. She watched the nurses move toward her, one on either side of the bed.

"Time to go to sleep," Margaret said, not so much to Emily but more to the worn-out body that now contained her.

They each pulled up a chair and sat watching her, waiting for the old woman to die.

I EAT THE DEAD

WILLIAM TOSS ROSE

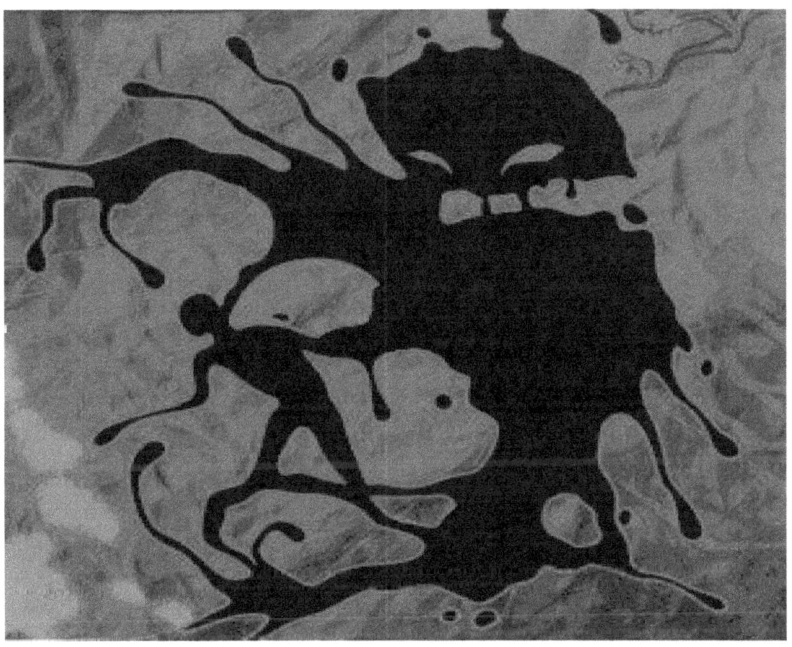

It's a little known fact that souls are greasy, and taste like gristle that's been marinated in bitter coffee and dusted with nutmeg. To look at them, one would think they'd go down easy. They seem almost like cotton candy, like something that can be pulled into long strands and allowed to dissolve upon the tongue, fine, gossamer filaments of pink, blue and orange, so delicate and tenuous they seem to teeter on the edges of reality. But even if you can choke down the bile that instinctively stings your esophagus, you still have to chew. And chew. And chew.

As your teeth grind and rip at the ectoplasmic treat, you also feel them screaming within your throat. Imagine a mouthful of flies, their wings buzzing and bristling to the point that the vibrations tingle your entire skull. Your eardrums quiver painfully and your eyes water as the vibrations take on tone and texture, and you hear the pain, you feel their torment, and taste agony as another incisor tears through their afterlife.

At this point, their defense mechanisms kick in and suddenly it feels like millions of needles are being rammed into your tongue. A foul stench, like a sewage treatment plant with slabs of rancid meat churning in the dirty froth, wafts from your mouth and your pulse starts to race as panicked thoughts dart through your mind. I'm going to choke, I'm going to die, get it out of me, get it out, oh dear God, GET IT OUT!

This is where most people fail. They end up with vomit trickling down their chins, coughing, retching, and gasping for breath between stomach spasms. They have to live with the shame, with the knowledge that they couldn't take it, that they couldn't please.

But not me.

I eat the dead and smile as I avert my eyes. I eat the dead and feel, for the first time in my life, pride blossoming deep within my chest. I eat the dead and am gloriously alive, every nerve tingling and sighing in a way that mere sex could never hope to replicate.

I eat the dead and readily accept more.

My feeder is blond, slender, and looks like a business woman who forgot that sheer lingerie isn't an acceptable part of the corporate dress code. She pulls her hair into a bun so tightly I can almost hear the roots scream in protest. Her makeup is impeccable. Light blush brings color to cheeks as pale as the finest cream and smoky liner makes her eyes twinkle like a pair of sapphires on display. When she leans over me, her breasts tickle my bare chest. I close my eyes, drinking in the aroma of spiced perfume while the warmth of her whisper caresses the little hairs within my ears.

"Eat for me."

Her fingers part my lips with the gentleness of a lover, sliding the piece of soul over my wet tongue while my mouth sucks at her fingertips.

"That's it...take it. Eat for me."

She's so patient, so kind and loving as her free hand traces swirling patterns across the expanse of my stomach. I arch my spine and pull against the chains that have secured me to the bed for the last seven months. Even the burning bedsores on my back are forgotten as I feel myself harden somewhere down beyond the rolls of fat that jiggle with my movement.

"Chew, baby...chew..."

I want so much to please her, to see the pride glimmer in her eyes, to hear her breathy voice tell me how good I am, how I'm the best gainer she's ever had. I want her to stroke my round face, to tickle me beneath the jowls, to reward me with a warm, soapy sponge as she lifts folds of flesh and washes the grit and grime from my crevices.

"Swallow...that's it, baby...swallow..."

She doesn't care that the bed sags beneath my weight or that my skin has begun to overlap the manacles on my wrists and ankles. She doesn't recoil in disgust at the way my man-tits sag with nipples as round as tea cups or how they overlap the stretch marks that streak my belly like dark scratches. No...she only sees all the souls I have eaten, all the morsels that have contributed to the bulk that quivers at her touch.

"Suck it all down..."

For her, I would gladly eat the dead until my stomach ruptured, until all the spirits spilled out like flies escaping a sun-bloated carcass.

"That's a good boy."

They stagger into the room from the brightness of the hallway. She's walking backward and leading him by his paisley tie as if it were some kind of a leash. After counting the ticks of the grandfather clock for hours in the darkness, my eyes have adjusted to the gloom and I see as clearly as if it were merely twilight, instead of three-thirty in the morning.

I can see his salt and pepper hair, the white Oxford half tucked in dark slacks, the gold band on his ring finger, and his glassy, unfocused eyes.

She giggles like a giddy schoolgirl and the smell of cheap booze floods the room like the ghost of an alcoholic as the door creaks shut behind them. The man fumbles in the darkness, his hands groping and tugging at shadows, his face as eager and excited as a child who thought he was simply taking a trip to Grandma's but instead found himself in Disneyland.

"Good God, you're beautiful, you know that? So very, very beautiful." His words are low and slurred and I remain still and silent, watching through the gloom as the scene plays out.

She's holding him by the shoulders, guiding him to the floor with gentle pushes.

"I want you right here, right now, baby." She makes a believable drunk, stumbling and staggering, her words sounding excited but coy at the same time. It's easy to believe she's never been picked up in a bar before, never taken a faceless stranger home for one night of passion.

He disappears from sight and I hear a zipper being undone, the shuffle of pants and underwear against floorboards as he squirms free. Still standing, she slips off the red dress she's been wearing, allowing it to slide down her body and gather at her feet. Her back is smooth and beautiful, her ass cheeks as perfect a runway model, and I catch a glimpse of her right breast as she turns slightly and opens her purse.

"Close your eyes, sweetie, and I'll take care of everything." She removes the Richter Cone, previously hidden amid makeup, business cards, and loose change. Its casing is shiny black, and I can just make out the series of buttons and levers lining its surface, can see her fingertip lovingly caress the controls.

My mouth is watering and my heart feels like it's fluttering in my chest as a stream of drool trickles from the corner of my lips.

"I'll take care of you like you've never been taken care of before," she whispers.

All pretense has been dropped. No trace of slur in her delivery, no shy tilts of the head. Her movements are as fluid and graceful as a ballerina as something shiny and metallic is fished from her purse. "I'll take care of you, all right."

Too drunk and horny and stupid to notice, the man just lays there as she squats over his pelvis. The hand holding the scalpel rises into the air and its blade gleams as it whooshes in a downward arc.

A sound like wet fabric being ripped fills the room. Gurgling, thrashing, heels kicking out a frantic beat against the floor, but I know she's got him pinned now, that he can only flop around like a suffocating fish as he grows weaker with every passing second.

I can hear the cone, the slow whir and hum that reminds me of the smokeless ashtray my aunt had when I was a child. I picture her pressing its base against his mouth as her other hand manipulates the levers, making minute adjustments in response to his struggles.

Operating the Richter Cone is an art. You just can't place it over the mouths of the dying and expect it to do all the work. It takes talent to operate, an instinct for how hard the soul is struggling, how badly it wants to stay within its fleshy prison. You have to ride it like a surfer on a metaphysical wave, feeling the peaks and troughs and responding to them almost instantaneously.

After several minutes, the scuffling stops and there's only the high-pitched whine of the cone followed by a sound almost like a popgun. The motors power down, dropping steadily in pitch and volume, until there's nothing but tiny clicks as the fan blades make their final revolutions.

She stands and turns toward me; her chest and face are freckled with spatters of blood and she's breathing heavily as her thin lips turn upward into a smile. The Richter Cone is cupped within her hands, a single LED pulsing like a fiery ember in the semidarkness. She's trembling with anticipation.

I wet my lips while she glides across the room like a phantom, watch as she positions the cone beside a porcelain bowl on the bedside table. Without a word, she fiddles with the switches and there's a whiff of ozone as the device hums with a tone so deep that it rattles the surface of the table. Fifteen seconds later and the captured soul is extruded from the top, curling and unraveling out of the apex as if it were a Play-Doh fun factory.

It plops into the awaiting bowl and creeps up the sides, piling onto itself as more and more soul is converted into solid mass. By the time the cone has fallen silent again, the bowl is overflowing and a quiver courses along my spine. There's enough for at least a week of feedings, a week of her warm approval, of her soft hands brushing my lips.

"Look what I've brought you. Are you a hungry, boy? Do you want something to eat?"

Nodding, I open my mouth with a wet smack as she tears off lengths of soul between pinched fingers. The blood on her hands will lend a bit of saltiness to the meal and make it more palatable, and being fresh it should still have the aftertaste of ionized molecules. It's a flavor that's more like a smell, like a beach ball fresh from its packaging or something between bleach and the air just after a lightning strike.

Not that it matters. Even if it were months old and shriveled like a mummified umbilical cord, I'd still open my mouth readily.

"That's a good boy."

It's been two years since the man with the salt and pepper hair. There were others after him of course, men and woman lured into the web of my beautiful feeder with the promise of easy sex.

I ate them all, wolfing down their souls like a starving man at a hamburger stand. Until recently, she kept telling me how proud she was, how she'd never seen anyone so voracious, how we were now on record as the top pair and no one was even close to our seven hundred pound achievement.

The manacles are entirely hidden beneath fat now and it looks like the chains sprout directly from my flesh, as if the bed and my body have merged into a single entity with metal links serving as connective tissue. Each breath I take is a struggle, something to be fought and won rather than an instinct. The weight of my body presses down on my lungs, squeezing air from them like a boa constrictor even as I'm gasping for another breath. Sometimes my left arm tingles as though it's gone to sleep and I wince at the twinge in my chest that feels like a jolt of electricity surging through my nerves.

But I still eat the dead, seeking those kind words that now seem further and further apart, the soft touch that means so much. Sometimes I feel like a puppy, so eager to please, wanting nothing more than a pat on the head as he does trick after trick after trick.

She's changed since we claimed our throne. My body's developed this sour odor from sweat dried beneath the crannies of flesh—flesh which no longer remembers the warm sponge and the tenderness with which she bathed me. Her encouragement has become more insistent, more like thinly veiled orders than playful teasing dripping with innuendo.

"I said eat it."

"Choke it down, Fat Boy."

"Swallow the damn thing for Christ's sake."

I hope to see that smile touch her eyes, to feel the napkin as she wipes my mouth and chin. Instead, her fingers plunge into my mouth faster and faster, shoving in chunks of soul with all the delicacy of a jackhammer. If I try to caress them with my lips, she pulls away as if I'd bitten her and immediately crams an even larger slab of spirit down my gullet.

Once the bowl's been emptied, once I'm left feeling dirty and violated and blinking back tears, once all of this has happened, she immediately wraps the measuring tape around me, jotting measurements into her little notebook, then silently uploading the data for the entire community to swoon over.

I try to talk to her and her eyes narrow into slits as she glares in my direction. For some reason, I feel as if I'm withering inside my massive frame, shrinking into something no bigger than a dried pea. Fat. Stupid. Ineffectual. Living only to eat the souls of the dead and further our fame within a very specific enclave.

What once would've lasted a week is gone in two days. The entrance to the bedroom has transformed into a revolving door as horny drunks enter and then are carried out in bulging trash bags.

She's going all the way with them now, riding them with soft sighs and throwing back her head, gyrating and bouncing faster and faster until, at the moment of climax, the scalpel finally begins its deadly descent. The entire time, I'm chained to the bed, eyes squeezed shut and face contorted into a grimace as I try to drown out her moans and gasps with songs from my childhood, mathematical equations, bits of poetry. Anything that will transport me out of this room, away from the hollow feeling that deepens with every pelvic thrust, away from the hot tears sliding down my cheeks.

Sometimes I fantasize about telling her it's over. I see myself breaking my chains like some movie strongman, rising out of bed and slamming the door behind me as she begs for me to stay, to forgive her, to please reconsider. I picture stepping out into the sunlight for the first time in years, how its rays would feel against my bone-white skin as the sound of traffic and passersby flood my senses. In this dream world she's left in the bedroom, holding a fresh bowl of soul as if it were a small baby, rocking back and forth, muttering over and over, I'm sorry, I'm so, so sorry.

Yet somehow I can't bring myself to tell her to unlock the manacles. I've tried, several times, but the words won't seem to come. In the back of my mind, I think it's only a matter of time. Sooner or later, someone will eat more souls than I could ever dream of. They'll rocket by my measly seven hundred pounds, leaving me looking like a half-deflated party balloon in the presence of a Macy's Day spectacular.

But maybe, once our notoriety has waned, things will go back to the way they used to be. Maybe if I can just weather through this rough patch, we'll emerge together on the other side, stronger for the shared experience of what we'll come to call our dark period.

This hope keeps me chewing, keeps me swallowing, keeps me eating ever increasing amounts of the dead—six, seven, eight times a day...by this point I've devoured the equivalent of a small cemetery.

But it's never enough.

I glance at the porcelain bowl beside the table. It's empty except for shadows, the once shiny surface now stained light gray from the souls it's collected. A crack runs down the side from where she dropped it and there's a chip on the rim...somehow, it almost looks lonely sitting over there and if I could reach out and touch it, just to let it know I'm here.

She'll be back soon. Back with another horn-dog frat boy, lesbian or two-timing businessman. She's got it down to a science now and has developed a taste for it, I think. She'll do her thing, the Richter Cone will fill the bowl with fresh soul, and I'll attempt to eat my way back into her loving graces.

Beads of sweat cool my forehead and it suddenly feels as if a boulder has dropped out of the sky and landed on my chest. I gasp, but this only causes a white hot bolt of pain to shoot up my arm, tensing my shoulders and breasts as if the muscles below all the layers of fat seized up in unison.

My heart races faster, thumping irregular rhythms in my temples, but this only serves to explode the pain into a million shards of molten glass that burrow into my chest and neck. Kicking, struggling, chains clinking as my hands try to press against my chest, I want to scream for help but there's no air, good God there's no air, and my windpipe is closing up, smaller, smaller still, and a ring of darkness creeps along the edges of my vision like an invading cancer.

Then, as suddenly as it struck, it's gone. Along with the bed, the little bowl, the table, the room. It's as if they all winked out of existence at the same time. Even the chains have dissolved.

I'm standing in what seems to be an infinitely vast field of darkness. Tendrils of fog swirl like an over-friendly cat weaving between the legs of reality, and it's cold. So cold that I can feel the chill in the marrow of my bones...almost as if it's actually radiating from somewhere deep inside me rather than seeping through the pores of my naked body.

"Hello?" My voice echoes in the silence, sounding tiny and forlorn.

"Is anyone there?"

I spin in a slow circle, but the same barren landscape greets me on all sides, nothing but darkness, fog, and the echoes of my voice mocking me.

"Hello?"

I long for my beautiful feeder, to have her by my side, for the reassurance of her presence.

"Anyone?"

My eye catches movement off to the side. Spinning around, I see a cluster of silhouettes emerge through the fog, packed together as if huddling for warmth, and I feel a flicker of hope.

"Thank God! I was beginning to think I was alone!"

The people are silent but continue walking toward me.

"Where the hell am I?"

Their feet shuffle and something about the sound makes me stiffen. I fight the urge to run, and wring my hands together as I peer through the fog at the newcomers. As they pass through the misty veil, their features begin to take form as if they were materializing from the very molecules of the air itself.

I know these faces, these men and women who were slaughtered before my bed as I looked on in silence, this parade of victims who walk silently toward me.

I know them well.

And they look famished.

THE DARKNESS THAT DEVOURS

KELLY M. HUDSON

I knew the lump of darkness in the corner of my bedroom was alive on the second night of my bedridden state. I saw it shimmer out of the corner of my eye and immediately let my laptop slide down the side of my thigh and stared into that pool of blackness like a man trying to solve a puzzle which made no sense.

I gazed into it for more than twenty minutes, expecting it to move again and when it didn't, the rational part of my brain tried to argue away what I'd seen, blaming the painkillers in my system or the tiredness of my eyes or any other myriad reasons, but deep down inside, despite all my rational protestations, I knew I had seen my imminent death. I understood, down to the core of my being, that I had witnessed my end, and it was coming for me as slowly and surely as cancer in a smoker's lungs.

I was stuck in bed because of sheer stupidity on my part. I had given in to a request from college friends I hadn't seen since we'd graduated, ten years ago. They were throwing a sort of reunion and it was to be held in Tahoe, where we would spend the weekend skiing and catching up on old times. I would not have gone had I not been personally contacted by Brenda, my first love, and I would be a liar to say my reasons for going were purely altruistic.

I had never gotten over her, even when she first left me for my old friend Ron and then, later, for Aaron Valmont, the man she eventually married. With her divorce just months finalized, I hoped for more than simply sitting by a fireplace and sipping hot cocoa and playing Pictionary. And the way she spoke, in that fiery, breathless excitement, I had the distinct feeling she, too, was interested in more than mere reminiscences.

Aaron had broken her heart almost four years into their marriage but she didn't know it until eight years in, when she visited her family physician and found she had a raging case of syphilis. When she confronted Aaron, he admitted he had cheated on her not once, and not for a year, but for four years, and with dozens of different women.

Divorce lawyers were called and they wrangled over the estate. In the end, Brenda came out pretty good, collecting half of the fortune Aaron made in the speculative markets during their marriage. Now she was free and on the prowl, and who better to turn to than the puppy she'd kicked so many years before? She could not know, however, I was no longer a puppy; I was full-grown and ready to have my own little romp.

That ended when I decided to show off and attempt to snowboard instead of ski. I had no clue to what I was doing and promptly crashed into a tree, snapping both my legs below the knees. Brenda didn't wait around, and after two nights in the local hospital, neither did I.

My leaving wasn't under the most pleasant of circumstances, but the doctors would have to learn to live with it, because I was not about to spend one more minute in that awful hospital. I decided to go back to the cabin I had rented for the weekend and extend my stay for a month, until I recovered.

It was there, all alone but for a nurse who stopped by once a day to make sure I was in a good state, I first encountered the encroaching darkness, and it was there where I learned the true meaning of terror.

I thought I knew, of course, because I already knew everything. I lost my parents when I was little and was raised by my Aunt. I put myself through college, working night shifts at a local diner, majoring in business and minoring in English literature. I went to work straight out of college for a firm that specialized in the investing markets overseas and within a few years, had worked my way to the top.

I ran the company now, had more money than I knew what to do with, and was generally satisfied in all aspects of life. Except for love. Damnable, hateful love. Was that not always the case, with poets and writers of all times? Love, the loss and the withholding of it, the driving furnace that fueled so many great works of art. I wanted Brenda back, the one woman who had understood me, who had been by my side more faithful than any friend or enemy ever could. Brenda, the woman who broke my heart when she needed something new. Brenda, who had been within my reach once again, only to slip away.

I picked up my cell phone. It was two in the morning and I needed someone to be with me. There was perhaps a chance she had not left yet, and I was willing to risk it.

She picked up on the fourth ring. She listened as I made my impassioned plea. She promised to come by in the morning.

I hardly slept the rest of the night, the visions of Brenda in my bed pushing away the phantoms of the dark corner.

The nurse checked in at ten, like she always did, preparing a couple of meals that she left in my room in a small refrigerator by my bed. She set my bedpans nearby and brought a couple DVD's for me to watch if I got bored. I had her leave the front door unlocked, telling her I had company coming. She gave me a frumpy look. This nurse wasn't the kind that fueled pornographic fantasies in men's magazines; she was the kind who made a man think twice about ever having sex again. She bid me a good day and left, eying me suspiciously.

Brenda arrived an hour later. She called up and I called down and as her steps neared my heart nearly exploded from my chest in excitement. She rounded the corner and stood in the threshold to my room, breathless and beautiful.

She wore her brown hair like she had in college, feathered to the sides and cascading down to her shoulders. Her face was classic porcelain, her features delicate and pale, her blue eyes shining through like a lighthouse in the dark. Time had not changed her at all.

"There you are," she said. She sat next to me and marveled at my legs, the casts running up both to the knees. "You poor thing."

She slid into bed next to me and melted against my side. As I held her in my arms, it was as if the ten missing years between us never existed. She slipped out of her clothes and somehow got me out of mine. We made soft, sweet love. When it was over, she wept on my shoulder and fell into a deep sleep. I followed her within moments.

I woke hours later, the sun having set and the room plunged into darkness. I was as content as I had ever been in my life. I was having insane thoughts of somehow wooing Brenda to go with me, to join me back in the Bay Area. I knew they were incredibly stupid thoughts, but once romance enters a man's heart, rational thought flees. She slept so quietly against me, so peacefully, if not for the beat of her heart against my ribs, I would have thought her dead.

I fell back asleep, as happy as I had ever been.

When I woke next, Brenda screamed and clawed my chest.

Rivulets of blood poured down my stomach as I bolted upright, confused and scared out of my mind. She slid to the floor, looking up at me, her face pale and her eyes pleading. Her mouth was open and the screech coming from it seemed inhuman. At her ankles, a pool of darkness blacker than the surrounding night had her in its grip.

It all came back to me then: the night before, the fears I'd buried, the sureness of my own impending doom. The darkness had returned, alive and murdering the love of my life.

The darkness gurgled and I heard something wet bubble out and hiss across the floor. These sounds were drowned out by the snapping of bones, like great trees felled by hurricane winds, and Brenda's even more harried cries for help. I watched as the darkness leaked over her in black tributaries, as if something wet had been spilled all across the top of her body. Her legs bent backwards and broke again and again, the bones splintering up and down as the darkness swallowed her. As the blackness poured over her, it dug in, like claws, tearing at her skin. I watched in horror as she was bent unnaturally backwards, her stomach thrust into the floor and her shoulders yanked up and back. Her spine snapped, sounding like a crunching bite taken from an apple, and her eyes rolled inside her head.

I knew in that moment she was dead.

My heart pounded in my chest so hard I found it hard to breathe and consequently I must have passed out because the next thing I remembered was lying on my side, my legs thrust out straight in front of me, bound in their casts, and my head hanging off the side of the bed. I watched, my eyes wide and bleeding tears, as the darkness devoured Brenda, pulling her slowly inside of it, gurgling louder, her bent and broken body sucked and dragged into its invisible, gaping maw.

At some point, I passed out again.

It was morning when I woke. The bed was empty next to me and I decided it all must have been some sort of strange dream. Brenda had left me during the night, running off to live her life after having her little fling, leaving me alone and helpless, waiting for my nurse to show up.

Still, with dread I looked over the edge of my bed and into the corner where the darkness had lived and pulsed. I saw nothing but the bland brown carpet covering the floor and the off-white paint of the walls as they converged to form the corner. Nothing was there; no clothing, no blood, no bones. Nothing.

It had to have been a dream.

By noon, I was sure of it. I even called Brenda's phone and left a message, telling her what a great time I had and I would miss her. I hung up, my chest hollow and my stomach rumbling. Where was my nurse?

She arrived half an hour later, a blizzard of curses and apologies. Her earlier client had a heart attack and died before she arrived and so she had to stay to deal with the police. She was her usual angry and bitter self. She made the bed, fixed me a meal, made a sandwich for later, and was about to leave when she turned and asked me the oddest thing.

"Where's your friend?" she said, one eye squinting and the other wide and inquisitive.

"She left," I said.

"Huh," the nurse said. "Did she walk off? 'Cause she left her car in the driveway and I had to park on the street."

My face turned white. I had been a fool.

The nurse, however, hardly noticed. She turned and swept from the room as she'd entered only an hour before, cursing and bitter. She was in her car and down the street before I recovered my senses enough to say to an empty room:

"Please. Take me with you."

The next few hours were full of white-hot panic. I tried to get out of bed without injuring myself but found the casts too large and cumbersome to deal with. I would get one on the floor when cramps would shoot up my other leg and my spine would seize up. The only relief was managing to get the leg off the floor and back into the bed.

I tried rolling on my stomach and sliding my torso down so that my hands held me up, but I found I had spent too much time at my desk when I should have been at the gym, toning my body. It was all I could do to get back up onto the bed.

I lay there, panting, my body coated in a thick sheen of sweat like I had been dipped into a barrel of thick, clotted oil. As the hours passed and the light outside grew dimmer, my eyes stayed on the corner where the darkness had appeared the last two nights and where surely it would return this one last time.

What was it? Why was it here? Why did it devour Brenda and not me? I had no answers. I knew my only hope was in escape, but how could I leave when I could barely move, much less get up and get in my car and drive off? And, what guarantee did I have that this thing would not follow me wherever I went?

I picked up my cell phone and made call after desperate call. No one answered. I tried the nurse first and got her voice mail. I called her again and again, leaving anxious messages, pleading with her to come back for me, until her inbox filled and there was nothing more to do.

I called colleagues back home but none of them answered, of course. I wasn't the most well-loved man in the company and had no real friends.

Next I called a couple of acquaintances from college, those who had invited me up for the weekend. None of them answered, either. Finally, I tried the police. They answered. And then they promptly laughed at my predicament. The lady on the phone signed-off by telling me to lay off the alcohol and get some sleep. I realized my tact had been all wrong; why would they believe a creature made of pure darkness was about to devour me? So I called back and made up a lie, telling the same lady there was a prowler outside my home and I needed help. She listened and when I finished, she paused. A long silence followed.

"Buddy, get some sleep. You call here again and I'll send someone out to arrest you," she said.

"Good! Send the cops! Arrest me! Please!" I screamed into the phone. She hung up. I dialed the police again when my phone beeped and died. The battery was drained.

Frustrated, I threw the phone across the room, watching with delight as it shattered against the wall, tiny fragments of plastic and computer chips showering to the floor. I realized how stupid I was when I turned and spied my phone charger, right next to my bed on the dresser.

The tears came then. They flowed free, hard and bitter. I sobbed like when I was a child, firmly in the grip of my wildest fears. When the crying passed, I fell into a deep nap. It seems ridiculous to state that, when I was at my lowest, when there was no hope for me at all, I simply went to sleep, but it does make a sort of sense.

My body shut down. It was an escape mechanism, a way for me to deal with the stress and terror I was experiencing. The slumber didn't last long, just enough for the sun to set and for the long shadows of night to creep across my floor like skeletal fingers, reaching out for me.

I came to with a start, my eyes staring directly into the corner where the darkness was to come. There was nothing there yet, just a small space filled with the normal blackness of night.

I turned on my lamp and laid it on its side so that the light beamed directly into the corner. Maybe all that was needed was to shine some light and the problem would be taken care of that easily.

"What are you doing?" the nurse said. She burst into the room a bundle of anger and incredulity. Her entrance shocked me; my heart stopped for an instant and I stared at her, mouth agape, feeling like a retarded child.

"What?" I managed to mumble.

"You didn't answer when I called you back," she said. "What's the emergency? You look fine to me. I'm supposed to be on a date tonight."

The thought of this sour lemon of a woman having a date was, up until yesterday, the strangest thing I had ever conceived of. I could not put a mental picture in my head of the kind of man who would see, or even worse yet, be seen with a woman such as her. I did notice she was dressed quite nice, with a blue suede coat covering a light blue dress and sheer stockings.

She had make-up that made her cheeks blush and her lips gleam a polished red, and eye-shadow just two shades lighter than a prostitute would wear. But she was my savior, after all, and I cleared my head of all such nasty thoughts.

"You have to get me out of here," I croaked.

"If you need the hospital, we'll have to call an ambulance," she said.

"No!" I screeched. My tone startled her. I tried to even my breathing and relax, but I couldn't. The fear of the growing dark was too much to overcome.

"Well?" she said, her hands on her hips.

"I think," I said, stammering for a moment. I had an idea, and it was desperate, but it was my last hope. "I think someone murdered Brenda last night."

"What?"

"The girl who stayed over," I said.

"What do you mean?"

"Her car is still here, but she's gone. I think whoever did it stashed her body in the house and is coming back tonight."

"That's absurd!" she said.

"It's the truth."

"Did you call the police?"

"Of course. They think I'm crazy," I said.

"Well, you are," she said. She didn't move, though. She placed a finger to her lips, thinking. "What makes you believe this?"

"I don't know. Call it instinct, but I think the killer is coming back, and I want to be out of here," I said.

She paced back and forth, chewing her bottom lip. I could tell I was getting through to her, that doubt was eating at her thoughts. What I did not notice, too caught up in watching my nurse, was the darkness as it grew in the corner, despite the light trained on it. The blob blurped and bubbled, doubling in size within seconds. When my eyes did fall upon it, when I realized again how doomed I was, my body froze with fear.

And as the nurse paced over next to it, I could do nothing but watch in horror as black tendrils whipped from the blot and lashed around her ankles.

She didn't notice at first. She was muttering to herself, caught up in her thoughts. When the darkness bit into her flesh, however, she screamed bloody murder.

It tugged her ankles and tripped her, the side of her head striking the corner of the dresser, splitting it open into a large gash, blood pouring from the wound. Everything happened in slow motion and I watched, mouth agape, as the darkness slithered along the floor, wrapping her left leg up into long tentacles of clinging blackness.

I heard and then smelled her flesh scald at its touch, hissing like a snake, as her screams filled the room so large and loud that they rung in my head, deafening me.

The tendrils curled and jerked, snapping back towards the dark mass. The skin on her leg tore and slid down, like she was removing pantyhose, exposing red, glistening, raw meat.

Her screams stopped as blood foamed from between her lips. I could hear the darkness eating the flesh it had taken, slopping it around in an imaginary mouth. I turned and vomited.

The nurse tried to crawl away, dust and dirt from the floor sticking on her wet leg, as she whimpered and looked up at me, eyes wild like that of a cornered animal. I stared down at her, helpless to do much of anything, as the darkness lashed out at her again, striking her back.

The tendril dug in and tore free a strip of meat, exposing her spine. She screamed once again, coughing out the blood in her mouth, as the tentacles of living darkness formed a hand and wrapped around her backbone.

With a sudden jerk, her spine cracked and the nurse stopped her screeching, her eyes glazing over with surrender.

The darkness yanked her spine with such strength that her head collapsed into her shoulders, stopping at the chin, as it pulled her entire body into its cold, black embrace.

While it busied itself with devouring her, I made my attempt at escape. Panicked, I threw my legs over the edge of the bed and tried to leap across the room. I figured if I could get my car I could drive away.

I stopped thinking altogether when my heels slammed into the floor and my legs screamed with unimaginable pain. I fell into a heap, white-hot agony burning through my body.

There was nothing I could do; I could not run, I could not even crawl, I was effectively paralyzed by a pain so intense it felt as if a hot poker had been shoved under my knees and then twisted for optimal torment. I could do little more than whine, my voice a keening cry to a world that no longer cared.

The darkness slid across the floor, slick and quick, gliding like a tilted pool of oil. It stopped and sat beside me, the size of an easy chair, tall and thick with its recent nourishment.

Somewhere inside of it, I could hear the nurse being digested, gurgling acids scorching her flesh and thousands of tiny teeth whittling away at the bones.

The pool of blackness quivered near to my face, not moving, until a tiny tendril, the width of my pinkie finger, wiggled out and touched my forehead.

My mind was flooded with thousands of images of torture, of animals dying, of pollution, of bombs and war, and of the most mundane of human antipathies to one another.

As these images played a psychotic loop of madness, a voice spoke over them. It was cold and distant and blacker than the space between the stars.

"For all these lies, mankind must die," it said. Over and over again, thousands of times, like a mantra to call down dark gods.

The blot of blackness revealed its nature to me. It was an anti-body, created by the earth to rid the world of disease. There were others like it, billions of them, forming all around the planet. These black-blood cells of the earth were scouring the globe and killing humans one by one. Brenda, the nurse, and I were just three of many thousands dying.

The small tentacle removed itself from my forehead and I stared at it, bitter towards my inevitable end. I did not think I deserved this, but I was helpless in the face of it.

Dozens of tentacles exploded from the pool of darkness, whipping my face and body. They tore my flesh and lacerated my nerves.

It was too late for me and for all of mankind and as I lay there, my end imminent, a strange peace finally came over me. There would be no more struggle, no more pain. This was truly the end.

With the calm serenity of a murderer facing the hangman's noose, glad to finally pay for his awful crimes, I closed my eyes and let the darkness devour me.

ABOUT THE WRITERS

Terry Alexander lives on a small farm near Porum, Oklahoma with his wife Phyllis. They have three children and nine grandchildren. His work has been published by Living Dead Press, Static Movement, Moonstone Books and at frontiertales.com. He is a member of the Oklahoma Writers Federation, Ozark Writers League, The Arkansas ridge Writers and The Fictioneers

David Bernstein wrote his first horror story when he was in first grade and even though some of the letters were backwards, his parents loved it. He's been writing since that time and has had numerous stories published in various anthologies and magazines. He lives in the NYC area, is working on his second novel, and wishes people would stop using their car horns so much.

You can visit him at davidbernsteinauthor.blogspot.com and email him at dbern77@hotmail.com

Eric S. Brown is the author of numerous horror books including Bigfoot War, War of the Worlds Plus Blood Guts and Zombies, Season of Rot, and the upcoming Bigfoot War II: Dead in the Woods to name only a few. His short fiction has been published hundreds of time. He lives in North Carolina with his wife, son, and crazy cat where he continues to write tales of walking corpses, blazing guns, and the things that lurk in the woods.

John C. Foster was born in Sleepy Hollow, NY, and has been afraid of the dark for as long as he can remember. A writer of horror and strange fiction, Foster spent many years in the ersatz glow of Los Angeles before relocating to the relative sanity of New York City where he lives with his lady, Linda, and their cat, Lucy. He can be reached at jfosterpro@yahoo.com.

David H. Donaghe lives and works in the high desert of Southern California. He has three passions in life: reading, writing and riding his motorcycle. David has several short stories published in anthologies published by The Living Dead Press and has two novels coming out. His short story collection, Monroe's Paranormal Investigations, also published by The Living Dead Press, is now available at Amazon.com and Barns and Noble. David invites you join his reader network at www.authornation.com/MCRIDER, to check out his author web page at http://dhdonaghe.weebly.com/index.html and to follow him on Face Book, My Space and Twitter. David is currently enjoying life on the high desert while working on his next novel.

Anthony Giangregorio is the author of 35 novels, almost all of them about zombies and has edited over 20 anthologies.

His work has appeared in Dead Science by Coscomentertainment, Dead Worlds: Undead Stories Volumes 1-7, and Wolves of War by Library of the Living Dead Press. He also has stories in End of Days: An Apocalyptic Anthology Vol. 1-5, the Book of the Dead series Vol. 1-6 by LDP, Zombie Zoology by Severed Press, and two anthologies with Pill Hill Press.

He is also the creator of the popular action/zombie series titled Deadwater and his action/ horror novel Dead Rage is being optioned for a movie.

Check out his website at www.undeadpress.com.

Michael D. Griffiths focuses primarily on writing Horror and Science Fiction, but has dabbled in odd Fantasy and even, gasp, literary works. He has won the Withersins 666 award, and several contests at Golden Visions. In the past, he has published two underground zines, been on over a hundred road trips, and has had his Skinjumper Series published in M-Brane magazine. He is currently a part of Abandoned Towers and Innsmouth Free Press magazines.

Check out his book: The Chronicles of Jack Primus published by LDP.

Dane T. Hatchell lives in Baton Rouge, LA. He has stories appearing in over fifteen different anthologies from Living Dead Press. You can contact Dane at Enadious@gmail.com.

Kelly M. Hudson was born in Kentucky and currently resides in California. He loves horror and has over a dozen stories published in various anthologies, as well as a novel called The Turning published by Living Dead Press and available on Amazon.com and other places. If you wish to know more about Kelly, please visit his website www.kellymhudson.com for links to other stories and news.

Joe McKinney is a sergeant in the San Antonio Police Department who has been writing professionally since 2006. He is the Bram Stoker-nominated author of Dead City, Quarantined, Dodging Bullets and Dead Set. His upcoming books include Apocalypse of the Dead, The Ninth Plague, St. Rage, Lost Girl of the Lake, and The Red Empire. As a police officer, he's received training in disaster mitigation, forensics, and homicide investigation techniques, some of which finds its way into his stories. He lives in the Texas Hill Country north of San Antonio. Visit him at http://joemckinney.wordpress.com for news and updates.

Rick Moore's stories have appeared in numerous anthologies, including 'The Undead: Flesh Feast', 'History is Dead' and 'Cthulhu Unbound' (Permuted Press), the Stoker Award nominated 'Horror Library 3' (Cutting Block Press), 'The Beast Within' and 'Harvest Hill' (Graveside Tales), 'Embark to Madness' (Coscom), 'Bound for Evil' (Dead Letter Press), and in several anthologies from Living Dead Press. Recently Rick joined 'Dark Moon Digest' as an associate editor. His story 'Kindread' appeared in the third issue of the magazine. Originally from England, he now lives in Phoenix, with his wife Ruth and their three cats.
Go to http://www.myspace.com/zombieinfection for updates on published works and to contact the author.

Jesus Morales is known as "Dark Riddle" in the business. A true Chicagoan, he metamorphosed from a popular graffiti artist to a horror writer and illustrator. The creator of odd and stylized books such as Knight Syndrome and Dark Love, he also writes science articles and science fiction. In occult circles he hails from the mysterious Chicago region of Gothicane and is known as the 7th Dark from BTB and the Synoptic Knight Templars.

Matt Nord lives in Central New York with his wife, Karen, two sons, Jacob and Judah, and daughter, Jordan. He is a fledgling horror writer with several credits under his proverbial belt, including several short stories published by Living Dead Press and Library of the Living Dead Press as well as stories in anthologies from Pill Hill Press, Wicked East Press and Static Movement Imprint. His most ambitious project to date may be the collaborative novel he is currently spearheading with 18 other authors, and will hopefully see published before his baby girl graduates college.

Mark Rivett grew up in Frankenmuth Michigan - home of the world's largest Christmas store. At the age of 18 he moved to Pennsylvania where he earned multiple degrees from The Art Institute of Pittsburgh. After four years as a multimedia instructor with a local college in Pittsburgh, he took a position as a web developer where he has prospered since 2005. Mark is fascinated by the macabre and his writing is inspired by the horror and suspense genre. In addition to writing Mark paints, builds models, plays poker, and continues to further his education.

William Todd Rose is a speculative fiction author currently residing in Parkersburg, West Virginia. His short work has appeared in magazines such as the now-defunct Twisted Nipples, OG's Speculative Fiction, and Macabre Cadaver as well as in various horror and zombie-themed anthologies. In early 2009, his debut novella "Shadow of the Woodpile" was released as the flagship publication for small-press publisher Fetid Press. His is currently at work on his next book, "The Dead & Dying: An Exostential Zombie Novel", which should be released in the coming year. Check out his LDP zombie novel "Sex in the Time of Zombies."

PLAYING GOD: A ZOMBIE NOVEL
by Jeffery Dye

It was supposed to be a regeneration virus to help soldiers on the battlefield— regrowing limbs and healing wounds— but a simple act of carelessness unleashed it on an unsuspecting world.

For the virus was not perfected, and once exposed, the host quickly dies, only to rise again as one of the undead.

As countries are quickly overrun, scientists and military teams battle to contain the outbreak.

There is no other option.

If the infection continues to spread, soon the entire globe will be consumed. And perhaps that will be a just punishment for a mankind that dared to try to play God.

DEAD HOUSE: A ZOMBIE GHOST STORY
by Keith Adam Luethke

The old mansion on the edge of town, aptly named Dead House, has a history of blood, pain, and death, but what Victor Leeds knows of this past only scratches the surface of the true horrors within.

But when his girlfriend is attacked by a shadowy figure one rainy night, he soon finds himself caught up in a world where the dead walk and ghostly wraiths abound. And to make matters worse, a pair of serial killers are fulfilling carefully made plans, and when they are done, the small town of Stormville, New York will run red. The last ingredient to open the gates of Hell, and plunge this small upstate town into madness, is rain.

And in Stormville, it pours by the gallons.

The Lazarus Culture
by Pasquale J. Morrone

Secret Service Agent Christopher Kearns had no idea what he was up against. Assigned on a temporary basis to the Center for Disease Control, he only knew that somehow it was connected to the lives of those the agency protected...namely, the President of the United States. If there were possible terrorist activities in the making, he could only guess it was at a red alert basis.

When Kearns meets and befriends Doctor Marlene Peterson of the Breezy Point Medical Center in Maryland, he soon finds that science fiction can indeed become a reality. In a solitary room walked a man with no vital signs: dead. The explanation he received came from Doctor Lee Fret, a man assigned to the case from the CDC. Something was attached to the brain stem. Something alive that was quickly spreading rapidly through Maryland and other states.

Kearns and his ragtag army of agents and medical personnel soon find themselves in a world of meaningless slaughter and mayhem. The armies of the walking dead were far more than mere zombies. Some began to change into whatever it was they ate. The government had found a way to reanimate the dead by implanting a parasite found on the tongue of the Red Snapper to the human brain. It looked good on paper, but it was a project straight from Hell. The dead now walked, but it wasn't a mystery. It was The Lazarus Culture.

BOOK OF THE DEAD
A ZOMBIE ANTHOLOGY VOL 1
ISBN 978-1-935458-25-8
Edited by Anthony Giangregorio

This is the most faithful, truest zombie anthology ever written, and we invite you along for the ride. Every single story in this book is filled with slack-jawed, eyes glazed, slow moving, shambling zombies set in a world where the dead have risen and only want to eat the flesh of the living. In these pages, the rules are sacrosanct. There is no deviation from what a zombie should be or how they came about. The Dead Walk.

There is no reason, though rumors and suppositions fill the radio and television stations. But the only thing that is fact is that the walking dead are here and they will not go away. So prepare yourself for the ultimate homage to the master of zombie legend. And remember... Aim for the head!

REVOLUTION OF THE DEAD
by Anthony Giangregorio
THE DEAD SHALL RISE AGAIN!

Five years ago, a deadly plague wiped out 97% of the world's population, America suffering tragically. Bodies were everywhere, far too many to bury or burn. But then, through a miracle of medical science, a way is found to reanimate the dead.

With the manpower of the United States depleted, and the remaining survivors not wanting to give up their internet and fast food restaurants, the undead are conscripted as slave labor.   Now they cut the grass, pick up the trash, and walk the dogs of the surviving humans.   But whether alive or dead, no race wants to be controlled, and sooner or later the dead will fight back, wanting the freedom they enjoyed in life.

The revolution has begun!

And when it's over, the dead will rule the land, and the remaining humans will become the slaves…or worse.

KINGDOM OF THE DEAD
by Anthony Giangregorio
THE DEAD HAVE RISEN!

In the dead city of Pittsburgh, two small enclaves struggle to survive, eking out an existence of hand to mouth.

But instead of working together, both groups battle for the last remaining fuel and supplies of a city filled with the living dead.

Six months after the initial outbreak, a lone helicopter arrives bearing two more survivors and a newborn baby. One enclave welcomes them, while the other schemes to steal their helicopter and escape the decaying city.

With no police, fire, or social services existing, the two will battle for dominance in the steel city of the walking dead. But when the dust settles, the question is: will the remaining humans be the winners, or the losers?

When the dead walk, the line between Heaven and Hell is so twisted and bent there is no line at all.

RISE OF THE DEAD
by Anthony Giangregorio

DEATH IS ONLY THE BEGINNING!

In less than forty-eight hours, more than half the globe was infected.
In another forty-eight, the rest would be enveloped.
The reason?
A science experiment gone horribly wrong which enabled the dead to walk, their flesh rotting on their bones even as they seek human prey.
Jeremy was an ordinary nineteen year old slacker. He partied too much and had done poorly in high school. After a night of drinking and drugs, he awoke to find the world a very different place from the one he'd left the night before.
The dead were walking and feeding on the living, and as Jeremy stepped out into a world gone mad, the dead spotting him alone and unarmed in the middle of the street,
he had to wonder if he would live long enough to see his twentieth birthday.

THE CHRONICLES OF JACK PRIMUS
BOOK ONE
by Michael D. Griffiths

Beneath the world of normalcy we all live in lies another world, one where supernatural beings exist.

These creatures of the night hunt us; want to feed on our very souls, though only a few know of their existence.

One such man is Jack Primus, who accidentally pierces the veil between this world and the next. With no other choice if he wants to live, he finds himself on the run, hunted by beings called the Xemmoni, an ancient race that sees humans as nothing but cattle. They want his soul, to feed on his very essence, and they will kill all who stand in their way. But if they thought Jack would just lie down and accept his fate, they were sorely mistaken.   He didn't ask for this battle, but he knew he would fight them with everything at his disposal, for to lose is a fate worse than death.

He would win this war, and he would take down anyone who got in his way.

MONSTER PARTY
Edited by Anthony Giangregorio

Zombies, vampires, werewolves and ghosts are just a few of the monsters in this anthology.

But this isn't any anthology, you see, this is a party.

Or to be more to the point…a *Monster Party*.

Ever wonder what would happen if a werewolf and a zombie squared off? Or perhaps a vampire and a Frankenstein monster? Or better yet, how about a world where every conceivable monster is real and humans are their prey?

If those burning questions have been driving you mad, then look no further than this book.

So go on over to the buffet table, grab yourself a plate (the shrimp looks good) and get yourself a drink, and enjoy the fun ride that is the *Monster Party*.

THE WAR AGAINST THEM: A ZOMBIE NOVEL
by Jose Alfredo Vazquez

Mankind wasn't prepared for the onslaught.

An ancient organism is reanimating the dead bodies of its victims, creating worldwide chaos and panic as the disease spreads to every corner of the globe. As governments struggle to contain the disease, courageous individuals across the planet learn what it truly means to make choices as they struggle to survive.

Geopolitics meet technology in a race to save mankind from the worst threat it has ever faced. Doctors, military and soldiers from all walks of life battle to find a cure. For the dead walk, and if not stopped, they will wipe out all life on Earth. Humanity is fighting a war they cannot win, for who can overcome Death itself? Man versus the walking dead with the winner ruling the planet. Welcome to *The War Against Them*.

DEADTOWN: A DEADWATER STORY
BOOK 8

by Anthony Giangregorio

The world is a very different place now. The dead walk the land and humans hide in small towns with walls of stone and debris for protection, constantly keeping the living dead at bay.

Social law is gone and right and wrong is defined by the size of your gun.

UNWELCOME VISITORS

Henry Watson and his band of warrior survivalists become guests in a fortified town in Michigan. But when the kidnapping of one of the companions goes bad and men die, the group finds themselves on the wrong side of the law, and a town out for blood.

Trapped in a hotel, surrounded on all sides, it will be up to Henry to save the day with a gamble that may not only take his life, but that of his friends as well.

In a dead world, when justice is not enough, there is always vengeance.

END OF DAYS: AN APOCALYPTIC ANTHOLOGY
VOLUMES 1-3

Edited by Anthony Giangregorio

Our world is a fragile place.

Meteors, famine, floods, nuclear war, solar flares, and hundreds of other calamities can plunge our small blue planet into turmoil in an instant.

What would you do if tomorrow the sun went super nova or the world was swallowed by water, submerging the world into the cold darkness of the ocean? This anthology explores some of those scenarios and plunges you into total annihilation.

But remember, it's only a book, and tomorrow will come as it always does.

Or will it?

ETERNAL NIGHT: A VAMPIRE ANTHOLOGY
Edited by Anthony Giangregorio

Blood, fangs, darkness and terror...these are the calling cards of the vampire mythos.
Inside this tome are stories that embrace vampire history but seek to introduce a new literary spin on this longstanding fictional monster. Follow a dark journey through cigarette-smoking creatures hunted by rogue angels, vampires that feed off of thoughts instead of blood, immortals presenting the fantastic in a local rock band, to a legendary monster on the far reaches of town.

Forget what you know about vampires; this anthology will destroy historical mythos and embrace incredible new twists on this celebrated, fictional character.

Welcome to a world of the undead, welcome to the world of *Eternal Night*.

DEAD HISTORY 2
A Zombie Anthology

Edited by Anthony Giangregorio

From the dawn of mankind, the walking dead have been with us.

The greatest moments in history are not what they appear.

Through the ages, the undead have been there, only the proof has been erased, documents destroyed, and witnesses silenced.

The living dead is man's greatest secret.

In this tome, are a few of the stories of what really happened all those years ago.

History isn't alive, it's dead!

INSIDE THE PERIMETER: SCAVENGERS OF THE DEAD
by Alan Spencer

In the middle of nowhere, the vestiges of an abandoned town are surrounded by inescapably high concrete barriers, permitting no trespass or escape. The town is dormant of human life, but rampant with the living dead, who choose not to eat flesh, but to instead continue their survival by cruder means.

Boyd Broman, a detective arrested and falsely imprisoned, has been transferred into the secret town. He is given an ultimatum: recapture Hayden Grubaugh, the cannibal serial killer, who has been banished to the town, in exchange for his freedom.

During Boyd's search, he discovers why the psychotic cannibal must really be captured and the sinister secrets the dead town holds.

With no chance of escape, Broman finds himself trapped among the ravenous, violent dead. With the cannibal feeding on the animated cadavers and the undead searching for Boyd, he must fulfill his end of the deal before the rotting corpses turn him into an unwilling organ donor.

But Boyd wasn't told that no one gets out alive, that the town is a death sentence.

For there is no escape from *Inside the Perimeter*.

THE BOOK OF CANNIBALS
ISBN 13: 978-1-935458-52-4   ISBN 10: 1-935458-52-3
ARE YOU HUNGRY YET?

LiViNG DEAD
PRESS
Books to
Die For!

www.ingramcontent.com/pod-product-compliance
Lightning Source LLC
Chambersburg PA
CBHW070947180726
48291CB00004B/1183